Ryan Kinzy

The New Frontier

Book I: The Cielo Space Chronicles

Library of Congress Cataloging-in-Publication Data Kinzy, Ryan.
[Fiction, English.]
The new frontier: Book I the cielo space chronicles/Ryan Kinzy
1st ed.
P. cm.
ISBN 978-1466421202

To my children

I may not be able to take you to space, but we can dream about it ...

Table of Contents

Part I: Brave New Space Station

Part II: The Treatment

Part III: A New Alliance

Part I: Brave New Space Station

Chapter 1

A New Beginning

"Look, there it is!"

"Where? I can't see it." The two girls stood on the ship's promenade deck, looking out the window. The younger girl squinted.

"That little speck out there. Here, let me zoom in." The older girl, Lauren, made a waving motion with her hands. The whole window zoomed in, revealing a complex of stations floating in space. She flicked her hand to the left until one of the stations was centered in the view.

"There. See?" she asked.

"Wow," said her sister Julia. "I couldn't have imagined that."

The girls looked at the space stations in awe. The magnificent structures sparkled in the blackness of space, slowly turning. The dust and debris of the asteroid belt formed the backdrop, with a blanket of brilliant stars sparkling beyond.

The station on the left looked like the oldest, four giant wagon wheels stacked on top of each other with an axle in the middle. The station's skin boasted giant swaths of steel that resembled patches on a worn out pair of jeans. It looked as if it had been haphazardly pieced together over the years.

Adjacent to the older station were two tubular stations. A smaller, completed one, and a larger behemoth that was half done. Unlike the wagon wheel station, these two had irregular shapes sprouting from their cylindrical bases making them look like pin cushions.

The larger of the structures, still under construction, sported gargantuan arms of steel jutting out into space on the unfinished part. The whole middle of the station was criss-crossed with massive cables that connected one side to the other. The other, smaller tubular station had the same shape as the bigger one, but was dwarfed by its larger companion.

“Look at that one!” Julia pointed to the incomplete station. “I hope we’re going to live there.”

“I think *that’s* where we’re going to live,” Lauren said, pointing at the smaller tubular station. “That should be Cielo Prime.”

“Oh,” Julia frowned slightly, looking back and forth between Cielo Prime and the larger station.

The new station bustled with activity. Ships scurried back and forth, bringing pieces and parts to the new station. Sparks flew as worker bots welded giant steel plates in place. The sisters stood silent for a moment, mesmerized.

“How big are the stations?” Julia cocked her head and crinkled her nose. It was hard to judge how big the stations were just by looking at them. They looked at least many miles long and several miles in diameter.

Lauren shook her head, as if coming out of a trance, and turned to look at her sister.

“I don’t know. Hold on.” She moved her hand to the bottom of the window and tapped on it. Words appeared above her fingers – Introduction, Location, People, Government, Economy.

“Here,” Lauren touched “Introduction.” A cloudy square appeared on the window, which brightened and then focused on a set of statistics. She could still see the station through the translucent text.

Cielo Outpost

Number of stations: 3

Station Names: Cielo Prime, Cielo One, New Cielo

Population: Cielo Prime: 250,000; Cielo One: 100,000; New Cielo: 250,000 (under construction)

. . .

Lauren's face crumpled and her shoulders slumped. "I'm sure I'm going to hate it. I bet they don't have anything I like to do there. I can't stand it already!"

She stomped her feet and growled, "We're out in the middle of NOWHERE! I can't believe we had to move! It's not fair!" She folded her arms and stared out into space, then glanced back at her sister, expecting validation for her anger over the atrocities they'd been subjected to by their parents.

Instead, Julia, who was used to these episodes, didn't pay attention and kept looking out the window.

Lauren rolled her eyes and folded her arms tighter.

Their family was headed to the Cielo Outpost—the furthermost stations in the solar system. It didn't matter to Lauren that her father had to move them for his job. She just missed home.

The trip was grueling and everybody's nerves were wearing thin. The family had been on the transport ship from Earth for almost 30 days, with just two more days to go.

The first two weeks had been exciting, as they met and played with other kids displaced by their own parents' tyranny. Of course, they kept up their schoolwork during the day, but there was plenty of time left over to explore all the nooks and crannies of the ship.

By the third week, it started to hit the girls that they really were moving. As gloom set in, the two sulked around the cabin complaining about the move. Julia fed off the emotions of her older sister, who increasingly grumbled in the last week. Now that they saw the outpost so close, it was final. The beauty of the incredible complex and excitement of living in space was overshadowed by the fact they had just left everything they knew behind them.

They turned around to face the crowd on the promenade deck and scanned the people with solemn faces.

The deck had small kiosk restaurants tucked along its back wall. Lauren thought it looked like a food court in a mall like they had back home. There were tables scattered about, families eating, and kids running around. She could almost forget they were in space.

They recognized a young girl who was sitting with her parents. The girl said something to her mom, then got up and weaved her way over to the sisters. She was one of the girls they ran around with on the ship.

"What are you looking at?" the girl asked. She wasn't quite as tall as Lauren, so she craned her neck to examine Lauren's face.

Getting no immediate answer, she looked down at Julia, whose curly blond hair encircled her head like a wreath. Julia's haphazard ensemble fit her personality, with clothes that sort of matched but didn't quite go together, topped off by a fanny pack she wore at her waist.

Lauren, on the other hand, had perfectly matched clothes with meticulously groomed hair.

"Hi, Heather. We're just looking at the station," Lauren finally said glumly.

Heather looked at the station in view. "It's that close now? Amazing! I can't wait. It's going to be great!"

Lauren tried to hide her disappointment. Heather stepped closer to the window, between the two sisters. She peered at the stations, watching them slowly turn.

"Where are you all going to live again?" she asked.

"Cielo Prime," Lauren muttered as she looked at the smaller cylindrical station.

Heather looked up, squinting at Lauren. "Oh, that's right, now I remember. We're going to be on the big station, New Cielo. My dad is working for some of the government people over there."

She paused, noticing Lauren's demeanor. "You don't seem too excited about it."

"I'm not," Lauren answered, barely audible.

"It'll be fun for you, Julia!" Heather looked down at Julia's fanny pack. Julia didn't go anywhere without it. "I've heard the asteroids have all kinds of new rocks and things nobody has ever seen before on Earth!"

Julia's eyes lit up. "Yeah, I know! My dad is going to bring back everything he can find from out there!" As she spoke she reflexively touched her fanny pack, where she kept her microscope and sample collections.

Lauren rolled her eyes and her body followed, exaggerating the exasperation. "I don't know why you carry that stuff around with you here, Julia. We're on a ship. You won't find anything here!"

"You never know!" was all Julia said, with a slight smile back at Lauren.

Heather looked back at the station as it was rotating. She pointed up at the window to the middle of the cylindrical station.

"Can you see where you'll live?"

Lauren made a counter-clockwise motion with her hand. The view of the station rotated and zoomed in. It looked like a weird, inverted city. All the buildings protruded off the surface of the station as expected, but all the writing and billboards were upside down.

The station was wrapped up and down, end to end with tubes where trains sped around, moving people from one end to the other.

The whole thing was surreal. It looked like something they'd only seen in movies, not in real life.

"Do you know what building you'll live in?" Heather asked.

"Hmm, let's see," Lauren said, tapping on the menu again. She found "Show landmarks," and touched it.

Little boxes of text appeared over the biggest buildings, labeling what the buildings were.

Lauren made a circular motion with her hand as if she were winding a yo-yo. As she did, the whole view of the station shot forward over the surface of the station. It looked like they were floating just outside it, looking in. One of the larger buildings was labeled, "Alpha Centauri Landing."

"I think that's where we are going to live," Lauren said. "I heard it takes some getting used to, with all the buildings upside down and all the grass and parks on the surface."

"Yeah, it's going to be strange," Heather said, raising her eyebrows.

Just then, Heather's mom waved to her. "Well, I gotta go eat. Good seeing you!" She turned and ran off to join her family.

Julia glanced up at the station on the window, then quickly looked at her sister and smiled. "It'll be OK. We'll have fun, you'll see."

Julia looked back at the window. The translucent menu was still there. "What's this?" she asked tapping on 'Introduction'.

The window transitioned to a panoramic view of the stations. Above them music started to play. The girls looked up and saw a cone shaped speaker that directed sound downwards so they were the only ones that could hear.

The music faded and a narrator started speaking, "People have been exploring space for over a hundred and fifty years building extensive civilizations on the moon and Mars. Yet until Will Thurmond III conceived the idea to build a civilization in the asteroid belt, nothing like it had ever been attempted. And now thousands of families, just like yours, immigrate here each year!"

The imaged changed to show a transport ship similar to the one they were on. The transport ship was shaped like a wagon wheel with five wheels sandwiched together. The whole ship spun as it moved, keeping a constant gravity for all the passengers. The narration continued, "Now, people lured by the drive to conquer this corner of the Solar System journey to Cielo as quickly as new immigration slots became available. Space is limited and only people who are invited can move to Cielo. You are part of the lucky few. These transport ships travel between Earth and the outpost eight times a year."

"Lucky?" Lauren questioned, frowning at the speaker overhead.

The window changed to show the picture of a bald old man with thin tufts of hair on either side of his head. "Cielo was the brainchild of an altruistic trillionaire from Earth who had a dream to build a new world in the heavens. He convinced investors from all around the globe to contribute part of the cost and he paid for the rest. Mr. Thurmond spent his entire fortune funding the project, but died knowing his dream had been realized."

The imagery shifted to show a construction zone in space with a wagon wheel station similar to the transport ship. "It took 20 years and many people's lives to build the first station, Cielo One. Soon after Cielo One was put into service the outpost blossomed. Cielo is strategically positioned next to the asteroid belt, where the inhabitants extract practically any minerals and metals they need to further extend Mr. Thurmond's dream."

The window switched to show Cielo Prime. "After Cielo One was built, architects dreamt bigger and better designs leading to Cielo Prime. Finally, the culmination of all we have learned went into the newest station, New Cielo, which is scheduled to be complete in two more years. Cielo is truly the pinnacle of human achievement. Welcome to the new frontier!" The final image showed New Cielo floating in space with the asteroid belt and stars glittering in the background.

"Huh. THAT was entertaining," Lauren said at the conclusion.

Julia glanced behind her at the doors. "We better get back to the cabin. It's almost time to eat."

The girls turned around and walked toward the exit. The window behind them flashed back to the original view with the station – a speck in the distance. The glass exit doors whished open before them, revealing the long hall.

Accommodations for the passengers were spread across the wagon wheels, with long spanning halls in the middle and doors on either side of the halls. At intersections, passengers could pass between the wheels and get to recreation centers like the promenade deck, the ship's school, hospital, and other necessities.

The cabins weren't cramped, but they weren't spacious either. The girls' cabin was barely big enough for a family of six. Much smaller than the home they came from on Earth.

As they walked, the girls reminisced about their old home which was in Austin, Texas, a bustling city of 10 million people. They had lived close to the city's center in a 14-story condo building. Their condo was spacious by condo standards, but it wasn't as big as the single-family houses around the corner from their building. Their mom always said she wanted a house with a yard, but at their dad's pay scale, that wasn't going to happen.

At 10 and 12, the girls didn't care for the cramped quarters much and craved the privacy they used to have back on Earth, so they spent a lot of time wandering around the ship trying to find quiet spots.

Lauren and Julia's cabin wasn't too far from the promenade deck. There was a single intersection between their wheel and the promenade deck's wheel.

In the hall, the floor noticeably curved in front of them with the shape of the ship. On either side of the corridor, the doors were indistinguishable from each other except for the numbers in the middle. Next to each door was a control panel that the inhabitants used to open the door with their handprint or where guests would announce themselves to the residents inside.

Lauren thought it looked like a utilitarian hotel. "They could have spruced this up a little, don't you think?" Lauren said to her sister.

"What do you mean?" Julia asked while she counted numbers on the doors. "Ten fifty two, ten fifty four, ten fifty six. Here we are."

"They could have put plants or something to make it look nicer," Lauren said.

"Yeah, I guess," Julia said as she put her hand on the panel beside door number 1056.

The door slid open. Their dad heard the door and came to greet them. "Back so soon? Did you see anything?"

Lauren's face soured. "Yes, we saw the stupid station. I can't believe we're moving there. Why are we going again? Oh, that's right, because you want to ruin our lives!"

Their mother looked up from the couch at their dad, heaving a sigh.

Their dad's faced softened. "Lauren, you know why . . . I have a great opportunity out there and we had to take it."

He continued, "Really, it's not going to be that bad. The place is growing like crazy. So you saw the new station? It's going to be twice as big as Cielo Prime! They need a lot of metal to build that thing, and that's why we're here."

"Yeah, we saw it, but it's still not home. I lived there my whole life! All my friends are there, my life is there!" She put her arms at her sides.

She moved toward him, counting on her fingers. "No more swims at Barton Springs, no more walks around Lady Bird Lake, no more rock climbing, no more bike riding on trails."

She paused, staring at him, then continued, "All the things I like to do—and there's NONE of that on the station!"

"I'm sorry, kiddo." He pulled her close and hugged her. "I know it will be rough at first, but you'll like it. I promise." She reluctantly hugged him back, closing her eyes and trying to hold back the tears.

Their two other siblings ran out of the back room. Evan was 8 and Maia was 6 now. She had just had a birthday the week before.

Their dad said, "I was just showing Evan and Maia where we're going. Do you want to see?"

He started walking to the back room, expecting the girls to follow. When he noticed they weren't coming, he yelled back, "Come on!"

Lauren folded her arms and looked at her sister. "Fine!" and went to see, with Julia close behind.

Hovering above the table in the middle of the room was a hologram of the solar system. Each rocky planet was a small dot, including Earth, and the gas giants were big balls with multi-colored bands encircling the globes. The hazy ring outside Mars, but inside Jupiter, was the asteroid belt. The planets looked strikingly real, as if they were looking at them through a telescope.

Their dad eagerly pulled up a chair in front of the table, "See, here we were on Earth and now we're waaaayyy out here." A red line showed a curved path from the third rocky planet out to the asteroid belt.

Maia hopped up on his lap and tried to grab the planets above the table. Her hand disappeared into Jupiter, and then she poked two fingers out the top to make it look like it had ears. The other kids laughed as she played.

"Let me do it," Evan said, shoving Maia aside.

"No, it's my turn. I did it first!" Maia insisted, and the scene erupted in violence.

"Come on, you two. Settle down." Their dad separated them then resumed his explanation zooming in on their destination. The detail of the asteroids and the stations sharpened. The stations were some distance away from the asteroids. They had a grid of small space buoys separating the stations from the asteroid belt.

The chaos of the asteroid belt was immediately apparent, as the real-life diorama showed massive asteroids hurtling through space, colliding with each other and exploding in a dazzling cloud of dust.

Their dad continued, “See here, this is the Cielo Outpost. We’ll live here and I’ll spend a lot of time out here.” He pointed to the asteroid belt some distance away from the outpost. “I’ll be supervising the operations out there.”

“What are those things for?” Lauren asked, pointing at the buoys.

“That’s to protect the station from the asteroids. They blow up any stray asteroids that come close to the station,” their dad said.

Lauren raised her eyebrows.

“How long will you be gone?” Julia asked.

“A few days at a time.”

“Can we go out there, too?” Julia asked next.

“It’s no place for kids. Lots of big machines floating around, and those stray asteroids.” He patted Julia on the shoulders. “Maybe when you’re older . . . for now, I’ll be sure to bring back lots of samples for you!”

That was good enough for Julia and she smiled her crinkled-nose smile back.

Their mother came in and put her hands on Juila’s shoulders. “I know this is hard, but I really think you’ll like it. How many kids your age get to live on a space station?”

“We’ll see,” Lauren said, not scowling this time.

“All right, time to eat! We have your favorite – Indian food.”

Chapter 2

Welcome to Cielo Prime

The family arrived at the outpost two days later. The transport ship stopped some distance away from the stations, and small ferries came out to pick up the passengers. The day they were to disembark was hectic. The family had to scramble to get to the transport dock for their scheduled moving time. Most of their possessions were already boxed up and had been moved to Cielo Prime while they slept and only their tote bags remained.

“Lauren, Julia, come on!” their mom barked while she picked up her bags. Lauren was moving slowly, having just rolled out of bed minutes before. Still half asleep, she struggled to stay awake as she changed out of her pajamas.

Their dad rounded up the last bags, then grabbed the younger kids. “We’ll go on ahead to get us a spot in line. See you down there,” he said as they headed out the door.

“Mom, hold on! I’m getting ready!” Lauren gurgled as she brushed her teeth.

“Your dad and the other kids are already going down to the dock. We need to get going.” As she spoke, Julia suddenly appeared, standing by the door.

“I’ll catch up with dad,” she said as she stumbled out the door, tripping on the doorframe. She recovered, brushed her clothes off in stride, then ran down the hall.

Lauren walked out several minutes later, surly, dragging her feet. “OK, I’m ready, let’s go.”

Her mom stood with her hands on her hips. “Why is it that you are always the last one out the door?” Lauren shrugged and walked out the door without answering.

Hundreds of people waited in winding lines for the ferry. Their dad and the three other kids were halfway up the line when Lauren and their mom arrived at the dock.

“Oh, no!” Lauren muttered. “We’ll have to take a different ferry. Or maybe not go at all. Too bad.”

Her mother just pushed forward into the line.

“Excuse me . . . excuse me,” she said, dragging Lauren with her up the line and around other passengers. Many gave her dirty looks as she passed.

One woman glanced back, seeing Lauren and her mother trying to get by, and shifted her bag to her side to block the way.

When her mother reached the lady, she tapped her on the shoulder. “Excuse me, we’re trying to reach the rest of our family.”

“Why don’t you ask them to come back to you?” the lady asked, frowning.

This time, her mother gave the lady a dirty look and pushed the bag aside.

“Hey!” the lady exclaimed.

Lauren’s mother didn’t respond and just kept shuffling up the line.

They reached the rest of their family and dropped their bags.

“Did you hear that woman?” their mom asked their dad.

“No, what did she do?” he asked.

Lauren's attention drifted as she looked out the window. A glass wall separated the waiting room from the actual dock. The ground personnel waited at the front of the line for the ship to come in.

She ducked down, peering through the window to see the ferry looming outside the ship, floating in space. It slowly maneuvered toward the dock.

She elbowed her sister. "Julia, look!"

Julia looked out the window, seeing the ship slip into the bay with its thrusters burning. It hovered for a moment, then came to rest on the deck. When it did, the bay doors closed. A loud whooshing sound erupted in the dock, pressurizing it with air.

The ferry looked like a twentieth-century bus to Lauren. Its boxy shape had windows along the outside and a couple doors on either end. There weren't any wings, and it had two large thrusters on the back. She could see the seats situated in rows all throughout the cabin. Towards the front, there was a large circular emblem which was a triangle with a line drawn through it.

"What's that?" Lauren asked her dad pointing to the icon.

"Oh, that's the seal for Cielo," he said. "It's on all their official documents."

"Huh," Lauren said staring at it.

Small doors along the back of the bay opened and bots automatically started loading large stacks of crates onto the ferry. At the same time, the passenger doors opened, allowing the crowd to spill into the bay. The crew on the deck opened the gates and waved the passengers out to the ferry. The family moved with the crowd and boarded.

On board, voices from overhead speakers repeated in a soothing voice, "Please take your seat. The ferry departs in 10 minutes."

Luckily, they were far enough up in the line that they found six seats next to each other. Lauren got the window seat and looked out the window to see the attendants stop the line right at the rude lady. She smiled slightly, then put her seat belt on.

Other families weren't as lucky and had to piece together their seats, spreading their families around on the ferry. Her siblings sat down and strapped themselves in. A few minutes later, the message from the voice changed to "Doors are secured. Please remain in your seats and secure your belongings."

Just then, the ferry lifted, hovering above the dock deck, turned 180 degrees, and moved slowly out of the bay as quietly as it had come in. As soon as they pulled away from the ship, the ferry twisted in space, shifting out of the transport ship's rotation, and gravity let go. Lauren got a sick feeling in her stomach as if she were falling in a really quick elevator.

Groans could be heard throughout the ferry as gravity released its grasp. "Oh, I'm going to be sick!" Lauren moaned, clutching her stomach. She reached in front of her seat for a throw up bag and put it over her mouth.

Maia had been flinging her water bottle around and accidentally sloshed it out by Julia. Without gravity the water droplets hovered right above Julia's lap. The spheres of liquid suspended harmlessly like floating silver balls until the ferry accelerated. The kids were pushed back in their seats and the liquid splattered all over Julia.

"Argh!" Julia shouted.

"Be quiet, you guys. We're not the only ones here!" Their mom tried to quell the impending disaster. "Julia, it's just water. Calm down."

"But, Mom, it's all over!" Julia frantically wiped the water from her fanny pack and scowled at her younger sister. "Maia, watch what you're doing!" She slapped Maia on the hand. Maia yelped and reached to pinch Julia.

"Do NOT touch each other!" their mom murmured through gritted teeth. The two straightened up, sat back in their seats, and continued frowning at each other.

Outside the window, they could see Cielo Prime getting closer as the ferry picked up speed. On either side, they passed several small satellite stations that mimicked the shape of the large station.

"What are those?" Lauren asked.

Her dad looked up from reading a message on his phone and glanced out the window. "Farms," he said absently.

"Farms? They don't look like farms," she retorted.

Her dad looked at them again. "They're farms, all right. See, they're spinning really fast. The plant roots grow toward the center of the satellite and nutrient water is sprayed on the roots. It's called hydroponics. That's how they grow food for us to eat here in space. And there're lights all around the outside, see?" He pointed at outside rim of the satellite.

Lauren creased her nose and made a face. "Does it taste good?"

"Yes, it tastes fine. You won't be able to tell a difference," he assured her. Skeptical, she watched the farms race by quickly as they got closer to the station.

Now in full view, the station was even more impressive than it had looked from the transport ship. The massive station dominated the entire view from the ferry. Lauren couldn't look anywhere out her window without seeing station.

Hundreds of buildings stood at varying heights rooted on the surface of the station. Several buildings clustered together, forming small skylines. Lights from all over the station glowed, shimmered, and flashed. Elevators went up and down buildings. Train lines wrapped around the station, looking like ribbons on a Christmas present. The trains sped back and forth, darting up and down.

Outside the station, ferry ships, cargo ships, and mining ships all waited in line to dock. Other ships sped away, headed for one of the other stations, a farm, or the asteroid belt. The passengers on the ferry sat gawking in wonder, as this was the first time most of them had seen the station.

Cielo Prime was rotating counter clockwise as the ferry moved to get in sync with the station. The ferry slowed down the closer they got. They could see the docking bay. Lights illuminated the landing spot their ferry aimed for and cargo lights shone on the bay, making it look like it was daytime.

The ferry landed with a thud and then sank down as it came to rest. Overhead, the soothing, almost mechanical voice returned, saying repeatedly, “Welcome to Cielo Prime. We hope you enjoy your stay.”

“OK, we’re here,” Lauren said, sighing and releasing her grasp on the armrests.

As the ferry came to a stop, everybody on board got up from their seats and stood in the aisles. The family unbuckled and gathered their carry on luggage.

“Let’s wait until it clears out a little,” their mom said, holding the kids back.

People shuffled by as they made their way out of the ferry. When it had thinned enough, the family got up and worked their way toward the door. Out in the bay, the crowd followed the yellow lines on the bay floor toward the far side.

Above the door, a sign read "Customs" next to the Cielo seal. Lauren and Julia looked around, absorbing every detail. They crossed into the customs area, which was a nondescript room with 10 lines of people in front of stalls. Each stall had a sign that read either "Residents" or "Non-Residents." The family moved to a line for non-residents and waited.

The residents whizzed by, simply placing their hands on the scanners at the Resident checkpoint booths and being waved through by guards. The non-residents waded through the winding lines.

On the side of each Non-Resident booth, there was a small pad tilted out from the side of the booth. In front of the pad was a line painted on the ground. When it was their turn, their dad stopped at the line and put his hand on the pad.

"Alex Michaels identified. Proceed." A green light flashed and he walked forward to a second line.

He stood with his arms at his sides, and a thin robotic arm extended out with an injection syringe. A small burst of air hit his arm. He flinched a little with the inoculation.

"Alex Michaels, you are processed. Please move forward," a voice commanded.

"Did that hurt? What was that?" Lauren asked with a look of panic in her eyes. She didn't like shots much at all, and her dad knew it.

"It's just a little shot," he said, trying to soothe her.

"No, No, NO! I'm not going to do it!" she insisted.

"Well, then they won't let you on the station. Everybody has to get one," he said, looking back at the disgruntled passengers who were next in line. "Come on, it doesn't hurt that much."

Julia jumped past Lauren and stopped at the first line. She got her handprint read and then stepped up for the shot. She flinched a little, too, and gave her sister an impish grin.

With puckered lips and a scowl on her face, Lauren stomped to the first line and placed her hand on the pad. “Lauren Michaels identified. Proceed,” the voice said. The green light flashed. Next, she stepped to the second line and out came the syringe. She covered her eyes, bracing for the injection.

The cold liquid jetted into her muscles. She flinched like her sister and dad before her, feeling strangely invaded by the inoculation.

“Lauren Michaels, you are processed. Please move forward,” a voice commanded.

“Processed? What am I an animal?” she screamed at the arm as she walked away.” She rubbed her arm where a weird feeling radiated from the spot. “What was in that?”

“Just something to make sure we don’t spread diseases to other people,” he said.

“Well, I didn’t like it. It didn’t feel like a normal shot,” she muttered.

“That’s it, let’s go.” The other family members went through without any issues, and they all followed the crowd to a set of escalators that took them up to the surface.

Lauren didn’t know what to expect. She assumed the station would just look like the inside of a building: drab, dull, and boring.

Immediately past the escalators were gates keeping hundreds of vendors outside the customs area. They were selling anything from food to everyday staples, like toothpaste.

Their dad turned to the family. “OK, just walk past them and ignore them.”

The family exited the gates and fought their way through the mass of people. The girls just kept their heads down, not talking to anyone.

The sea of people parted, revealing a grand mall with shops, restaurants, and lots more people. A dazzling array of plants and flowers invited them in. It almost looked like a rainforest, with sprawling trees supporting hanging vines, orchids growing on trees, moss clusters nestled on branches, and fragrant smells from the gardens wafting by. A thin mist permeated the area from a picturesque waterfall in the middle of the space.

Far above their heads was the ceiling of the station. It was a web of steel and glass intertwined with strips of lights. It almost looked like clouds had formed around the lights.

Massive cable bundles shot up into the ceiling every thousand feet or so, holding the station together. Although the station was curved, it wasn’t as noticeable as on the ship. There were so many trees and the ceiling was so high that the gradual curve of the station was barely noticeable.

The mall was bustling with activity. There were restaurants, and people reading, talking, and on the go. It was much busier than the ship. A breeze flowed by and the sisters took deep breaths.

Julia looked around, squinting.

“What are you looking for?” Lauren asked.

“That breeze! Where is it coming from? How do they do that?” Julia asked.

“I don’t know, but being on that ship I almost forgot how nice it was to feel a breeze. This almost feels like Earth,” Lauren said.

There were even squirrels running around, jumping from tree to tree. Lauren watched as two small squirrels chased each other around the trunk of a large tree. They looked like they were playing tag, as one would hide from the other in the crook of the tree, surprise the other one as it approached, then start the chase over again.

Birds flew in the massive open air space. There was a flock of parakeets flying in unison as they dipped and swooped, eventually landing together on the top of a tree and chirping loudly.

The waterfall was on the other side of the mall. It flowed into a giant hole surrounded by a railing. The girls walked over to the railing to see where the water went. The hole opened to the floor below, where there were more shops and restaurants.

Evan ran up to the railing and climbed halfway up it, looking down.

“Evan!” their mom cried. Lauren grabbed Evan by the back of his pants and slung him to the ground.

“What?” he asked, and wandered back to his dad.

“Evan, don’t do that. You scared the daylights out of me,” his mom said.

“All right, let’s go find our apartment!” their dad blurted out, completely oblivious to what had happened.

He had most of the luggage stacked on his back like a pack mule, and their mom carried one bag and held Evan’s hand. Their dad grabbed Maia’s hand and all four of them started walking toward a different set of escalators on the edge of the courtyard. The sign above the escalators read “Central Station.”

Lauren and Julia followed, stumbling as they both glanced back at the mall to see what else they could see before they went down the escalator.

In the train station at the bottom of the escalator, doors opened and closed, and people got on and off. Rectangular white tiles lined the walls, and blue square tiles formed the station sign, which read "Central Station," recreating a nostalgic scene from Earth's ancient New York subways.

On the side of a wall, an electronic map showed the network of rail lines. The rail lines went up and down the length of the space station and around the circumference as well. They were positioned about a quarter of a mile apart, forming a nice uniform grid. The rail lines were color coded, with the express lines labeled in green and local lines in blue.

"We're at the Alpha Centauri Landing. It's a ways away from here," their dad said.

The family dropped their luggage and huddled together while their dad tried to figure out where to go.

He started toward the map and was cut off by a worker bot darting around sweeping the floor. As he stepped forward, the bot swerved around him, catching him off guard.

When he reached the map, he said, "Grid 21, Alpha Centauri Landing."

The map highlighted the rail lines that would take them where they wanted to go, showing the moving trains outlined in a slightly darker color. Their dad pointed up at the map with one hand on his chin. "OK, we take this express line to here, then the local line here, then . . . Looks easy enough!"

As he spoke, the outlined green dot on the map blinked. Overhead they heard "Express line approaching."

"This is it," their dad said, picking up some of the bags and slinging them over his shoulder. "Let's go," he said as he headed toward the train. The family followed him to the platform. Lauren and Julia helped their mom with the remaining bags.

The express train pulled up and the doors opened. A sea of people got off pushing and shoving. The family forced their way onto the train, slipping in just as the doors closed.

Lauren noticed the Cielo seal on the side of train as she boarded. They symbol seemed to be on anything municipal.

The express train darted out of the train station and plummeted down a few floors. The train moved so fast that the walls and buildings outside were indistinguishable.

Evan, who didn't heed the warnings about standing without holding the railing, fell into his mom. The force of his falling knocked his mom down, and she slammed into his dad, who lost his footing and fell with the bags he carried, bumping another passenger down and another like dominos.

"Oh, sorry," their dad said, standing up.

"Evan, pay attention," their mom grumbled as she righted him and then herself.

Lauren watched in horror, turning to the side and pretending not to know them.

Maia jumped up and down laughing.

Julia didn't notice a thing, as she was looking out the window.

The train cleared the inner tunnels where it was surrounded by buildings and shot out into a clear tube that was suspended below the buildings. The clear tube allowed them to see the bottoms of buildings fly by above them. A few minutes into the journey, the train approached a mini skyline. As they got closer, the train dove down into the heart of the buildings into another tunnel. Above, the speaker rang out, "Approaching Grid 45." Then all of a sudden the train slowed down and came to a stop.

After two more trains and another 15 minutes, they hopped off at a fairly small station and the train zipped away out of view. A couple other passengers exited the train and a handful of passengers got on the train. Three halls – left, right, and center – and a set of stairs stood before them. Electronic signs adorned the walls describing where each hall led. The sign on the stairs was labeled "To Surface." There was a hanging sign in the center of the station that read "Grid 21".

"Here, this way," their dad said, and walked to the hall on the left, which flashed "Alpha Centauri Landing." They went through the corridor and walked for about a minute before reaching an elevator. The elevator whisked them down to level 4. A short walk from the elevator, their dad stopped.

"This is it!" he said. They were standing in front of their new apartment.

The door opened. "Welcome, Michaels' family," a calm voice said overhead. Inside, their belongings had been delivered in big metal boxes that sat in the middle of the living room. All the walls were bare. The girls excitedly rushed in to take a look, dashing into each room, laughing. After a cursory glance at each room, Lauren came out with her hands out to either side, her elbows tight into her hips.

"That's it? Where's the rest of it?" she asked.

Evan came out. "There are only three bedrooms! I have to share a room with Maia?!" Maia giggled and went to hug her brother as he tried to push her away.

Their mom was looking around, peering into each room. She came out with a smirk, "It's definitely cozy . . ."

Their dad defended the apartment. “Now, it’s just for a little while, until we can find a permanent place. I know it’s smaller than what we’re used to. It’s not that bad.” He showed them each of the rooms. “Look—Lauren, you and Julia share this room. Evan and Maia share this other room. Your mom and I share that room, and there’s a small playroom over here.”

He circled the kitchen, waving his arms. “And the living area and kitchen are right here.”

Julia came up to her dad and wrapped her arms around his waist, “I LIKE it!” She looked up with a smile.

“Thank you, Julia. That was nice.” Julia seemed genuinely appreciative.

Lauren frowned, muttering under her breath, “You think you’re SOOO smart, Julia,” and stomped off to their new room.

“OK, let’s get started . . .” their mother said, as she opened one of the boxes.

Chapter 3

Life on the Station

It had been four weeks since they moved to the station and the new apartment. Things were settling into a routine. The kids started school which was a short train ride away. In fact, they could ride their bikes if they wanted, as the surface had well-maintained bike paths, but they elected to ride the train most days since they were usually running late.

The older sisters were enrolled in a couple of after-school activities, as were the younger ones, making their mother's life frenzied. Lauren had tennis Tuesdays and Thursdays. Julia had tennis on Monday and music on Thursday. Evan and Maia were both in swimming once a week and in swim meets on the weekends.

Complicating life further, their father started his regular trips out to the asteroid belt. He was gone Tuesday through Thursday each week. It was rough on the family, but they had known that would be the case. On Earth, their dad traveled, but not quite this much. He promised that when things settled down, he wouldn't have to be gone as much, but their mom was skeptical.

After four weeks, the apartment began to look more like home. Their mom painted the girls' room a soft green and arranged their furniture along the walls. She situated their beds parallel to each other, just like in their room on Earth. The room was a little smaller, but it was at least comforting that it resembled their room back home.

Evan and Maia had separate rooms on Earth, but here they had to share a room. They couldn't agree on a color, and their mom got so frustrated that she split the room down the middle and painted one side pink and the other side blue. Each time Evan walked into the room, he put his hand to the side of his face, hiding the pink walls from view.

The girls' room reflected their personalities, with Lauren's side neat and tidy and Julia's side a little disheveled. Julia was a budding scientist and her experiments sprawled all over her desk. She had a rock collection on the shelf above the desk, a few terrariums, and a number of experiments in progress.

The terrariums were clear boxes where she grew various things. One terrarium housed some exotic plants she brought from Earth and a few insects. Others just had strange substances growing. Julia regularly studied her rocks and plants, periodically looking up information about them on the Internet.

She had a makeshift laboratory at her desk with her prized possession—her new microscope. It was the last thing she bought on Earth before the move. The microscope was about the size of her hand, and it was circular with a black rim around the outside and a screen in the middle. When she held it over something, she could twist the bottom of it to zoom back and forth, then the image would show on the screen. A detached stand allowed her to hold the microscope steady over whatever she was looking at, but she could also take it off the stand and carry it with her wherever she went.

Lauren's side was covered with artwork she had created over the years. She loved to paint, use pastels, and sculpt clay when she had the chance. She swapped out the pictures on her wall periodically and would put the rest in an overstuffed drawer. She only kept the ones she liked best, and the others she would take pictures of and either give them away or recycle them. Some of her pictures were angry, others happy, some pencil drawings, and some still lifes. She tried it all.

She also tinkered with computers, but there was nothing visible to show for it except that she had two screens on her desk instead of one, like Julia. She also had a visor she often used when working on the computer.

This Thursday morning, Julia woke up early, as she usually did, and was checking her experiments. She shuffled through some of the rocks on her desk, clanking them together.

"Ugh!" Lauren grunted. "Why are you making all that racket?"

Lauren rolled out of bed, hair tangled. She struggled to open an eye while the other stayed closed. She stumbled into the bathroom to brush her teeth, mumbling something to Julia, who wasn't paying attention to her.

From the bathroom, Lauren yelled, "I said, why do you have to wake up so early?"

Julia turned her body, kept reading, and then slightly turned her head to acknowledge Lauren. "What? Did you say something?"

Yelling from the bathroom while she was brushing her teeth, Lauren repeated, "I said, why do you have to wake up so early?"

Julia absently responded, "Oh, I don't know. I'm just reading stuff," and then went back to reading. She read something on the screen, then looked at one of her experiments, read again, then back to the experiment.

Lauren frowned as she came out of the bathroom and sat down at her desk. Her monitor automatically turned on. It displayed her schedule for the day, which started with school at 8 AM and ended with tennis after school at 4 PM. Her homework assignments due that day flashed on the screen, as well as messages from her friends. She had tried to keep up with her friends since the move, but it was a little awkward because messages took so long to get back and forth. With a several minute delay she couldn't chat with them real-time and none of her friends had the patience to wait.

This morning she had five messages from friends back on Earth. Each week she got fewer and fewer messages. Here on the station, she tried to make new friends, but it was hard after living in the same place all her life. She never had to make new friends before. They were just always there growing up.

Their mom stuck her head in the room. “Girls, time for breakfast.” The girls hopped up from their desks and wandered out to breakfast.

“Wow!” Their mom looked astonished. “I only asked once! What would you all like for breakfast?”

“Waffles,” they glumly said in unison. Neither was excited about going to school that morning.

As their mom toasted some frozen waffles and brought them to the table, Evan and Maia ran into the kitchen like a whirlwind. Evan was screaming, “Stop touching me!” Maia chased after him.

“Maia, stop,” their mom ordered.

Maia stopped, but kept smiling. Evan sat down with his arms crossed and mouth pursed.

“You know, your dad comes home today,” their mom said as she sat down at the table with a cup of coffee.

“We know,” Lauren responded in a monotone.

“Where’s my breakfast?” Evan said sternly, still scrunching his lips together.

“Excuse me?” their mom asked.

“I want my breakfast!” Evan said again.

“You can go get it yourself. And make some waffles for your sister, too!”

Evan looked astonished, but then grabbed two waffles out of the box his mom had left on the counter, stuffed them into the toaster, and frowned over the counter at his sister. When they were ready he walked the plates over and slid one out of her reach.

Lauren shoved Maia's plate back to her.

Maia grinned at Evan, rubbing it in, then gobbled her waffle down.

Evan bumped her and Maia screeched.

"You two stop it!" Lauren screamed at them before her mother could react. "I'm tired of listening to you!"

Evan and Maia froze, and their mom stared at Lauren. Then she laid her hand on the Lauren's arm. "Lauren, are you OK?"

"OK? I don't like it here, Mom. I'm not meeting anyone, and since we didn't grow up here, we're different."

"What do you mean?" their mother asked.

"I mean exactly what I said! I don't like it here," she said, sitting back in her chair.

"Do you like it, Julia?" their mother asked.

Julia shrugged, chewing a mouthful of waffle and looking unaffected by the drama around her. "Sure."

"I'm not sure what to say, Lauren. We're out here already."

"I like it!" Evan said.

Lauren rolled her eyes at her brother.

"OK, clear your dishes and finish getting ready. Time to go." Lauren's mother looked at her with concern. "Please keep trying,

Lauren. I'm sure it will get better. Something interesting will happen. I'm sure of it."

She reached down to wipe Maia's mouth as the girl squirmed away from her.

They walked to the train station together. School was one train stop up the station, so it wasn't too far. The local trains came every few minutes, and Lauren and Julia both had their phones out, staring at them while they waited.

Evan had gotten over Maia bugging him and chased her around a post as the train tore into the station.

When the doors opened, the kids hopped on and found seats, waiting for the other passengers to board.

Their mom sat down with Lauren on one side and Julia on the other. Lauren looked up at the advertisements that lined the top of the car. The ads weren't allowed to have sound, but they were definitely flashy.

"Looking for a change?" one read, and then flashed a photo of a woman with cat-like eyes. "Come visit us for the best mod of your life."

"Mom, what's a mod?" Julia asked.

"What?" Her mother looked up, catching the last part of the ad. "Nothing you'll ever need! And if you try to get one, I'll kill you!" she said to Julia.

Julia raised her eyebrows, staring at her mother. Just then, the train came to their stop. The kids jumped off the train, running through the maze of hallways to get to school with dozens of other kids.

Their mother stopped short of going in at the doors to the school, as did many of the other parents.

"Bye kids, have fun at school!" She waved at their retreating backs.

The kids turned the corner out of sight of their mom and walked to their respective classrooms.

School was computerized on the station. They had a teacher, but all the lessons were done electronically. Each child had his or her own tablet computer to work on and all the rooms had large blackboards that were actually screens the teacher could write to from his or her desk. Then, when the kids were called on, they could write on their own tablets and have it show up on the blackboard.

Lauren sat in Geometry class trying to pay attention. Most of the time it was interesting to her, but today she just didn't care. She slumped down, staring at the board in the front.

The bell rang for lunch. She sprang up, stretching to shake off her sleepiness.

She brought her lunch most days, but today she was eating in the cafeteria. She stood in line with the rest of kids, waiting to get her food.

"Hey." The girl behind her poked her in the back.

Lauren turned to see the girl. "Yes?"

"You're new here, aren't you?" The girl said it more than asked it, since she already knew the answer.

"Yes."

"You're in my History class, aren't you?" the girl asked.

"I think so." Lauren shuffled further in the line.

"You're in my tennis class, too, after school."

"Yes," Lauren answered, moving again.

"How long have you been here?" the girl asked.

"About a month, I guess."

"That's not very long."

"No, it's not."

The girl shuffled along with Lauren, drumming her fingers on her tray.

"Have you heard the stories on the station?" the girl asked.

"What stories?" Lauren looked at her.

"About the 'mind control' creatures." She put air quotes around "mind control."

"What do you mean?" Lauren asked.

"Just people say there's something here on the station that controls our minds," she said.

Lauren rolled her eyes, piled her food on her tray, and walked off to a table to sit by herself.

The rest of the day was almost as long as the first half for Lauren. Her mother waited for outside the school, as she did most days, so Lauren briefly stopped by to see her and her siblings and then walked to tennis center which was fairly close to school.

She hadn't been at this center very long, but she had already made an impression. On Earth, she had gone to several tournaments, getting to the semis or finals in a number of them, but here on the station things weren't as competitive so she just tried to have fun with it. She was a pretty strong and agile kid, having spent her younger years in gymnastics, but then transitioning to tennis when she got older.

Lauren stood at the baseline, hitting the balls as hard as she could, trying to take out some of her frustration. It was a good outlet. She simply put her headphones on, the ball machine fed her the balls, and she hit away. As she hit them, a little bot hopper scurried around after the balls, sucking them up and returning them to the ball machine.

The girl from the lunch line stood at the side of the court twirling her racket. She watched Lauren hit a few forehands. Lauren hit a crosscourt shot that hugged the outside baseline and the girl clapped, “That was really good!”

Lauren acknowledged her with a fleeting glance and a smile that said “Thank you.” The girl smiled back and wandered off to another court. The tennis center had 16 courts total with four on each floor. They were completely enclosed, different from the centers Lauren had grown up with on Earth, which were all outside. Here they had mostly hardcourts, but there was a grass and clay court for people looking for a change of pace.

After tennis, she felt better. Today was Thursday and her dad was getting home early, so she decided to cut practice short and hurried to get back home.

When she got home, her dad was in the back room talking to someone on the phone. He sounded angry. The other kids were in their rooms.

“What’s wrong with Dad?” Lauren asked.

“I’m not sure. Why don’t you get your homework done before dinner,” her mom said as Lauren set her bags down.

“Ugh!” Lauren groaned. “I just got home! Can’t I relax a little?”

"Just for a second," her mom smiled.

Lauren went straight to her room, where she found Julia working at her desk. Lauren retreated to her desk and began mindlessly perusing the Internet.

Their dad got off the phone and walked out of the back room. They could tell he wasn't happy, even from the other room.

"Everything OK, Alex?" they heard their mother ask.

"I can't believe they make us bring these useless rocks back."

Julia perked up at the mention of rocks from space and crept out of the bedroom to see what her dad was talking about. As she peeked around the kitchen doorframe, he took a box of various-sized round rocks out of his bag and set them on the table. "I can't find any reason for them to want these things. We're not making any money on it, and it's costing a lot to get them back here."

Their mom picked up one of the rocks, glanced at it, and said, "Well, why don't you just tell them you can't do it anymore?"

"We can't! It's part of the deal. Since they're letting us out there, they said we have to bring them back. Must be some covert operation—nobody seems to know what they use them for."

As her parents were engrossed in conversation, Julia snuck up to the pile of rocks and swiped one of them. She went back to her room and sat at her desk.

She put the small rock under the stand of her microscope, moved the microscope into position, turned it on, and then turned to her computer. The rock came into view on the computer screen. It was unusually round, but it's surface looked similar to some of the basalt rocks she had brought from Earth.

She zoomed in on the rock 100X and started to see some differences. The surface was porous, as she would expect with a basalt rock, but it also appeared to be moving. Julia intently looked at the screen, trying to discern what was moving on the rock.

She zoomed in even further. Now the surface of the rock looked like Swiss cheese with holes and pockets all over it. The things moving on the surface were some sort of microorganism, but none she had seen before. She isolated one of the organisms and tapped on the screen. The screen showed, "Searching . . ." and then after a few seconds displayed "Unidentified organism."

Some of the organisms were clinging to the inside of the holes on the rock. She zoomed in closer to the surface. It looked like they were eating the rock and then disappearing into the holes.

"That's strange," she mused out loud to herself.

"What's strange?" Lauren asked.

Julia quickly turned off the screen and swung around to see her sister. "Oh, nothing."

Lauren rolled her eyes and put her hands on her hips. "It's just a rock, Julia. Why do you keep looking at those things?" Lauren frowned at her sister. "Why don't you clean up your desk? And while you're at it, throw away some of these things—they stink!"

Lauren made a move toward Julia's desk.

"No! Don't touch them!" Julia shrieked, grabbing Lauren's arm and pinching it.

"Arghh! Fine! I won't throw them away, but at least put them away where I can't smell them!"

"OK, I'll put them away, just don't touch them." Julia started gathering her experiments and putting them in containers.

Lauren spun around and walked out of the room. As soon as she had left, Julia turned on her screen again, looking closely at the organisms. She wanted to get a closer look, so she pulled out a small hammer to break away some of the rock. The first few taps on the rock yielded little, so she smashed the rock as hard as she could.

With a crash, the rock crumbled. As she sifted through the debris, Julia noticed the center of the rock was made up of a crystalline structure. Fascinated, she swept up the pieces and put them under her microscope.

To her amazement, the organisms seemed to be building the crystal structure from the basalt material they were eating. She could see the organisms frantically trying to repair the smashed crystal, like ants rushing to repair a broken mound in the wake of an attack from a kid's wayward foot.

The crystal didn't look like a normal crystalline structure. It seemed to be a complex organic structure with intricate facets. It was like nothing like she had ever seen on Earth.

Lauren burst into the room again. "Are you still playing around with those rocks?"

Startled, Julia didn't say a word, searching for a container to put the rock crumbles in. She found a partially used container that had some jelly-like residue stuck to the inside surface from one of her previous experiments.

She wiped the rock crystals off her desk into the container, then put it back on her shelf. Intrigued, she turned to her computer to research crystals that grew in basalt rocks.

Chapter 4

Exploring the Station

The next day, the kids went to school as usual. School got out at 3 PM each day, and parents picking up their kids waited for them in the atrium in front of the school. At their school on Earth, the kids' parents waited outside the school doors with the other parents, and each grade had a pickup zone where the kids met their parents.

On Cielo, things were a little different. For one, the school was smaller with fewer children so there were zones, but things were much less chaotic because there were fewer kids. Also, here on Cielo, there were chaperone bots for younger kids of families where both parents worked or for single parents who worked or for parents who were busy.

The bots were robots that would pick up kids and lead them to wherever they needed to go, like after-school activities or back home. Lauren and Julia's mom didn't like using the chaperone bots and would only use them when she was in a pinch and had an appointment that prevented her from picking the kids up.

That Friday, their mom stood waiting for them to come out of school. When the bell rang, the kids spilled out into their respective zone and waited. Chaperone bots navigated the crowd, found their assigned children, and guided them off the premises. The kids who were going home with their parents sought them out in the crowd.

Outside the school, Lauren looked for Julia. Julia was standing with her class chatting with a few classmates. Lauren ran up to her. "Are you ready?" she asked, grabbing Julia's hand and tugging her in the opposite direction.

"Sure, let's go!" Julia said as they went to look for their mother.

"Let's ask mom if we can stop at the plaza before home, OK? Lots of the kids in class were talking about going up there after school," Lauren said.

Their younger siblings had gotten out of school earlier. Lauren and Julia found their mother talking to some of the other parents. Evan leaned against her, moaning that he wanted to go. Maia was wandering around close by. The sisters ran up to their mother. "Mom, is it OK if we go to the plaza before coming home?"

"Hmm. I don't know," she said hesitantly. "For how long?"

"Not long. A bunch of kids were headed up there, and I wanted to go check it out. Please! Can we go?" Lauren pleaded.

"Well, OK. But don't stay too long. I'm taking Evan and Maia home right now, so just be home before dinner."

The girls nodded and then trotted off to the stairs to go up to the plaza. Their local plaza was on the surface at the top of the stairs. It was much smaller than the one at Central Station. It only had a few restaurants, but there was a nice playground for younger kids and a pond with park benches and tables for the older kids.

The entire surface of the station was covered with parks and plazas. Each plaza was a little different from the others, with a mix of restaurants, playgrounds, parks, water gardens, and rocky knolls. Below the surface there were malls, apartments, offices, warehouses, and even factories on some parts of the station.

The kids from school were hanging out at the tables talking, doing homework, and playing games. The sisters tried to fit in the best they could. They approached a group of girls from some of Lauren's classes. The girl from the lunch line and tennis practice was in the group.

One of the other girls looked them up and down with a slight scowl. "You're in my grade, aren't you?"

Lauren timidly replied, "Yes."

"What's your name?" the girl said, folding her arms and staring at the sisters.

"Lauren. And this is my sister, Julia," Lauren managed.

"Are you new to the outpost? Or did you come from one of the other stations?" the girl interrogated.

Julia piped up with a smile, oblivious to the girl's argumentative disposition. "We're from Earth! We just moved here last month."

"Ohh, you're from Earth. Doesn't that make you special?" the girl smirked. "I was born here, and so were they. Why don't you go find some Earth girls to hang out with?"

The girl from the lunch line pushed in front of the rude girl. "Sorry about her."

"No problem!" Julia said, still oblivious.

"You can hang out with us if you want." She invited them to sit down, to the disappointment of her bad-mannered friend. "I'm Alyssa."

The sisters sat down at the table next to them and scanned the plaza. They had come here a few times since they'd been on the station, but most days they had their after-school activities.

In the plaza, there was an ice cream shop that had pumpkin ice cream, the girls' favorite. Next to that was a pizza shop that had Chicago-style deep pan pizza, where their whole family loved getting a pie with pepperoni and black olives. There were a few other shops around the corner as well. Beyond the plaza was a park with rolling hills, trees, and a big grassy area where they would go play sometimes.

All of these things made it feel almost like Earth to the girls, helping them grow more comfortable with station life as the days went on.

"I'm going to go get some ice cream. Do you want some, Julia?" Lauren asked.

"Um, yes. Pumpkin!" Julia enthusiastically answered, rubbing her belly.

Lauren ran off to get the ice cream. In her absence, Julia tried to talk to the other girls, but they just weren't interested, so she opened her fanny pack and started looking at some of her rocks with her microscope.

This piqued Alyssa's interest. "What are you looking at?"

Julia replied, "Just some asteroid rocks my dad brought back."

"So your dad works out there?" Alyssa said.

"Yeah, he's gone a lot. But he brings back some cool things." She put a few pieces of the broken rock out on the table. "These are basalt—like volcanic rock from Earth. See?" Julia held the microscope over the rock and showed Alyssa.

Alyssa looked through Julia's microscope. "That's really cool."

Lauren carefully walked up with two scoops of ice cream on waffle cones. Julia set her microscope down and reached for her cone. Lauren handed it to her and looked at the microscope with horror. The last thing she wanted was for her sister to embarrass her in front of these new girls.

Her fear subsided when she realized Alyssa seemed genuinely interested, but just in case, Lauren said, "Why don't you put that back in your pack, Julia, so it doesn't get lost."

Julia nodded and put it back in with her free hand. After that, neither of the girls said a word and just dove right into their ice cream, periodically wiping their mouths.

About halfway through their cones, the mean girl started patting her pants and looking in her backpack. "I lost my phone." She searched around her, patting the ground. "Where is it?" The girl glared at Julia. "I bet you took it! Let me see what's in that stupid pack on your waist!"

Julia looked surprised and then scowled and spat back, "I didn't take your stupid phone. Leave me alone." As she turned away, she put her free hand on her pack.

The girl reached for Julia's fanny pack and got her hand on it. "Give me that!"

As the girl grabbed for Julia, Lauren's blood began to boil. She threw the remaining ice cream cone to the ground and stood up between the girl and Julia. "You don't TOUCH my sister!"

The girl ignored Lauren and reached around her. Years of sports had strengthened Lauren's wiry frame. Lauren seized the girl's shoulders with both hands and tossed her to the ground. Surprised, the girl just stared up blankly at Lauren. The other girls didn't offer much help to their mean-spirited friend.

"Come on, Julia, let's get out of here." Julia dropped the remainder of her cone on the ground next to the girl. Lauren grasped Julia's hand, and they ran off together toward the park.

The girls ran deep into the park, past the edge of the fields, beyond the rock ledges that formed the boundary of the park and into a grove of trees. Not many people ventured beyond the rock ledges, as the thicket of trees wasn't maintained and the undergrowth formed a significant barrier. This didn't stop the girls. They found some obscure paths cut by animals and crawled on their hands and knees through the brush, eventually finding the perfect hiding place nestled between two new understory trees.

“This is good, right here,” Lauren said. There wasn’t a soul around. When they stopped moving, they could hear the rustle of the trees and chatter of squirrels. Lauren heaved a deep sigh. “This almost feels like we’re back home.”

Julia nodded, “Yeah, I miss home. I miss it a lot.” Lauren agreed without saying a word, reclining back on a bed of leaves. They closed their eyes and listened to their surroundings. They could hear the clanking of metal on metal faintly below. They assumed there was some sort of factory below the surface, as they were nowhere near a residential grid.

After several minutes of daydreaming, the two heard a rustle of leaves that didn’t sound like an animal. They peered out of the branches that hid them to see what it was. Two men walked through the woods with slow robotic footsteps. They entered some dense undergrowth and disappeared.

The girls waited for them to come out, but minutes passed without any sign of them. Intrigued, the girls wanted to find out where they had gone. They walked right into the undergrowth, only to find a large rock wall on the other side of the bushes.

“Where’d they go?” Julia asked. Lauren didn’t have an answer and shrugged.

Julia studied the rock wall and reached out to touch it. As she reached, her hand went right through the rock. Frightened, she tumbled back, then cautiously crawled back to do it again.

“What—?” Lauren asked in shock as Julia’s hand disappeared into the wall.

To her horror, Julia stood up, stepped forward, and disappeared into the rocks. She heard a shout from behind the rocks, "Come on!"

Apprehensive, Lauren stepped gingerly into the wall.

Beyond the illusory boulder wall was a small rock enclave with a prominent metal door nestled between the rocks. The girls nervously approached the door. Julia reached out to touch it. Lauren did the same. It was solid steel with a red light above it and a nook that looked similar to the one in front of their apartment door. Suddenly, the door started to open.

Lauren grabbed Julia's hand and pulled her behind some rocks.

The door opened and two men walked out, continuing beyond the false rocks.

The sisters looked at each other and, without a word, leapt through the open door, just before it shut behind the men. They looked around to find themselves in a small corridor, standing on a steel grate.

They ran down the corridor as fast as they could. At the end, the corridor opened onto a ledge that looked down into an expansive warehouse. The girls peered over the railing and saw hundreds of people operating large equipment.

Conveyer belts carried huge rocks into a crushing hammer that pounded them with such explosive force they were smashed into rubble. The crushed rock was collected into giant bins at the other end of the conveyer belt. Huge lifts whizzed overhead, picking up the bins and carrying them through a doorway at the other side of the room.

The workers moved in the same robotic fashion that the two men outside the entrance did, almost like they were sleepwalking. The workers shuffled back and forth between machines, pushing buttons and moving things. They didn't notice the girls up on the ledge, doing their best to stay out of sight.

To the right of the ledge was a corridor that looked as if it spiraled down to the floor of the factory. Lauren motioned to Julia to move down the corridor, but when they got about halfway down, they heard footsteps. There wasn't anywhere to go, as the sides of the corridor only had a handrail. The girls froze and huddled against the rail like scared animals.

The footsteps got closer and closer until they saw a man their father's age come up the hallway. He approached, but ignored the girls entirely, plodding along almost as if he were in a trance. He slowly trudged up the hall, passed the girls, and kept going.

Their hearts pounding, they wondered what had just happened. The girls stood up and another man approached, oblivious to them. Lauren moved in front of the man and waved her arms. The man didn't notice her, so the girls continued down the spiral walkway to the factory floor.

Still cautious of being seen, the girls hugged closely to the wall, out of sight. On the floor, the machines sped by, barely clearing over the heads of the working men. There was a large bay door that had been out of sight to them when they were standing on the ledge, but on the floor they saw that it opened onto a space dock. Inside the bay doors were six giant bins filled with rocks. Enormous grapples clasped the rocks and transferred them to the conveyer belt.

As the rocks sped down the conveyer belt, they were pulverized by hammers and then collected in the bins at the far side of the warehouse. The girls stayed in the shadows close to the wall and snuck over to the bins.

Julia peered over the side of one of the bins to take a peek at the crushed rock. It contained the crystals she had discovered in the rocks from the asteroids. Amazingly, the crystals weren't smashed with the other rock fragments. They were completely intact. She was so fascinated, she didn't notice another bin hovering right above her. Lauren lunged for Julia, knocking her out of the way before the bin came smashing down beside them. They both fell to the ground. Julia looked up, dazed.

"Be careful!" Lauren said.

"I didn't even see it!" Julia stuttered, quivering from fright.

She stood up, dusted off, grabbed a few crystals, and put them in her fanny pack.

"Let's get out of here," Lauren said, and they made their way to the spiral corridor, careful not to be noticed.

Outside the entrance, the girls stood for a moment in a daze, wondering what had just happened.

Lauren pulled her phone out of her backpack. "5 missed calls," it blinked at her.

"Mom's going to kill us," she said, and they quickly headed toward home.

Chapter 5

Getting Really, Really Sick

Back at home, the girls snuck in, hoping their mom wouldn't notice how late it was. Unfortunately, their mom was waiting in the kitchen, talking on the phone. As soon as the girls came in, she looked up.

"Here they are," she said with relief to their dad on the other end of the phone. "I'll call you back." She put the phone down and then turned to the girls and demanded, "Where have you been? I tried calling you several times. I've been calling half the station trying to find out where you were! Your dad is out there looking for you."

Lauren stammered, "We were just in the park. Some girls were mean to us in the plaza, so we left and were playing in the park." Then she added, "I guess I had my phone in my backpack and didn't hear it."

"And you didn't think about calling me and telling me you were OK?" Their mom stood up from the table and walked stiffly to the counter. "Here." She shoved two plates of cold mac and cheese in front of them on the table. "Eat this and go straight to your room. You two are in big trouble."

The girls bowed their heads and sat down. The cold mac and cheese wasn't very appealing, but they ate it without complaint.

"How could you not think that I would be worried sick about you?" their mom asked. She was visibly shaken and trembled slightly when she spoke. The girls felt bad for scaring her and sat eating with their heads down, guilt ridden.

When they'd finished choking down the cold food, they went to their room and shut the door. Once in their room, their mood changed.

"What do you think that was?" Julia said excitedly as she took her new treasures out of her fanny pack and set them on her desk.

"We've got to tell somebody about that place," Lauren said.

"Who would we tell? Mom and Dad are so mad at us right now, we couldn't tell them. They'd see that place and ground us for life!" Julia said.

Julia swiveled around in her chair to look at her desk. "I've seen these crystals before." She held one up to her microscope and looked at it. It refracted the light as beautifully as the ones from the asteroid belt.

"They're the same ones that Dad brought back." She looked at it, and then pulled down the box where she kept the other crystals.

She opened the box with the crystals, but she didn't immediately recognize the crystals she had put in there. One was roughly the same size as they one she'd dropped into the box, but it was a much different color and had a strange glowing green growth all over it. The residue that had been on the perimeter of the box had all but disappeared.

"Lauren, come look," she said, as she reached in her drawer for some tongs.

Lauren walked over to look. Julia reached for the crystal with the tongs to pull it out of the box. As she touched it, a horrible stench permeated the room.

"What is that smell?" Lauren coughed. Julia coughed, too. "Put it back!" Lauren shouted. The two coughed uncontrollably.

"Turn the fan on," Julia shouted to Lauren as she put the crystal back in the box and sealed it.

Lauren reached for the fan switch and turned it on. Within seconds, the smell dissipated from the room.

"What was that?" Lauren demanded.

"I don't know," Julia responded innocently. "They were the same crystals we just found. They're the same as the ones Dad brings back."

"Well, keep them in there! I never want to smell that again! Ugh, I feel sick." Lauren rubbed her stomach as she spoke.

Their mom opened the door. "Lights out, you two," she said sternly and then started to close the door. She stopped and came into the room, where she wrapped her arms around Lauren's shoulders. "Listen, I was really worried about you two today. We're in a new place that I'm just getting to know, and I had no idea where you were. I was just worried."

She stroked Lauren's hair a couple of times and then walked over and gave Julia a hug, too.

"We know," Julia said. "And we're sorry."

The girls quickly got their jammies on and hopped into bed.

* * *

The next morning, Julia awoke with a sharp pain in her stomach. She swiftly jumped up and ran to the bathroom just in time to lose last night's mac and cheese in the toilet. Lauren was close behind.

"Watch out!" She was holding her mouth. Julia moved over and Lauren threw up, too.

"Unghh, I feel awful," Lauren said, wiping her mouth.

"Oh, my stomach." Julia heaved again just as their mother came in to wake them up.

"What . . . ?" Their mother saw the two girls crowding around the toilet. "What's wrong with you two?"

"I don't know," Lauren said, wiping her mouth again. "We just got up and felt sick."

"You must have caught something at school," she said, putting her hand on Julia's forehead.

The listless girls scarcely heard what she was saying. They both suddenly felt groggy and barely made it back to bed before falling back asleep.

What seemed like only a moment later the girls woke up to their mother's voice, telling them a doctor was here to figure out what was wrong with them.

Behind her, a man wearing the white doctor's coat came in and smiled at them.

"How are you two feeling?" he asked.

"Not so good," Lauren said, pulling herself to a seated position in her bed.

"My stomach hurts," Julia added.

"OK, let's see what we have here." The doctor took his medical device out of his pocket. It almost looked like Julia's microscope, but it had a handle grip allowing him to hold it steady with one hand and a larger screen above the handle. "Open your mouth and say ahh," he said to Lauren. He moved the apparatus up and looked through it at Lauren's mouth. Then he looked at her eyes.

"That looks OK. Now, can you give me your arm?" Lauren cautiously stretched out her arm. When he took hold, she flinched, pulling her arm back.

"It's not going to hurt. I just need to check your blood," he said.

He tapped a button on the device's screen and held it over Lauren's arm. Lauren peeked at the screen and saw her blood flowing through her veins. A circle appeared highlighting something floating in her blood. The doctor pulled back the device to read the screen.

"Hmm. Some unidentified microorganism. They probably picked it up at school."

Their mother looked worried. "Is that bad?"

"No, we see that a lot out here. Most of the time antibiotics will take care of it. They don't seem too sick. Their bodies are just fighting it off."

He turned to examine Julia.

"Same thing," he murmured after looking at her mouth and eyes and running the same test on her blood. "Let's start them on some antibiotics."

He pushed some buttons on his medical device.

"We'll also watch them for the next few days. There are some sensors in the room that will monitor their vitals," he waved his hand in the general direction where the sensors resided in the ceiling.

Their mother thanked him and left the room to show him out. A few minutes later, the doorbell rang and the girls heard a robotic voice request, "Please take the bottle."

Julia pushed halfway out of bed, suspecting that the voice was coming from one of the robotic medical delivery carts she'd seen in the halls. She wanted a closer look, but she was too fatigued to stand up.

Their mother came back into the room with a bottle of purple syrup and gave each girl a dose. Before she was out of the room, they were asleep again.

* * *

Deep in the girls' minds, they were struggling in an identical dream so vivid they felt as if they were living it. Together they journeyed to a foreign ship, floating in space. It loomed in front of them. Arms grew from its center, making it look like a giant spinning starfish.

In a flash, they found themselves in a hall on the breathing ship. Around them, the walls were alive. The humid air was heavy and thick and rocked rhythmically like waves in the ocean.

Julia reached to touch the spongy wall. It recoiled as she touched it. The two were transported down the hall, not knowing where they were going or how they were moving. The hall branched, and they were propelled down corridors, twisting and turning to the point that they had no idea where they had started.

People emerged from the shadows, slowly walking through halls, dazed like the people they'd seen in the factory on Cielo Prime. Intermingled with the people were ashen-faced hominoid creatures the size of a young adult. The two drew closer to one of them. In the shadows, they could scarcely make out the details of the creature. A cold chill overcame them as they neared it.

They floated deeper into the ship to the very center. An enormous mass pulsed in front of them. Flashes of colored light shot through the mass as it glowed. It was alive. Surrounding it were the crystals from the asteroid belt, shimmering with a multicolored glow when the blob flashed.

The closer they got to the mass, the more they could feel it tug the life out of them. Slowly, methodically, it felt like it was overtaking them.

Suddenly, Julia woke up in a cold sweat with her heart pounding, whimpering.

"Julia!" Lauren was at her bedside shaking her. "Wake up! Are you OK?"

Julia opened her eyes, blinking the sweat off her eyelashes.

"Lauren? You're OK? I thought . . ." Julia stammered.

"It was a dream, Julia, you had a bad dream. I did, too." Lauren reassured her.

"What was yours about?" Julia asked.

"It was awful. We were on some living, breathing ship."

Lauren felt a tremor go through her sister, then Julia said, "That's where I was in my dream . . . that thing, that pulsing thing, it felt like it could look right into me, like it was cutting something out of me. It was horrible. Then, all of a sudden we were ripped away from it and I woke up."

They both sat still for a little while until the door opened and their mom appeared, blinking and with sleep-mussed hair.

"Are you two OK? I heard a scream."

"Yes, I just had a bad dream," Julia answered quickly. She met Lauren's eyes, and the girls silently affirmed to each other that they would keep the dream a secret.

Their mom walked into the room and put her hand on Julia's head. "You're burning up. Here, let me take some of the covers off. Do you feel OK?"

"Yes, just a little hot, but feeling better." Julia said.

"I'm going to be awake for a while to make sure you're OK, so if you need anything, let me know. Try to get some sleep." Their mom walked out of the room, briefly stopping at the doorway and looking back at them, then closely the door softly behind her.

"Let's just keep that between us," Lauren said.

"I'll try, and I never want to see that again." Julia said. She turned over and closed her eyes.

Chapter 6

Strange Things Are Starting to Happen

The girls finally felt well enough to go back to school. It had been a week since they got sick, and they still felt a little queasy. Their father had to go back out to the asteroid belt for a few days, came home again, and then had to go back out for some emergency. However, their mother was there to help them fully recover.

The first day back at school was uneventful. They hadn't missed enough days to get too far behind. By the end of the day, they felt better, and when they met their mother and Maia and Evan after school, their mother surprised them.

"How about we go get some ice cream?" she asked.

The girls perked up a little bit. "Yeah that sounds good," Lauren said.

The five of them headed up the stairs and out to the plaza. At the plaza, the mean girl and her crew were sitting in the same place Lauren and Julia had seen them last time. The mean girl glared at Lauren when her mother wasn't looking, but Lauren didn't care today.

Lauren and Julia got their favorite pumpkin ice cream and sat at a table, eating their cones while their mom watched Maia and Evan try to eat ice cream and play on the playground at the same time. Alyssa approached their table.

"Hi, Lauren, I missed you at school and tennis," she said.

"I haven't been feeling well for about a week," Lauren responded. "Julia and I got a really nasty stomach bug."

Alyssa continued, “Hey, I wanted to apologize for Kara being so mean before. She has issues.”

“Seems like it,” Lauren replied.

“You really surprised her! Nobody treats her like that. I think she got what she deserved.” Alyssa smiled as she spoke.

“Yeah. And nobody treats my sister like that,” Lauren confirmed.

“Well, I’ll be at tennis tomorrow. See you then!” Alyssa walked off.

“What was she talking about?” their mother asked. She had been close enough to hear the conversation.

“Nothing. We took care of it,” Lauren said.

“Hey, what’s that?” Julia said, tugging at Lauren’s shoulder with one hand and pointing with her ice cream cone in the other. “I haven’t seen one of those things before.”

Their mom looked toward where Julia was pointing. “What? I don’t see anything.”

“Right there, Mom. It looks like a raccoon or something,” Lauren added.

Lauren and Julia could clearly see a creature perched behind the wall where Alyssa and the other girls were sitting. It almost looked like a raccoon, but it was larger and its hands were more like a monkey’s hands.

As they were watching, it stood up on its hind legs and looked over the wall. A second creature came up beside it and seemed to whisper something in the first one’s ear. It disappeared behind the wall again.

“Mom, can’t you see it? There were two of them there just now,” Julia probed her mother.

"Julia, I don't know what you're talking about. I don't see anything," her mom insisted.

Julia turned to Evan and Maia, who had run up sweating from the playground. "Can you guys see it?" They ignored her, eating their ice cream.

The mean girl, Kara, rummaged through her backpack and then left it sitting on the ledge. One of the creatures ducked behind the wall and reappeared next to Kara. The girls in the group didn't notice the creature as it put its hands right inside her backpack.

Lauren got up and ran over to the girls. "Look!" She pointed at the creature. "Julia didn't take your phone. It was that thing!"

The girls turned to look where Lauren was pointing with blank looks on their faces.

"What are you talking about?" Alyssa asked Lauren. "There's nothing there."

As she spoke, the creature looked directly at Lauren and Lauren looked at it. Locked in a stare, the creature didn't know what to do. It blinked, then grabbed something out of Kara's backpack and ran off.

"There it goes!" Lauren shouted. "And it took something from your backpack."

Kara grabbed her backpack and looked. "You! You took my wallet? How did you do that? Give it back!"

Alyssa held Kara back. "Kara, she didn't take anything. She's been over there the whole time."

Just then, Lauren's mother came over and grabbed her by the shoulders. "I'm sorry, girls, she's still not feeling well. Lauren, come on." She dragged her daughter away as Lauren stared in disbelief.

"Lauren, what's wrong with you? There's nothing there." Her mother put her hand on Lauren's forehead.

Lauren grabbed her hand and flung it down. "Nothing's wrong with me! Julia saw it, too!"

"Maybe we better go back home and take a break. I don't think you two are better yet." Their mother led them back to the stairs to go down to the train.

Back at home, Lauren and Julia flung their backpacks onto the rack and then retreated to their room with the door closed.

"You saw those things, didn't you? I'm not crazy, right?" Lauren asked.

"I did! I don't know why everyone looked at us like we were weird," Julia said.

"Hmm. Maybe they're right. Maybe it's just because we were sick," Lauren mused.

Julia turned her attention to her experiments. She wondered what the substance was on the crystals that had made them so nauseous. She pulled the box out of the drawer and set it on her desk.

"Don't open that thing again!" Lauren said insistently.

"I know," Julia said, and immediately turned on a vent above her desk and opened the container. The substance was still on the crystal. She positioned her microscope above the crystal, being careful not to touch it, as that was what had triggered the horrible smell last time.

Under the microscope, she could see the strange oozing material encasing the crystal. It had started to form a crust, but was still wet in some parts. Strangely, the microorganisms were still moving around, but they looked different. They were larger than last time, and a different color.

Looking closer, she saw that the organisms were eating the crystals and depositing the oozing material out the other end. There was more of the ooze now and much less of the crystal.

She carefully closed the lid of the box and put it back in her shelf, wondering what the substances could possibly be.

* * *

The next day, the girls got up and got ready to go to school. They had agreed not to say anything about the raccoon-like creatures again except to each other until they figured out what was going on. In fact, they tried not to think about the creatures at all. Over the next few days, they simply went to school, then to any after-school activities, and straight home.

After several days of this schedule, they began to think maybe they had just been seeing things because they hadn't seen the creatures again.

That Friday, the family decided to go to the plaza after school. Lauren and Julia had all but forgotten the creatures. Then, coming up the stairs from the school, they were talking with each other, their mother, and their brother and sister when one of the creatures darted across the path right in front of the family.

Lauren and Julia stopped with wide eyes and a gasp. Lauren's arms flew open as she stopped the family suddenly. The girls looked at each other, but didn't say anything.

Their mother stopped. "What's wrong, girls?"

"Nothing, nothing," said Lauren. "I forgot something at school. I'll get it Monday."

They kept walking. Julia looked to see if she could see where the creature had gone, but it was nowhere in sight. Lauren simply looked ahead, pretending not to have noticed it.

They walked to the courtyard and sat down. Their mother asked, "What kind of pizza do you want?"

"Pepperoni and black olives!" Julia shouted.

"OK," their mother said. "Maia, you come with me. You three stay here and wait for your father."

A few moments later, they saw their dad coming up the stairs to join them. One of the creatures was walking right beside him. He didn't notice it in the slightest. Lauren looked at Evan to see if he noticed anything strange. He was just looking at his dad with a grin.

"Evan. Do you see anything next to Dad?" she asked.

"Oh, sure. I see something walking next to him," he said, squinting to get a better look.

"You see it?" Julia asked elatedly.

He put his fingers up next to his eyes and started pinching them together in front of his face. "There, got it. I squished it."

Immediately recognizing he was making fun of them, Lauren blushed red. Angrily, she smacked him on the back of the head.

"Hey! That hurt," he said. "You two are crazy! Totally insane. There's nothing there." He ran to greet their dad.

As Evan charged out toward his dad, the creature was startled and lay down on the ground in front of him. Evan didn't notice the creature at all and tripped over it, falling to the ground.

"Whoa. Are you OK?" his dad asked, picking him up. Evan stood up, brushing off his pants. He looked around to see if anybody was watching. He saw his sisters smirking. He shot them a glare, then walked back to the table with their dad.

"Did you all have a good day at school?" their dad asked as he sat down.

"Yes, fine," was all Lauren said. Their dad had grown accustomed to these short answers and decided not to pursue it.

A short while later, their mother and Maia came back with pizza. Everybody took a couple pieces and the platter was empty in seconds.

After dinner, out of the corner of her eye, Lauren spotted another one of the creatures lurking around Alyssa and her friends. The girls didn't notice the creature and, again, it was rummaging through their bags.

Lauren kneed Julia under the table. "Ow!" Julia blurted out and rubbed her leg.

"What's wrong?" their mother asked. Lauren caught Julia's attention and nodded in the direction of the creature.

Julia said, "I just banged my leg."

Julia spotted the creature and hatched a plan in her head. Rather than finishing her whole pieces of pizza, she saved the crusts in a napkin in her lap. She motioned to Lauren to do the same.

Their mom noticed they were acting shifty. "You girls are acting weird. Are you sure you're feeling OK?"

"We're fine, Mom. It's Evan that has problems," Julia said, trying to divert the attention away from the two of them.

"What? You two just asked me . . ." Julia kicked Evan under the table before he could finish. "Ow!" he yelped.

Their dad cut him off. "I've got to get home to do some work. Are we ready to go?"

Lauren quickly answered, "No, no, we're going to stay here for a little while." She grabbed Julia's arm.

"OK, don't stay too late," their mother said. "Remember what happened last time? Make sure you keep your phone on this time." She narrowed her eyes at them for emphasis.

After the rest of their family went down the stairs, Lauren turned to Julia and whispered, "We have to find out where those things are coming from." Julia nodded.

As Lauren and Julia walked toward Alyssa, Lauren asked, "What are we going to call those things?"

Julia thought for second. "How about rackey? Because it looks like a raccoon and a monkey!"

Lauren frowned. "No, that sounds silly. How about monkoon?"

"That's a good name," Julia said, smiling.

Chapter 7

A New Species

"Hi, are you feeling better?" Alyssa asked Lauren.

"Yeah, much better," Lauren said, a little distracted. She was looking past Alyssa at her bag.

"Are you sure you're better?" Alyssa asked, looking at Lauren, who still hadn't made eye contact with her.

"Sure. Much better," Lauren said unconvincingly.

Julia was even less cordial. Her full attention was centered on the creatures. She pulled a piece of pizza crust out of a napkin and tossed it close to one of the creatures. It quickly picked up the crust, cupped it in its hands, and nibbled on it.

She threw the next one closer and the creature ventured nearer to her. One more piece and the creature was almost eating out of her hand.

Alyssa saw Julia tossing crust out of the corner of her eye. It appeared odd to her that there wasn't a squirrel or other animal anywhere in sight.

"Julia, what are you throwing that to?" Alyssa asked her.

Julia glanced at her uneasily, "Oh, nothing, I thought some animal might eat it later. I mean, I wasn't eating it, so maybe something else will."

Alyssa clearly wasn't buying Julia's argument, but she didn't ask anything else.

Lauren watched as the creature ate the crust and then turned and ran off into the park. She looked distracted, so Alyssa shook her arm.

“Lauren? What are you looking at?”

“Oh, nothing,” Lauren responded.

Lauren and Julia were intently focused on the creatures that had plagued them for the past week. They could still see the one that was taking food running off into the park. They started to run after it.

“Wait!” Alyssa shouted. “Where are you going?”

The girls turned, and Lauren shouted back, “To the park! We’re just looking for something.”

Alyssa shook her head and went back to talking with her other friends.

The sisters ran as fast as they could, trying to stay with the creature. They thought they lost it a few times as it darted in and out of the trees, but it would reappear almost as if it invited the chase. The girls stopped to catch their breath.

“I can’t believe they run that fast,” Lauren gasped as she leaned over, placing her hands on her knees.

Julia didn’t say a word, just nodded in the direction of the creature and started running again. The creature ran past the park and into the woods. They ran after it, following its tail. Once in the woods, they came upon the grove with the secret entrance where they had been earlier.

The creature continued beyond the entrance to the backside of the rocks and then vanished.

“Where did it go?” asked Julia.

"I don't know. I thought I saw it go into these bushes, but now it's gone," Lauren said.

"It has to be around here somewhere." Julia jumped down on all fours and started patting the ground while Lauren peered behind some bushes.

"Here. I think this is it!" Lauren found a hole in the ground that was masked by the bushes. The hole was barely large enough for a small kid to climb in, but not big enough for an adult.

"I'm not going in there," Julia said, staring at the hole doubtfully.

"Fine! I'll go first. Do you have a flashlight in that fanny pack?" Lauren asked, looking down at it.

Julia smirked. "I thought you made fun of my fanny pack, and NOW you want something out of it?"

"Just give it to me," Lauren snarled.

Julia rummaged through her fanny pack and pulled out a flashlight. "Here you go."

Lauren snatched it from her hands. "You're welcome," Julia muttered under her breath.

Lauren bit down on the flashlight as she held it in her teeth, then got down and crawled cautiously into the hole. Julia hesitantly followed, wondering what might await them in the tunnel.

After a few minutes of crawling behind Lauren and being unable to see anything, Julia asked, "Are you sure we can find our way out?"

"I hope . . .Whoa!" Lauren called back, but was interrupted as she stumbled into a large chamber.

Julia tumbled after her. They rolled to a stop on hard metal unlike the earthen tunnel they had just climbed through. The flashlight slipped out of Lauren's grip and bounced on the floor, clanging as it rolled to a stop and shined directly back in their eyes.

"Ah, get the flashlight," Julia shrieked as she covered her eyes. "That thing is bright."

Lauren reached for the flashlight and waved it around. A myriad of lost and stolen items littered the room—shiny objects, electronics, jewelry—no doubt collected over several years. The floor was warm to the touch, with large metal plates and rivets aligned in square patterns.

Julia immediately began rummaging through the objects. Lauren was a little more cautious, preferring to scope the situation out before diving into the loot.

"Julia, where are the creatures? Wouldn't you think they'd be here?" she asked.

"I dunno. We probably scared them off. What does it matter? They look harmless enough," Julia muttered, and she went back to looking at the treasure. She found a small, shiny piece of metal she couldn't identify, so she pulled out her microscope to get a better look.

Lauren scanned the back wall with the flashlight. A lone tunnel led out of the room. From the tunnel, she saw eyes peering back at her.

"Julia, look," she said quietly as she pointed to the tunnel.

Julia looked up, squinting at the tunnel and setting her microscope down for a moment. Lauren moved forward, flashing the light deeper into the tunnel.

One of the creatures came into view. The creature stared at the girls and the girls stared back, not knowing what to do. The standoff ended when it left the tunnel and slowly approached Lauren.

Julia moved forward, pulled out some pizza crust, and offered it to the creature. In return, the creature simply sniffed the crust and then rolled over on its back.

The girls were taken aback, not knowing what to do. Then Lauren reached down to scratch the creature's belly. The creature immediately responded by licking her hand. Tension broken, the girls laughed.

With the girls' attention diverted, Julia didn't notice another creature that came out of the darkness, fixedly looking at her microscope. In a flash, the creature grabbed her microscope and darted into the tunnel, alerting Julia with its movement.

"Hey! It took my microscope!" she gasped as she pursued the animal.

"Wait!" Lauren yelled and jumped after her in the tunnel. The two didn't have time to wonder where the tunnel led. After several feet, the tunnel curved to the left. At the bend, there was a dim light shining. The creature leapt toward the light.

Lauren scooted into the tunnel, trying to catch up to Julia, but she was already way ahead. As the tunnel curved, there was a small opening in the wall. When Lauren caught up to Julia, she was staring out of the opening. On the other side of the hole was a steel girder the creatures used as a walkway. Down below, Lauren saw the floor of the secret factory where they had just been a few weeks before.

The creature sat in the middle of the girder fondling the microscope. Julia tried to coax the creature close to her, but it ignored her gestures. She started sniffling, worried she had lost her most prized possession.

Lauren looked out the opening and saw the men down below walking around like zombies just as they did the other day. This opening breached the ceiling far above the floor, overlooking the massive processing operation. It was well concealed by the girder, so the people had no idea it was there.

Lauren looked down at the workers. Some of them didn't look quite right—they were smaller than the other people, about half their size. Immediately she recognized the hominoids from her dream. It sent shudders down her spine. At closer look, she realized they were telling the zombie men what to do. She looked back at Julia to see if she saw the hominoid people, but she didn't. She hadn't taken her gaze off her microscope.

There were only a few of the hominoids, and they were preoccupied with directing the workers, so maybe that's why they didn't notice the girls before when they were on the floor. She tried to look more closely, but couldn't make out any details. She couldn't think about it now, as she had to get Julia's microscope back.

"Hold on," Lauren said as she cautiously climbed through the hole and out onto the steel girder.

"Lauren, be careful!" Julia called out to her.

"It's OK, I've done this a thousand times before." She confidently walked along the girder with her arms straight out to her side to help keep her balance, her body remembering the years of balance beam practice in gymnastics. As she approached the creature, it dropped the microscope on the girder and ran off.

The creatures seemed to leave behind them small pebbles and twigs that had clung to their fur in the forest. Some of that debris was on the girder, and Lauren carefully maneuvered around it. She got to the microscope, carefully reached down to pick it up, and put it in her pocket.

As Lauren turned around, she lost her footing as she stepped on some loose pebbles. Julia called out to her sister. Lauren bobbled her arms and knocked loose a pile of pebbles that tumbled far below to the ground. Seeing where they were going to land, she picked up the pace to get back to the opening. The pebbles landed directly on one of the short hominoids down on the floor.

It looked up just as Lauren reached the opening. Heart pounding, Lauren climbed in and looked back down at the floor. The hominoid was looking up at the girder and another was pointing up to where the rocks came from.

The girls peeped out of the opening when one of the human-like creatures pointed right in their direction. Time stopped. The girls froze. They could see directly into the hominoid's eyes. Julia shrieked as she and Lauren suddenly recognized the creature from their dream. Both Lauren and Julia froze.

They could see the hominoid point toward them. Its snarled, wrinkled face was an ash gray color, its eyes yellowish gold with slits that looked reptilian. Canine teeth protruded over its bottom lip, and as it spoke, spittle blanketed anyone in its vicinity. Just then, the monkoon that had stolen Julia's microscope bounded back into the opening. The hominoid looked at it, then turned and started walking toward the stairs.

"We have to get out of here," Lauren said. "I don't think they saw us, but we still need to get out of here."

Without hesitation the girls crawled as fast as they could back to the chamber. The monkoon stared up at them innocently, but the girls didn't notice. They scurried as quickly as they could to the other side and into the tunnel. Racing through it, they reached the end where the bushes were. Once there, they stopped and waited to see if the hominoid creatures would come out.

Chapter 8

Escaping from Aliens

Just as they feared, a couple of the creatures appeared at the entrance to the cave and started looking around.

One of the creatures approached the clearing with his hands on his hips, glaring to see if he could spot anything. His clothing hid most of his body, but he appeared to be about Lauren's height, though stockier. His gaze seemed to look straight through the bushes. Just as he was about to look the girls' way, one of the monkoons ran out in front of him and off into the woods.

One of the ash-faced hominoids waved his arms, picked up a rock, and threw it toward the monkoon, missing it, but scaring it enough for it to run off further. He followed the monkoon toward the woods. Just then, the girls noticed they had lost track of the other hominoid. Curious, Julia poked her head slightly out of the hole, trying to catch a glimpse of where he went. Lauren sat up on her haunches to peek, too.

Suddenly, the missing hominoid jumped in front of the two sisters. As quickly as he appeared, he grabbed Julia by the arm. She shrieked and squirmed to get away from him.

The other hominoid rushed over to help. Startled, Lauren fell back and gasped for air. She felt her lungs deflate like a popped balloon. Her eyes contracted as if she were looking through a tunnel. The hominoid was pulling and tugging at Julia. She had to do something.

A rush of adrenaline overtook Lauren. With all her strength she pulled back her legs and donkey kicked the hominoid in the face.

This time it was his turn to shriek. He pulled back, letting Julia go to clutch his own face as he reeled in pain. Lauren's blow had hurt.

They knew they didn't have much time. Quickly, they turned and crawled back down the tunnel. They could hear the hominoids talking to each other, but they couldn't understand what they said. They just knew the creatures were coming after them.

As soon as they got to the small treasure-filled cavern, they looked around to see if they could find anything to slow the hominoids down. Lauren started grabbing anything she could get her hands on and stuffing it into the tunnel.

She grabbed a small stick and poked at the roof of the tunnel. "Here, help me with this," she said as she grabbed another stick, giving it to Julia.

Julia whacked at the tunnel. Big chunks of rock and dirt fell as the tunnel partially collapsed. The girls wheeled around to find the monkoon simply staring at them, blinking. The girls jumped to the tunnel at the other side of the cavern, moving as fast as they could.

"Hurry, hurry," Lauren said, stuffing Julia into the tunnel. Julia rushed, bumping her head as tried pushed forward into the tunnel.

She stopped to rub her head.

"No, don't stop, keep going," Lauren forced her on.

Remembering their predicament, Julia crawled as fast as she could. Unexpectedly, a monkoon jolted by both of them and stopped further in the tunnel, looking at them.

As they crawled on, the creature kept slightly in front of them, keeping pace with the girls. "I think he wants us to follow him," Lauren said.

"Fine with me. He's the only one of us that knows the way," Julia said, crawling after the creature.

They passed the juncture to the factory ceiling and kept going as the tunnel twisted and turned in the darkness. There were several offshoots that the creature navigated through, making sure the girls were right behind him. The girls could hear the creature shuffling ahead of them, but not much else. Julia paused for a second and Lauren bumped into her.

"Ow. Why'd you stop? We need to keep going," Lauren insisted.

"Hold on." Julia reached into her fanny pack and pulled out the flashlight.

"Not yet. Let's get a little further and then you can turn it on," Lauren said.

They continued for another several minutes and the creature stopped. It started chattering frantically. Julia turned on her flashlight to look around. The girls could see a small opening that went down into the station.

"Shh. What's that sound?" Lauren asked. Julia paused and listened intently.

They could hear a slight whooshing sound in the distance out of the opening, which seemed to be getting louder. A few seconds later, a full blast of air hit them as a train sped by. The two could see the train below and realized the opening was a vent to one of the train tunnels.

"Hurry, when the train goes by, let's jump down there," Lauren commanded. The train passed. "OK, now."

Lauren jumped into the tunnel with cat-like precision, landing firmly on her feet. She looked up to see her sister shove herself out of the opening, hanging frantically with her legs dangling.

"Julia, just let go. It's not that far," Lauren shouted up to her.

"No, I'm scared! I don't want to," Julia said as she wildly kicked her legs. Finally, her grip gave and she plopped on the floor of the tunnel.

"Come on," Lauren said as she helped Julia up.

The walls were solid steel and the tunnel almost pitch-black. Far up ahead they could see a light where the train disappeared. They both started running toward it, fleeing the hominoid creature they were sure wasn't too far behind.

"What's that?" Julia asked as she felt a cool breeze pick up. The breeze rapidly grew from slow to a full-blown gust.

"Hurry, jump up here against the wall," Lauren said anxiously as she heaved herself up onto a ledge. She offered Julia a hand to pull her up.

As soon as they both got up, the next train sped by at full speed. The blast of air wisped their hair about their faces and tore at their clothing. It was gone in seconds.

"Come on, let's get out of here before the next train comes," Lauren shouted to Julia, jumping down between the rails.

The two ran as fast as they could up the rail line, eventually coming to their familiar station, close to their local plaza and school.

A post blocked them from view of the other passengers waiting to get on the train. They hopped up out of the rail tunnel and into the station. Looking around the post, they nonchalantly strutted out, pretending nothing had happened.

An older lady caught a glimpse of the two easing away from behind the post. She hobbled up to them, "You two, you know how dangerous it is over there? You could fall on those rail lines and get hit by the train. If I knew your mother, I'd tell her all about this," she said, wagging her finger.

Lauren shyly looked at the older lady, not knowing what to say. Julia hid behind her sister, hoping not to be noticed.

"I'm sorry, we didn't realize how dangerous it was," Lauren said, looking down at the floor.

The old lady looked the two sisters up and down. Unlike her usually composed appearance, Lauren looked more like a street urchin. Her hair wrapped wildly around her head and she had dirt and grease smudges all over her face and clothes. Julia wasn't as dirty, but not by much.

The old lady shuffled off to wait for her train. When the next train pulled into the station, the two tousled girls boarded it, sitting down next to each other. They were safe for now. They sat shuddering in disbelief.

"What are we going to do?" Julia stared blankly at the other side of the train.

"I have no idea," Lauren said, distraught as well. "We need to tell someone, but we're the only ones that can see them. Nobody will believe us."

"You know, those people-like things . . . they could see the little creatures, too, so we're not the only ones that can see them," Julia mused.

"You're right." Lauren thought about when the hominoid threw a rock at the monkoon. "Why can't anybody else see them?"

Things had happened so quickly, the girls hadn't had time to stop and think about the whole situation.

"When did we start seeing all these things?" Lauren asked, staring at one of the other passengers at the back of the train, a lady who was reading something on her phone and didn't notice the girls.

Julia thought for a minute and then said, "Well, it was right after we got sick."

Lauren looked puzzled. "That's right, but why would that have made a difference? Didn't the doctor say it was just some strange organism?"

Julia seemed perplexed.

"What is it?" Lauren asked her.

"I didn't tell you this before because I didn't think you cared, but those crystals had some strange organisms on them," Julia said.

"You mean the crystals in those rocks that Dad brought back from the asteroid belt?" Lauren asked.

"Yes, and they're the same crystals that were in that factory." She pointed back to where they came from. "The rock had some organism on it that the computer couldn't identify, just like the doctor couldn't tell us what the microorganism was that made us sick."

"Why didn't you tell me before?" Lauren questioned.

"I didn't think about it. When I put them in the container, the crystals turned a strange color and got that funky stuff all over them." She paused. "Then, when I opened that container and touched them, it had that horrible smell . . ." She trailed off in thought.

"Do you think that oozing stuff has something to do with this?" Lauren asked.

"I don't know. We got so sick I kind of forgot about it. I guess it could have made us sick, some bad reaction between the two," Julia thought out loud.

"Well, we need to find out. If that was the key, then it will help other people see these things and they won't think we're crazy," Lauren said

"OK, so we'll get the ooze and expose Mom and Dad to it so they can see," Julia suggested.

"Yes, that's what we have to do. I sure hope it works . . ."

The rest of the way home, they didn't say a word to each other. They both just sat expressionlessly on the train with this weight on their shoulders.

Part II: The Treatment

Chapter 9

A Spoiled Plan

"Are you ready?" Lauren looked at Julia as they readied themselves to enter the apartment, both knowing what had to be done.

"Yes. I'm ready," Julia said, tucking her curly hair behind her ears and wiping her face on her shirt sleeves.

Lauren waved her hand beside the door. It opened before them. With the fervor of soldiers, the two marched into their room to retrieve the strange substance that allowed them to see these new, strange creatures.

Julia went directly to her shelf and pulled down the box where she'd left the crystals. Both girls stood over the container in anticipation. Julia pried the lid open and discarded it on her desk. To their amazement, the container was completely empty—wiped clean!

Julia's jaw dropped.

Lauren's eyes widened.

Neither could speak as they stared at the empty container.

Julia opened another container —not there! Then another—empty! She opened all the containers on her desk but didn't find the rocks in any of them.

"No!" Julia shrieked as she opened the last container.

Terrified, Lauren asked, "Where could it be?"

Julia didn't answer, starting in dismay at all the empty containers.

In desperation, Lauren overturned both of their chairs and pulled the covers off their beds, looking anywhere she could, but it was no use. The strange ooze that could free them from their burden was nowhere. A few moments later, the girls stopped and sat in the middle of the room.

Their mother came to investigate, having heard the noise.

“What in the world?” She stared at the mess. Almost everything was scattered about the room. Oblivious to their mother, the girls sat unresponsive.

She turned to reprimand the girls and then gasped, taking a step back. The pair looked like two she-devils smudged with dirt head to toe.

Julia’s usually crazy hair was wilder than ever.

Lauren’s normally impeccable hair whirled around her head in all directions.

The two younger siblings, Evan and Maia, ran to their mother’s side, peering into the girls’ room with eyes opened wide.

“What in the world?” Evan repeated.

Maia ran past their mother to join in. She opened a drawer, giggling, and started pulling clothes out, throwing them in the air. Then she tousled her hair with both hands.

“No, no, no,” their mom said. “Maia, go back to your room. Evan, you go with her.”

Evan turned and slowly walked toward the door, looking back with each step. He didn’t want to miss any of it. He stopped just outside the door and peeked back in.

“Go,” their mom said, waving Evan back.

Maia hopped off the bed, running to join Evan.

Their mother snapped her fingers in front of their faces. "Girls, what's going on here?"

Lauren spoke first. "We're looking for one of Julia's experiments." She looked up at her mother, about to cry. "Did you take it?"

"No," their mother said. "Why would I do that?"

"I don't see how it could have disappeared," Julia murmured.

"Why is it so important? What is wrong with you two? You've been acting really weird lately."

Lauren ignored her mother, saying, "We just need it! Did anyone come in here?"

"No, we just got back 10 minutes before you did," their mother said, frowning. "Clean this up. Now! And go take a shower or something!"

Julia ran across the room and grabbed her mother in a big hug.

"What is that for?" Their mother looked perplexed.

"Nothing, nothing. Just glad to see you." Julia let go of her mother and went back to her bed.

Their mother just sighed, shook her head, and then turned and left the room.

As soon as she was gone, Julia said, "Well, SOMEBODY was in here,"

"Or something."

"Exactly," Julia agreed. "But there's no way to prove it or figure it out because nobody can see them except us."

"We have to get that ooze and fast, so other people can see these things. It seems to be some sort of treatment . . ." Lauren started picking up some of the mess they had made. Julia started to help.

"So, what exactly was this stuff on the crystals?" Lauren asked as she put her bedspread back on her bed.

"That's just it, I don't remember. It was something I did on Earth for extra credit in science. I didn't spend a lot of time on it . . .," Julia mused.

She continued, "Let me think . . . I think it was the genetic modification experiments. I know I was trying to get something to glow neon green . . ." Julia put her finger to her mouth, staring at the ceiling in thought. "If I remember, I had inserted some protein from some jellyfish into some simple single-celled organisms . . ."

"I have no idea what you're talking about," Lauren cut her off. "Did you keep a log of what you were doing? Maybe we could recreate the experiment?"

"We could try. Hold on, let me look." Julia went to her desk and the screen flashed on.

She spoke to the screen, "Show my blog."

The screen flashed Julia's personal blog on the screen, with a picture of Lauren and Julia hiking at a local state park back in Texas as the homepage. There were entries for "What's going on in my life? Experiments. Family. Friends."

Julia looked back at Lauren smiling, "Remember that?"

"Yes, that place was a lot of fun."

Julia turned and tapped on the entry for "Experiments."

The screen showed a tiled view of active experiments Julia was working on with the name of the experiment and a small graph detailing what she was tracking.

She scrolled down the list and clicked on the last tile titled "Archive."

The screen showed another tiled view of what looked like cardboard boxes stacked on top of each other with labels on the front. Each label had a number and a short description of what was in the box. She scrolled down the stack and tapped on Box 12.

The screen flashed back, “Entry corrupted.”

“That’s strange,” Julia tapped on another bin entry.

The same result. “Entry corrupted.”

She tapped on another entry that cataloged her rock collection.

Lauren said, “Is any of it there?”

“No, none of it! All my experiments are gone!”

Lauren asked, “What possibly could have happened to it? Nobody can write to your blog can they?”

“I don’t think so, but I have no idea. They were just on the station system. I moved them over there when we got here. I didn’t think they were important,” Julia said, staring at the screen.

“You didn’t protect them?” Lauren asked astounded.

“It was just my blog! It wasn’t important. First that treatment stuff is gone and now this? What is going on here? Who would want to do this?” Julia wondered aloud.

“I don’t know, but somebody sure doesn’t like what we’re doing,” Lauren answered. “Hold on, scoot over, this is my domain now. Let me dig around a little bit.”

Lauren motioned in front of the computer to take control of it, then whipped her hands back and forth like she was conducting an orchestra.

“What are you doing?” asked Julia.

“I’m going to find out who did this,” Lauren said as she continued her cryptic motions. The screen flashed picture after picture too fast for Julia to keep up with.

After a few more gestures, Lauren clapped and stopped. “This is the strangest thing. I can’t figure this out. The blog entries are just gone . . .” She peered at the screen, furrowing her brow, “Hmm . . . wait . . . there! Gotcha!”

“What? What is it?” Julia asked.

“There! See that?” Lauren pointed to the screen.

“No, what is it? It just looks like numbers to me,” Julia said, unimpressed.

“That, Julia, is evidence someone or something was poking around here. It looks like it left a tracer here to alert them when you add logs,” Lauren said triumphantly.

“What? So anything I do, they’re going to find out about it?” Julia asked, shocked.

Lauren smiled an impish smile. “They have no idea who they’re dealing with.”

“What are you going to do?” Julia was out of her league with computers, just as Lauren was with biological experiments.

“I’m going to put a Trojan horse here that will get picked up by their tracer, then it will tell us exactly who they are,” Lauren declared.

“Lauren, this is getting scary. I don’t like this,” Julia said, feeling even more alarmed than she already had. “We need to tell somebody.”

“Who would we tell? Nobody would believe us, and they’d put us in the loony bin because they’d think we were crazy! We need that treatment, fast!” Lauren glared at the computer. “Is there anywhere else you kept your entries? Or did anyone else help you?"

"Well, I guess the teacher would have kept my notes and report," Julia said. "I could try and get in touch with her."

"OK. Give me a minute and then we'll send the message," Lauren walked over to her desk and rummaged through her drawer. She pulled out a pair of strange glasses that had full blinders around the rims, and then sat down at her desk.

After a minute, Lauren started waving her hands around. Julia simply watched and waited.

"There, done," Lauren said after a few minutes more, setting her glasses down.

"What did you do?" Julia questioned.

"So, I put a Trojan horse on your blog that will trace who's trying to access these files. Looks like their tracer picked it up as soon as I changed it. Then I changed the system to make the tracer think it was monitoring your activities when it's really monitoring somebody else's blog."

"Who is it monitoring?" Julia blinked at her sister.

Lauren smiled "A fake person named Ima Hogg."

Julia laughed, remembering the name from Texas history as one of a former governor's daughters.

"Well, now, contact your teacher and start trying to recreate that treatment from memory. This redirect won't fool them forever and we need to move fast," Lauren commanded.

Julia was already getting set up to record a message to her teacher. She started speaking to the screen, "Mrs. Montgomery, I seem to have lost my experiment logs from when I was in your class last year. Can you find my report on genetic modification I did a few months back? If you have any of my notes, please send them to me as soon as possible. It's important." She was about to sign off the message, but then added, "Oh, also please encrypt this message. I don't want anyone else reading it!" She smiled at the camera and touched the screen to send the message.

"OK, we'll just have to wait now." Lauren looked at Julia straight lipped. "Do you think you could try to make it again from memory?"

"It's going to be really hard. I don't even have the right equipment or the DNA I need."

"Hold on." Julia turned to her screen and said, "Find gel electrophoresis chambers for sale on the station."

After a second, the system flashed back with an intricate three-dimensional model of the station. A blinking red dot appeared at the girls' location, their apartment. The system zoomed into a closer view of their apartment, hovering far enough back so they could recognize the main landmarks. It then proceeded to trace a path from their apartment to the location of the store they needed to go to. At the destination, a tag displayed "Morison's Genetics Shop."

"Wait," Lauren stopped Julia. "Whoever is watching us could watch your search, too. I didn't put anything in there to mask your searches—it's a lot more difficult."

"OK. I guess they'd have everything else we need," she said, focusing on the screen. "Wow, it's all the way at the end of the station. Over in Grid 2," she muttered under her breath.

"Uh, oh. Grid 2. There's no way Mom would let us go down there," Lauren said.

"What's wrong with Grid 2?" Julia asked.

"I'm not exactly sure. I've just heard it's a pretty rough part of the station," Lauren answered.

"We still need to go. It's the only place on the station that has it," Julia said.

"We'll have to figure something out . . . anyway, electro-what? What is that?" Lauren asked with a contorted look on her face.

"It's something I need to isolate the neon green gene from the jellyfish," Julia answered, half paying attention. "There are better ways to do it, but we have to do this pretty cheaply."

"OK. Whatever that means! What else do you need?" Lauren questioned.

"Well, I remember I needed the jellyfish gene, then I needed a virus to put the gene on to insert it into the microorganism." Julia looked at the screen, then shifted her gaze to Lauren.

"If I search for the other things, I bet whoever corrupted my blogs would know what we were up to," she continued. "So why don't we go to this store and see if they can tell us where to get the rest of the stuff."

"OK, let's go after school tomorrow. We'll have to figure out something to tell Mom, though, because there's no way she'd let us go down there . . ."

Julia sat down at her computer, trying to piece together what she remembered from the experiment.

Lauren turned to her own computer, putting her strange glasses on. "I'm going to try and hide our tracks. They can trace us anywhere with our phones and biometric scanners on the station and I don't want those weird creatures following us."

Chapter 10

The Experiment

The next day, Julia awoke with vigor, ready to get through school and get to the store. She got up early and plotted out their course down to Grid 2.

Lauren woke up a little while later as she always did, enthusiastic as her sister. In their room, they collaborated on what to tell their mother about where they were going.

First thing, Lauren logged onto her computer to check email and look at her schedule. The screen flashed on and an alert popped up saying, "Blog tracker—no results."

"Shoot. I was hoping it would have returned something by now. Oh well, we'll just have to wait," Lauren said, then turned to her sister.

"How about we tell Mom we need something for one of your projects at school," Lauren suggested.

"Yes, that's kind of true. I did need it for a project six months ago . . . and I don't have the equipment now!" Julia agreed.

The two mustered up the courage to talk to their mom and walked out to the breakfast area.

"Mom," Lauren said, with innocent-looking eyes as big as saucers. "Julia and I need to go get something after school. It could take a little time. Is that OK?"

"What do you need to get?" their mom absently asked as she blocked Maia's hand from dipping into Evan's cereal bowl.

"Oh, just something for school," Lauren responded.

"Where is it?"

"Oh, I think it's over in Grid 2," Lauren mumbled.

"Where? Grid 2! Absolutely not! You know what's down there?" Their mom froze and stared at Lauren in disbelief.

Lauren smiled broadly. "I'm just kidding, it's in Grid 11."

"You better be kidding! Grid 2 isn't any place for kids," their mother said. "Well, Grid 11 is still on the other side of the station. What do you need to go there for?"

"Like I said, it's for a school project. It's Julia's project," Lauren explained.

"Can't you just have them deliver it?"

"No, I'm not sure what I need and I need to look at it," Julia said, shifting her eyes.

Lauren shot Julia a glance to get her to stay quiet and leave the talking up to her. Julia fell silent.

Suspicious, their mother looked at Julia to see if she would crack. Julia held her own, simply returning her mother's stare.

Lauren felt their permission slipping away and tried one last plea. "Mom, she really needs the equipment. She can't do her extra credit experiment without it."

Their mother stood thinking for a second, "OK. You can go, but try not to be there too late. Leave your phone on so I can make sure you're OK."

Their mother felt secure they would be safe, knowing that the phone would track their movements. Plus, as the girls' dad had reminded her when they had been out late before, the safety net on the station was second to none. At a moment's notice when anybody was in trouble, all they had to do was yell and police bots would come detain all the parties involved for the police to sort out.

"We promise," they both said and headed out the door for school. Unbeknownst to her mother, Lauren had already changed their phones to send out a false signal from a different location.

They got to school a little early to hang out with their friends before class. It helped to distract them a little from thinking about the experiment, but not fully. Lauren's first class was math. She slouched down in her desk, struggling to pay attention. Around the room, her fellow students answered questions as the teacher called on them.

There were 20 students in the advanced math class. The teacher wrote on the board in the front, and most students were following along on their tablets.

Lauren's friend Alyssa sat behind her, and they'd frequently get in trouble for talking when they were supposed to be listening.

But today, Lauren wasn't paying attention for an entirely different reason.

"Lauren!" her teacher called her name.

"What? Huh?" she said.

"What's the answer? $X + 10Y = 300$, where $Y = 1/2X$. What is X?" The teacher pointed to the board at the front of the classroom.

"Uh, I'm not sure."

"Lauren, think. You can do this."

Lauren looked up toward the ceiling, "Um, 14 something?"

"Try again," her teacher said, glaring at her.

Lauren took a pen and wrote on her tablet. While she wrote, it displayed on the board in front of the class, "Um, 50?"

"Yes, that's right. See how she did it?" The teacher pointed at her work on the board, but Lauren had tuned out already.

Her friend Alyssa tapped her on the shoulder.

"What's wrong with you? Where are you?"

"I'm right here," Lauren defended.

"No, you're not. You're out there in space." Alyssa pointed to a window where stars shown in.

"Girls," their teacher looked at them, "pay attention."

Lauren sat straight in her seat, staring ahead with a blank look on her face.

Fifteen minutes later, the bell rang.

"Finally, lunch!" Alyssa said. "Are you ready?"

"What?" Lauren said again.

"Come on, space cadet! Get up, let's go eat." Alyssa grabbed Lauren by the arm.

They walked through the halls toward the lunch room. Kids ran around, scurrying to class or lunch. They got to the cafeteria and waited in line.

When she smelled the food, Lauren started paying attention to the here and now.

"I hope we get Mexican food today," Alyssa said.

"Mexican food? No way, I want Indian food," Lauren protested.

"I'm tired of Indian food," Alyssa complained. "I've had it twice this week already."

As they reached the trays, they could see what it was.

"Mmm, Mexican food!" Alyssa said.

"Ah, man! I don't like it here. They can't make it right. It's a lot better at home," Lauren said.

"What are you talking about? You all don't make it, it's prepared for you!"

"Maybe . . . but there's still something different," Lauren said.

They got their food and Lauren sat down.

"So, what is going on with you?" Alyssa asked as she sat down. "You've been in la-la land all morning."

"Oh, nothing," Lauren said, hiding her gaze.

"It's not nothing. You're up to something," Alyssa said. "And I'm going to find out!"

A couple other girls joined them at the table, distracting Alyssa from her grilling. But at the end of lunch, Alyssa reminded Lauren, "I haven't forgotten about it!"

Throughout the rest of the day, Lauren tried to focus, but just couldn't manage to do it. At 3 o'clock when the bell rang, she sprang out of her seat, sprinting to the door.

On the way out, Alyssa tried to stop her "Lauren, want to go to the plaza after school?"

Lauren slowed down briefly to answer her friend. "No, not today. Julia and I are going down to Grid 2 to pick some things up."

"Grid 2! So that's what you were thinking about all day. Do you know what's down there?" She looked at Lauren in amazement. Then she grinned slyly. "What kind of mod are you getting?"

"What kind of what?" Lauren asked, not understanding what Alyssa was talking about.

Surprised, Alyssa asked, "You really don't know what's down there, do you?"

"I've heard it's not really a place for kids our age," Lauren admitted. "But the place we're going is right on the edge of Grid 2. It's not in the middle where all the bad stuff is."

"Where is it?" Alyssa asked.

"I think it's just a couple blocks off the local line 2," Lauren said.

"OK. What's the place?" Alyssa continued.

"It's called Morison's Genetics Shop," Lauren answered.

"Genetics? Then you are looking for a mod! I knew it! What kind?" Alyssa appeared startled.

"It's something for Julia. She's doing an experiment or something," Lauren said, vaguely hoping Alyssa wouldn't ask more than that.

To Lauren's relief, Alyssa dropped her interrogation. "Huh. A 10-year-old doing genetic experiments . . . your sister is pretty smart."

"Yes, she's something else!" Lauren grinned as she fondly thought of her quirky sister.

"Regardless. You guys are new on this station and don't know how things work around here," Alyssa said confidently.

Lauren could tell Alyssa was trying to entice her to ask more, and she knowingly took the bait. "Why, do you know that area?"

Alyssa could hardly contain herself. “Sure do! I used to go down there with my older sister. She would go down there to meet some people and took me along a few times.”

Lauren wasn’t feeling too sure of herself and thought she could use the help. “Would you like to come with us? I don’t know the area and it sounds like you do.”

“That’d be great! I need a little adventure. Let me go tell my mom when we get outside.”

She started toward the door.

Lauren grabbed her before she could get very far, “Alyssa! Don’t tell her we’re going to Grid 2. I told my mom we were going to Grid 11.”

A slight smile crossed Alyssa’s mouth as she said sarcastically, “Really, Lauren, do you think I was born yesterday? Of course I wouldn’t tell her where we were going.”

Outside, the two approached Julia. Surprised to see Alyssa, Julia gave Lauren a questioning look.

Lauren reassured her, “Alyssa wanted to come down there with us. She’s been there a few times and said she could help.”

Julia looked relieved, “Good! We could use the help. I’ve heard it’s not a place for kids. I guess we’re taking the train?”

“Yes. We’ll take the express line down the station, then it’s just one local train over there. Where we are going it’s not too bad,” Alyssa said with a nod.

The two sisters were glad to hear that. “OK, let’s go tell Mom that we’re off.” Lauren moved in the direction of her mother with Julia following.

Alyssa did the same, walking over to her mother.

Lauren approached her mother quickly. "OK, Mom, we're off!"

"Hold on, you two," her mom said, holding her finger up behind her back as she finished a conversation with another mom.

"All right, Kathryn, I'll see you later tonight," their mom's friend said as she waved and walked away with her daughter

"Mom, we're going to go get the stuff Julia needs. We need to go! Alyssa's going with us and she's waiting."

"Grid 2, right?" their mom asked, trying to catch her daughter.

"What? Grid 2? No, we're going to Grid 11," Lauren said as certain as she could.

The two turned to walk away and Alyssa walked up to join them.

"Well, hello, Alyssa," Lauren's mother said.

"Hi! How are you doing today?"

"Fine," their mother folded her arms in front of her. "I hear you all are going on an adventure down to Grid 10."

Lauren grabbed Alyssa's arm and drew her closer.

Alyssa looked confused. "Grid 10? We're going to Grid 11."

Their mother's frown gave way to a smile. "OK, kids, be careful."

Lauren felt bad about lying to her mother, but she knew how important this was. If they didn't get that equipment, they couldn't recreate the experiment and they'd never be able to get the truth about the creatures out.

The three adventurers headed toward the train station.

Chapter 11

A New Ally

On the train ride down to Grid 2, the two sisters shifted in their seats, looking around at the other passengers. Julia drummed her fingers on the seat next to her while Lauren fidgeted with her phone. The sisters had heard so many bad things about Grid 2, they didn't know what to expect.

Alyssa was calm, casually looking out the window, unaware of how the girls were feeling until she caught a glimpse of Julia's long and expressionless face. Her eyes were focusing on the advertisements above her. "Are you nervous?" Alyssa asked her.

Julia blinked and then looked at Alyssa. "No," she insisted crumpling her face and almost acting offended.

Lauren knew it was a facade. She squelched her own apprehension and tried to reassure Julia. "It's going to be OK."

Julia gave Lauren the same offended look. "I know."

Alyssa chimed in, "It's not as bad as you've heard. And we're not going to the middle of Grid 2."

"I sure hope Mom doesn't find out about this. She'd kill us," Julia blurted out. Then, more quietly she muttered, "Unless we die here first!"

"Don't worry. It's almost like a circus down there. The people there are a lot different than from where we live, but they're still nice just the same," Alyssa said.

"What do you mean they're different?" Lauren asked.

"Well, you know why this genetic shop is there?" Alyssa asked the leading question.

Julia looked up, "Why?"

"Well, it's a mod shop . . . that's where people go to get genetic modifications," Alyssa said, staring into Julia's eyes.

"What is a genetic mod? You said that before and I have no idea what you're talking about," Lauren said.

"Your parents haven't told you about that? It must not be a big thing from where you come from." Alyssa continued, "Well, have you ever wanted cat eyes or whiskers or something? You can go to the mod shop and inject yourself with the serum to get the mod you want."

Lauren looked horrified. Alyssa fed off the emotions, adding, "Yep. It's true. Here on the outpost it's a big thing. That's what my sister wanted to do down here. She wanted a mod for cat eyes. She got the serum to do the mod and had it at home. Mom and Dad found it and flipped out."

"So she didn't do it?" Lauren questioned.

"No, she didn't, but she still wants to. So as soon as she moves out of our apartment, she said she's going to do it." As Alyssa finished, the train came to a stop.

"Looks like we're here." Julia got up and moved toward the doors. The two other girls followed.

They could immediately tell they were somewhere different—very different. A young man wandered in front of the girls, walking toward the bathroom. At first, he didn't look any different. But then they noticed his neck had five slits that flapped slightly open with every breath he took. When he reached into his pocket to pull out his phone, the girls noticed his fingers were webbed.

Julia gawked, not believing what she was seeing. Alyssa quickly stepped in front of Julia, obstructing her view. "Don't stare. These people just want to be treated like everyone else. I know it's hard not to, but just don't make it obvious."

Julia and Lauren looked down at the ground trying to hide their astonishment.

"Let's go. It's this way," Alyssa walked through a hall straight in front of them.

As she walked, Alyssa described the surroundings. "Grid 2 is like a labyrinth. You can get lost down here very easily. So stay close. And your GPS doesn't work down here either. They disabled it somehow."

"Why is that? How did they do that?" Julia asked.

"Not sure. And nobody really cares because it's Grid 2. People come down here to get lost," she said.

The girls followed, trying to concentrate on not staring, but that only made it more obvious they didn't belong there. As they plunged deeper into Grid 2, the mods got more and more unusual—a person with rabbit ears, another one with what looked like wolf hair covering his body. Then the ultimate mod they couldn't help but stare at was a man who had hooves for feet beneath his jeans and small knobbed horns on his head, reminding the girls of a legendary Greek satyr. The sisters fell further behind Alyssa as they gaped at the strange sight.

The man stopped and stomped his hoof. "What are you looking at?"

Julia turned her head, pretending not to look.

Lauren stepped back. "Nothing, sir. We're not looking at anything."

"You don't belong here," he said, clomping away.

Alyssa noticed they weren't behind her and stopped to drag them along. "Lauren, Julia, come on. We need to get going."

Julia and Lauren snapped out of it and continued following Alyssa through the twisted halls. The halls got darker and smaller as they forged ahead, darker than any of the halls where they lived.

Many of the lights were dim, blinking, almost out. Others were completely smashed. Incredible graffiti murals adorned the walls, with scenes of demonic lands and strange symbols that they could only imagine was a language the folks here made up.

They finally arrived at the shop. Above the store entrance, "Morison's Mods" was scrawled in paint.

When the three girls walked in, all eyes shifted toward them. They knew they did not belong. As they walked up to the counter, the patrons' glares followed them.

It was as dark in the store as in the halls outside. The bald man behind the counter turned to address them, and the girls noticed his skin was smooth, glossy, almost scaly. His eyes were reptilian.

Julia shrieked, reminded of the horrible hominoid creatures that haunted her dreams. She spun around to avoid looking at him directly, as she had with the hoofed man.

"What," the man hissed, "haven't you ever sssseen a reptilian mod before?" He pointed his hairless boney arm to a back shelf. "If you'd like to take the plunge, the mod kit is right there." A sly smile crossed his face. His forked tongue lapped the air after he spoke.

On learning the man had a mod, Julia pulled herself together, "I thought . . ."

The man hissed, "What, that I was one of them?"

Julia and Lauren looked astonished, "One of who?" they questioned.

"You know, one of them . . . ssss," the man said, waving his hand in the air, looking around.

Gathering her confidence, Lauren followed up by asking, "You've seen them before? You know about them?"

"Of courssss . . . we all know about them down here . . . ssss," the man added.

Alyssa smirked, "Ya, right. That conspiracy theory has been around forever."

"What? What are you talking about?" Julia asked.

"Them . . ." the man replied. "The creatures that control our thoughts—the Zebs. They're here, among us, controlling us."

Julia and Lauren couldn't believe what they were hearing. Finally, somebody who knew their secret!

Alyssa stood with arms folded. "Except that nobody has ever seen these things . . . it's just ridiculous."

Ignoring Alyssa, Lauren interrogated the man further. "You've seen these creatures—what did you call them?"

"Well, no . . . ssss . . . we just know about them," the man admitted, but then continued, seeing the girls leaning his way. "Dr. Eduardo . . . sss . . . Zebellum first came across them 10 years ago." He paused, licking his lips. "He was a ssssycologist. Many people came to the doctor with horrible nightmare . . . ssss. The doctor found a way to ssssee. He said he wasss going to set us free, then he disappeared. Nobody has sssseen him ssssince."

The sisters stared at him in fright, wondering if they would be next in line to disappear. After all, someone had removed all of Julia's research—someone knew that the girls knew too much. Remembering what they had come there for, Julia wanted to get what she needed and get out. “I came for an electrophoresis chamber.”

“What do you need that for, little girl? You going to make your own mods?” The man laughed as spittle spewed from his mouth.

“No, I just need it . . . and do you have any jellyfish DNA? The kind with bioluminescence?” Julia continued.

“Big words for a little kid . . . ssss . . . how old are you?” The man frowned.

“Old enough,” Julia shot back with a glare.

The man furrowed his eyebrow-less temple. “You better know what you’re doing, kid. I could get in big trouble sssselling you this sssstuff. You know mods are sssstrictly regulated here. Rogue mods are illegal . . . ssss.”

Lauren put a wad of money credits on the counter. “Just give us what we need and don’t keep any records of this.”

Julia slapped a list of equipment next to the money.

Alyssa gaped at the mound of money credits on the counter. “Where’d you get that?” The credits were untraceable cards that people used when they didn’t want anyone to know what they were buying.

The man’s frown shifted into a smile. “Sure, kids, whatever you want. Give me a second to get all these things.” He picked up the list, stared at it for a moment, and walked to the back of the store.

A short while later he walked back carrying a bag, placing it on the counter. Julia opened the bag and made sure all the equipment was there.

“OK, it’s all there,” she said, nodding to the other two girls.

"All right, let's get out of here." Lauren led the others out of the store.

"Thankssss girlsss. Come back and ssssee usss," the man waved as they left.

Out of the store, Alyssa grabbed Lauren by the arm, "Is that what this is all about? About you thinking strange things live on this station and control us?"

Lauren faltered, looking around and avoiding eye contact with Alyssa.

Alyssa couldn't help herself. "Ha! Are you kidding me? You think you've 'found' the secret?" She waved her arms in an exaggerated circle.

"Uh . . ." Lauren stopped herself before revealing anything, obviously embarrassed.

The three blazed their way through the maze of halls. It was getting late and now along the way, they saw more and more people with bizarre mods walking about. A few times, the three had to catch themselves from staring too much.

Back at the train station, Alyssa continued her tirade.

"Lauren, we're not finished with this! What are you all doing with this stuff?" she asked.

The train pulled up, empty, and the girls got on, Lauren and Julia keeping quiet.

"I can't believe you two!" Alyssa flung herself into a seat.

Julia had enough. She leaned over and grabbed Alyssa by the shoulders, staring straight into her eyes. "Look! If we told you, you wouldn't believe us."

"Try me," was all Alyssa said.

Julia burst into the story. "You have no idea what we've gone through. Did you know there really are creatures living on this station? We don't know what they do or why they're here, but they're living among us. You remember that day we saw you at the plaza and your obnoxious friend accused me of taking her stupid phone?"

Alyssa smirked. "Yes."

"It was some sort of fuzzy little monkey-raccoon creature. They live here, too!"

"I don't believe you," Alyssa said, putting her hand up.

"Did you know they have a factory on this station where they harvest these?" Julia reached into her fanny pack, pulling out a small crystal sample.

"Did you know we went to that factory? They saw us! They chased us down tunnels. We crawled through those tunnels like rats and almost got run over by a train!"

Alyssa's mouth dropped open.

"They DO live here. They KNOW who we are and NOBODY would believe us." Julia stopped, heaving out a big sigh.

Alyssa just sat blinking, not knowing what to say. Then she asked, "So you think this genetic stuff will help you?"

"I think so—it better. These, what did he call them? Zebs? The station needs to know about them." Julia slumped back in her seat, reflecting on the story. Both sisters were noticeably relieved now that they had shared the story with someone else, even if Alyssa thought they were crazy.

Less skeptical, Alyssa seemed to accept the story, or at least that the girls thought they had been through something. She consoled them, “Wow, you two have been through a lot. That explains why you were acting so weird lately . . .”

“Yes, we didn’t know who we could trust or who would believe us,” Lauren said.

“Well, I definitely wouldn’t have believed you before we came down here and I saw how serious you are about this!” Alyssa confirmed. Then she continued, “Can you show me these creatures?”

“You wouldn’t be able to see them,” Lauren said, “but we could maybe show you at the plaza.”

“Where is their lair?” Alyssa asked.

“It’s by the plaza, way past the park and deep into the woods,” Lauren told her.

“That’s a good place to put it. Nobody ever goes back in there,” Alyssa contemplated.

“We can’t show you tonight, we don’t have enough time, but we can go tomorrow after school,” Lauren said.

“OK, let’s do it. If what you two say is true, all of the outpost could depend on this . . .”

Julia didn’t need to hear that. She was already under enough pressure. But she could take solace in knowing someone else shared their burden now. At the next stop, the three separated, with the sisters going one way and Alyssa going another.

Chapter 12

Making the Treatment

Back at home, their mother greeted them as they entered the apartment. "Did you get all the stuff you needed?"

"Yep, got it," Julia said with a smile, masking her true feelings of angst. "Now I need to go get it set up," she said, heading toward her room.

"Don't you want to eat and say hello?" her mom asked.

"Oh, yeah, almost forgot." Julia went to the kitchen counter and grabbed her plate. Juggling the bag and the plate, she retreated to her room.

"That's not exactly what I meant . . ." her mom sighed, but didn't stop her.

Lauren noticed her mom's frown. "I'll stay out here with you, Mom. Let Julia go work on her project. She's really excited about it."

Evan and Maia were intently focused on a block construction project in the playroom. Evan noticed his oldest sister was back and came out to talk to her.

"Where have you been?" he asked.

"Just getting some things for Julia," Lauren responded.

"No, I mean for the past several months. Ever since we got here, you've been doing stuff and you never play with me or talk to me anymore," he protested.

"What do you mean?" Lauren asked.

"He is right, you know," her mom said, reclining on the couch.

"Well, I'm busy!" Lauren defended.

Lauren sat down on the couch beside her mother. "What did you do all day?"

"Well, after I picked up your brother and sister, I came home, helped them with their homework, read a little, and now you're home," her mom said, surprised that her daughter actually took an interest in what she was doing.

"That's great," Lauren responded, looking straight through her mother as she answered.

"Did you hear a word I said? You're doing it again."

"What?" Lauren said shaking her head. "Oh, yes, you got Evan and Maia and came home. You do that every day." She shrugged, leaning back.

"Come see what we built," Evan said, grabbing Lauren's hand.

"Not now, maybe later," Lauren said.

"Hmmpf." Evan grunted and stomped back to the playroom.

"When is Dad getting back?" Lauren asked, unfazed by her brother's reaction.

"You know you're ignoring your brother. He misses his sister," her mom said.

"I know. I'll do something with him this weekend. But when is Dad coming back?"

"Tomorrow. He's probably going to get back earlier than usual, he said."

The family had grown used to their father being gone frequently, and the two older girls had grown accustomed to their newfound freedom, given that their dad wasn't around and their mother was consumed with the day to day needs of a family of six.

Behind them in the hallway, Maia snuck out of the playroom and slipped into Lauren and Julia's room.

"Did you do your homework yet, Lauren?" her mom asked her.

"No, not yet. I don't have much, though," she mumbled.

"OK, well, you better go get it done."

"Sure," Lauren sighed as she got up to retreat to her room.

Back in their room, Julia had the contents of her bag scattered about on her desk. She was hunched over parts and pieces, carefully putting the apparatus together when Maia strolled in.

"Whacha doin'?" Maia asked, dancing up to her sister.

"Something for school," Julia said automatically.

"Do you need any help?" Maia asked.

"No, I'm almost done," Julia responded. "Once I get it set up, I'll get started."

Maia picked up one of the pieces of the apparatus and fondled it.

"Put that back," Julia commanded.

Maia tossed it over her shoulder onto Julia's bed.

"Arrgh," Julia said, reaching for the part.

Lauren walked in and plopped on her bed, pulling her tablet computer out of her backpack. She tapped on it and it brought up her homework assignments: Geometry, Literature, and Science. She tapped on Geometry. It showed the Pythagorean Theorem definition and some problems below it. She tapped on one of the problems and it brought it up with a blank space below the problem description. She pulled out a stylus and started working through the problem.

Maia sat down on the bed beside Lauren. "What are you doing?"

"Homework," Lauren said.

Maia looked over Lauren's shoulder at her tablet. "Can we read together?"

Not really wanting to do her homework, Lauren tapped on it and brought up a book. "Sure."

Maia smiled brightly and started reading aloud to her sister.

Julia arched her back, stretching on the chair and exhaling a big yawn. "OK. Here we go!" she said, ready to dive into a long night of research.

* * *

Hours later, Julia was still sitting at the desk under her lone light. Maia had returned to her room and Lauren had gone to bed hours before. Julia pounded her fists on the desk, waking up her older sister.

Lauren pried open one eye to see what the racket was.

"I just can't figure it out," Julia leaned over on the desk and closed her bloodshot eyes.

Lauren pulled herself up to sit in bed. She rubbed her face with both hands. "You've got to figure it out!" She rolled her legs off the side of the bed, stood up, and walked over to Julia. "What else can you remember about it?"

"Nothing! I thought I had the steps right, I just can't remember all of it. It's too complicated," Julia said, looking up at Lauren.

Concerned, Lauren tried to encourage her. "You have to! I know you can do it . . ."

"I can't! I just can't remember all the steps! I've been working all night on it."

Lauren glanced at the clock on the screen at Julia's desk: 7:17AM.

Lauren patted Julia on the back, "Come on, we have to get ready for school. Maybe after you stop thinking about it, you'll figure it out."

Julia tried to pull it together. She brushed her teeth and splashed water on her face, hoping that would wake her up a bit. She found some crumpled clothes on the floor and threw them on.

Once she was somewhat refreshed, she walked out to have breakfast. Her mom glanced at her, then paused to get a better look. Julia's normally quirky attire was punctuated by bleary eyes and unusually messy hair.

"What happened to you?" her mom asked, walking over to put her hand on Julia's forehead.

Julia brushed her mom's hand away, clearly irritated, "Nothing. I didn't sleep much. I was trying to get that project to work."

"Well, you'd better hurry. We're already late." Their mom pushed them along.

On the way to school, Julia could barely walk straight. Her mom didn't notice much because she was dealing with the younger kids, so Lauren helped Julia along.

As they split, with Lauren going to her class and Julia going her way, Lauren paused to watch her sister meander down the hall.

In class, Julia plopped down at her desk. She grabbed her computer out of her bag and immediately propped her head on her arms and pretended to read her computer.

“OK, class, we’re going to do some independent reading this morning on your history lessons, then we’ll take a test,” her teacher said.

Julia wasn’t paying attention. She had dozed off already.

After what seemed like a few minutes, she awoke when her teacher shook her shoulder. “Julia. Julia!”

Julia’s head dropped, landing her forehead in a puddle of drool that had accumulated on her computer.

“Julia, are you feeling OK?” her teacher asked.

“Yes, fine.” Julia sat up in her seat.

“OK, well, you need to take your test.”

Julia tapped on her tablet and the test appeared. There was a timeline with key dates highlighted. The top of the timeline had the title “Cielo’s Story.”

They had been studying the short history of Cielo in school. Many of her classmates had grown up on the station and knew the history intrinsically, but Julia did not. She tapped on the first highlighted date.

A bubble graphic appeared with the question, “Who was the first governor of Cielo?”

She had no idea what the answer was. Guessing, she wrote, “Grover Cleveland.”

The rest of the test went about the same way. At the end of the test, her score came up, "20%".

Her teacher immediately walked back toward her.

"Julia, you're not well. You've never performed like that before. Go to the nurse's office."

Julia got up, bowing her head, and walked out the room. She took her time getting to the nurse's office, shuffling down the halls. Once in the office, she slumped down in the seat, waiting her turn. Another kid was waiting before her.

The nursed poked her head out the door. "OK, John, come on in."

The kid next to her went in the office and the door closed.

Julia leaned over on the seat next to her and promptly fell asleep again.

"Julia? Julia?" she awoke once again to somebody shaking her.

"What? Huh?" She sat up, rubbing her eyes.

"Come on in."

She got up and walked into the office.

"Let's see," the nurse pulled out a handheld device, waving it up and down the length of Julia's body.

"Hmm," she said looking at it. "Doesn't look like anything's wrong."

"Nothing's wrong! I'm just tired! I didn't sleep very well last night!" Julia insisted.

"Hmm. Is everything OK at home?" the nurse asked.

"What do you mean?"

"Is everything OK? Are your mom and dad OK?" she asked.

"Yes! Of course they are," Julia snorted back at the nurse.

"OK, well, get back to class and try to pay attention."

Julia didn't say anything else. She just got up and slowly made her way back to class.

By the end of the day, she was ready to get out of there. But her teacher was concerned enough to address her mother out at the pickup line.

"Kathryn, Julia didn't have a very good day today," her teacher said.

"Oh, really? I wondered. She said she stayed up late working on a science project," her mother said.

"Science project? What science project?" her teacher asked.

Julia looked up. "It's a surprise."

"Well, it better be after today! I'm looking forward to it, Julia. You should have told me," she said, then got distracted by other student's parents.

Her mother squinted her eyes, "Surprise, huh? What are you up to?"

"It is! I don't want to talk about it. It wasn't working."

Lauren joined them a minute later, "Hey, how'd your day go?"

"I DON"T WANT TO TALK ABOUT IT!" Julia screamed.

"Fine! You don't have to be so rude." Lauren glared at her sister, then turned to her mom. "Can Alyssa come home with me after tennis practice and have dinner with us?"

"Sure—I'm glad you're making friends, Lauren," her mom answered.

"All right. See you later!" Lauren called as she jogged away.

Julia's shoulders sagged. "I don't want to go to music today. Can I please go home and take a nap?"

"Sure, honey," her mom answered, rubbing Julia's neck. "I'm worried you're getting sick again."

Julia grunted in disagreement but didn't say anything else while she went with her mother to drop off Evan and Maia at swim practice and then barely made it home and into bed before she fell asleep.

* * *

When Lauren got home with Alyssa in tow, the girls barged into the bedroom and found Julia sleeping soundly. They tiptoed back out and went to the kitchen.

"Are you two ready to eat?" Lauren's mom asked.

"Sure, what are we having?" Lauren asked.

"Beef stroganoff."

"Mmm . . . I love that!"

"Umm, do you have anything vegetarian?" Alyssa asked.

"Vegetarian? You aren't vegetarian, are you? I've seen you eat fish, at least." Lauren said.

"Yeah, but I really don't eat beef," Alyssa replied.

"Why?"

"Have you ever seen a cow up here?" Alyssa asked.

"You know, come to think of it, I haven't."

"So how do you think this beef got here?" Alyssa asked.

"Umm, I'm not sure," Lauren said.

"It's cultured beef, that's why."

"What's that?" Lauren asked.

"You know, like a Petri dish? They take cells from a cow, then grow them on a fake bone and make meat."

Lauren gagged, faking to throw up. "Uck! I'm not eating it, Mom!"

"Fine, I'll make mushroom stroganoff, would that be better?"

Alyssa smiled shyly. "Yes, ma'am, I'd like that."

After a couple minutes, their dinner was ready and the kids dished their plates and sat down at the table. Evan and Maia came out of their room when they smelled it.

"Where's Julia?" Evan asked.

Their mom looked toward the room where Julia slept. "Let's just let her sleep a little longer."

After dinner, Lauren and Alyssa went back to her room.

"I can't believe she's still sleeping!" Lauren complained. She shook Julia lightly.

"Julia!" she whispered. "Julia, we need to get back to work."

Julia shifted and slung her arm up above her head. She smacked her lips and mumbled something unintelligible.

"Julia!" Lauren shook her harder.

Julia blinked her eyes then rolled over, burying her head in her pillow.

"Julia!" Lauren tugged on her arms and then her hair.

"What!" Julia finally answered, turning over.

"We have to keep trying," Lauren insisted.

"Trying what? What are you talking about?" Julia moved around a little, kicking her legs, then snapped into consciousness.

She sat up. "I thought I was dreaming," she whimpered.

Lauren sat down next to her. "No, I'm sorry, you're not."

Julia rubbed her face, trying to organize her thoughts. "OK, OK. I'm getting up."

She swung her legs around, feeling for the floor with her feet. She walked over to her desk and sat down, not even noticing Alyssa.

"OK. Let's see . . ." Julia's screen flashed on as she sat down. Her email showed several new messages.

The first message in her inbox was from her teacher back on Earth. She excitedly opened it, hoping it might have the answers that had eluded her for the past few days.

"Lauren, look, Mrs. Montgomery responded," she said as she tapped on the message. Julia's report was attached to the message. She opened it immediately and scanned it.

"There!" she exclaimed. "That's it! How could I have forgotten that!"

"What!" Lauren asked.

"What is it?" Alyssa asked.

Julia turned around, noticing Alyssa for the first time. She blinked. "I didn't remember this step." She pointed to the report on the screen. "OK, I think I can do it now."

Julia pulled out the equipment and started moving some of the parts around. As she worked, she spoke to herself. "Put this here, and there. Now this. OK. That should do it."

She tinkered with the equipment a little more and then looked at her monitor, squinting, then yawning.

"What? WHAT?" Lauren asked anticipating big changes.

"There, doesn't that look better?" Julia asked, looking up at Lauren and Alyssa.

"I can't tell a difference," Lauren frowned.

Alyssa shrugged.

"We just have to wait now. I'm going to bed," Julia retorted, then got in bed and was sound asleep within seconds.

Lauren looked at Alyssa, frustrated that there wasn't a more immediate result. She sat down at her desk and her monitor flashed on.

"Hmm . . . that wasn't very exciting," Alyssa said.

"Let's see what the tracer brought back for me today," Lauren said. "Show tracer activity."

Instantly, an alert flashed on her screen: "Tracer reported activity . . . location found."

Alyssa walked up to Lauren and looked over her shoulder. "What is it?"

Lauren's heart throbbed in her chest. She touched the alert message with her finger. "I set up a tracer on Julia's blog. It should show us where the attack came from."

A map of Cielo Prime appeared with a blinking red light at Lauren and Julia's room. A thin line re-traced the bounces the message took, rotating the three-dimensional map as it zipped through the station. Finally, somewhere in Grid 15, the line launched out into space, landing on New Cielo, darting in and out of the station and finally resting in a new construction zone. The line sat blinking, then the screen flashed, "Trace complete . . ."

Lauren stared contentedly at her screen, "Gotcha."

"That's where it's coming from? New Cielo?" Alyssa asked.

"Looks like it."

"I guess you need to figure out a way to get over there!" Alyssa said.

Lauren sat thinking. "I have no idea how we'd get over there alone."

"Well, I need to get home. I'll try to think of something."

Lauren got up to walk Alyssa out, then went back to her room to read a book before going to bed.

* * *

The next morning, Julia felt much better after sleeping for 12 hours.

Lauren, unusually, had been awake for a while and was ready for school.

The first thing Julia did when she woke was check the experiment. It seemed to be coming along nicely.

The two got ready and left for school with their mother and siblings. Their dad was working out at the asteroid belt.

"Let's walk today. We're early enough," their mom said.

"Ah, Mom, I don't want to," Evan said.

"Come on, Evan, what's wrong?" Julia chided her brother.

"Fine, I'll walk," he accepted.

On the way, Lauren and Julia walked ahead.

"How are we going to get to New Cielo?" Lauren asked.

"I have no idea. First, I need to get the treatment going again. You figure out how we get to the other station," Julia said.

The two walked, pensively concentrating, both with furrowed brows, not saying a word. Lauren thought about how to get to New Cielo and Julia thought about her experiment.

School was difficult to sit through again, given all that was on their minds. Both girls were distracted and had trouble concentrating on their schoolwork.

At lunch, Alyssa sat with Lauren, trying to pry bits and pieces of the puzzle from her. They sat away from the other students.

"So, tell me about these creatures again?" Alyssa asked.

"Well, they're about this big." Lauren held her hand above the floor about a foot and a half. "And they're furry," she laughed, "They have long bushy tails. And they chatter."

"Wow, I wish I could see them," Alyssa said.

"Hmm, maybe you can't see them, but what about feeling them?" Lauren said.

"What do you mean?"

"Well, Julia and I have fed them. They practically come up and eat out of your hand. Maybe we can watch them and tell you when to feed them," Lauren said.

"Oh, that would be cool. Let's do it," Alyssa said.

After school, the three of them met. They asked their parents if they could go to the plaza. Up in the food court, the girls scoured the shrubs for the little creatures.

Eventually, one of the creatures popped its head up over one of the planters. Julia saw it first and slapped Lauren on the arm.

"Over there!" she pointed.

The three slowly walked over and sat down on the planter ledge. Lauren picked up an old piece of pizza crust and handed it to Alyssa.

"OK, now pretend you're not doing anything. Hold the pizza crust down here," Lauren said.

Alyssa held the pizza crust steady. After a few minutes she asked, "Are they coming?"

"There's one that's interested. Just keep holding it," Julia whispered.

The creature cautiously approached Alyssa.

"OK, look down," Julia said.

Alyssa looked, but didn't see anything. Then, suddenly, something grabbed the pizza crust and it disappeared into the bushes.

"Ah! Awesome! They really are there!" Alyssa blurted out.

"Shhh!," Lauren motioned to be quiet.

"That was so cool!" Alyssa said, more subdued.

"We told you!" Julia couldn't help herself.

"OK, I believe you now. There's something there," Alyssa said.

"Now, I need to get home and check on the treatment," Julia said.

The sisters agreed to keep their friend updated as they departed.

"I'm glad Alyssa finally believes us," Lauren said later that evening as they got ready for bed.

"Even though she hasn't had the treatment, she's listening. That's a start," Julia said as she settled down to go to sleep. She rolled over, burying her head in her pillow and pulling her covers up.

Lauren held up her tablet to read it, but didn't last very long. After a few minutes, her tablet slid onto the floor and she was sound asleep.

A loud, screeching, grating sound rumbled through their bedroom. Lauren and Julia awoke at the same time.

"What was that?" Lauren asked with her hands wrapped tightly around her covers.

"I don't know!" Julia said, a little scared, from her bed.

Again, the noise penetrated the room. This time it sounded a little further away, out in the hall of the station.

Lauren jumped out of her bed. She stood at her door in her jammies, listening.

Again, the screeching noise riveted them, sounding a little further away.

"Come on, Julia," Lauren said, running out of her room and to the front door. Their parents and siblings hadn't awakened. Lauren waved her hand in front of the door. It opened.

Julia tiptoed up to her sister, cautiously peering around her.

They heard the noise again, around the corner in the hall, still further away.

The two stepped out into the hall. Their door closed behind them.

The noise rang out again, this time sounding closer, with thumping footsteps.

They turned to open the door. It didn't open. Lauren tried again, waving her hand in front of the door. It didn't open.

The footsteps came closer. A dark, ominous shadow filled the hall around the corner. The sound came again -- a hoarse, rasping screech.

"Let's get out of here," Lauren said, grabbing Julia's hand and running down the hall in the opposite direction.

The sound got closer. The shadow followed them, obscuring any details of what was behind it.

Down one hall, then over another, they both ran as fast as they could.

The screech came again. This time it hurt. They could both feel it in their ears. Reflexively, they both cupped their ears, trying to shun the noise. The noise pierced their ears again.

They ran faster.

Again, it was right behind them—the noise pounding in their heads. Julia looked back. The shadow was closing in fast.

The noise again . . . it was painful, almost too painful. Julia stopped, grabbing her ears, tears streaming down her face from the pain.

Lauren looked back. Blood dripped from her sister's nose and ears. She reached for her sister, but it was too late, the darkness enveloped them. All went blank.

Julia awoke, gasping for air. Lauren did the same. The two were back in bed, sweating profusely, their beds were soaking wet.

"Lauren?" Julia asked.

"I'm here," Lauren responded.

"What was that?" Julia asked.

"I don't know," Lauren said, shuddering.

They both sat silent in their beds, reflecting.

"What do we do?" Julia asked.

"I think we just need to get that treatment done."

Chapter 13

New Cielo

It had been a week since Julia started growing the treatment and since their last strange dream. The dream still haunted them, but Julia felt better knowing the treatment was almost ready. She could tell because when she cracked the lid, that familiar, funky smell seeped out. Meanwhile, Lauren and Alyssa hatched a plan to convince her parents to go to New Cielo for a short trip. Alyssa talked about an amusement park on New Cielo that she thought was really cool. They thought maybe they could get Alyssa's parents to take them over there on an upcoming weekend.

Lauren was on her bed staring at the ceiling, contemplating the options, and Julia was tending the crystals when they heard the front door open.

Their father barged into the apartment after a long, late work day. He was not in a good mood. The girls thought they were lucky it was almost bedtime, and they stayed in their room pretending to do their homework.

Without apologizing for the being late, their dad jumped right in complaining to their mother. "I just don't understand it. We can't keep bringing these rocks back! We're losing so much money on it, we just can't keep doing it."

"What do you mean?" their mother asked. She turned to the two younger kids. "Evan and Maia, why don't you go to the playroom?"

Maia hopped up and ran into the other room.

"Ah, Mom!" Evan said, then stomped into the playroom with his shoulders slumped.

"Well, what can you do?" their mom continued.

"I have no idea . . . I have no idea," their father admitted, staring at the kitchen table.

"And another thing," he continued. "We're bringing back WAY more metal than is being used at New Cielo. I don't know where it's all going. We're working as fast as we can, but the appetite for metal is insatiable."

Their mom patted him on the shoulder. "I wish there was something I could do to help. Is there anyone you could talk to?"

"Maybe," he said. "If I went to New Cielo where the government seat is, I could maybe talk to the governor's office."

"What would you get by talking to them?"

"Well, if I explained how much money we're losing on this and show them the numbers, maybe I can convince them to actually start paying us to bring it back."

He sat thinking, then continued, "I'm not trying to make money on it . . . I'm just trying to make sure we don't lose TOO much money."

"Why can't you do that on a conference call?" she asked.

"It's better in person. It'll be harder for them to tell me no in person," he said. "I guess I'll go ahead and go to New Cielo tomorrow to try and talk to the governor's office."

Lauren and Julia had been quietly listening from their room. Lauren whispered, "If we're going to get to the bottom of this, we need to go with Dad to figure out where that tracer came from."

Julia added, "Plus, we need to stay close to him with the treatment. As soon as it's ready, I want to expose him to it."

The two went out to the kitchen. "Can we go too? We haven't seen New Cielo before."

"What? You all have school. You can't go," their mom dismissed them.

"Mom, it's just Friday. We won't get behind. All the tests are done for this session and, at least in my class, we were planning on watching a movie half the day, anyway," Lauren mentioned.

"A movie?" their dad questioned. "What kind of movie?"

"Oh, some space cowboy movie. Why?" Lauren said sensing it was the right thing to say to get her way.

"Oh, I don't know." Their dad was too preoccupied to care. "Well, I'm OK with it if you are. If all they're doing is watching a movie, might as well have them tag along and see the other station."

Their mother thought about it for a minute more. "Well, OK. But what are you going to do with them there?"

"My meeting should only go through the afternoon, and then we could stay an extra day to look around," he said.

He turned to the girls. "Well, if you're going to go, you better get to bed so you're rested for tomorrow. We have to leave early in the morning. Go pack and then get to bed."

Back in their room, Julia checked the experiment for the treatment. She looked at Lauren. "It's coming along. We should have enough in the next day or so."

Thinking, Lauren said, "I need to call Alyssa and tell her. She's probably trying to convince her parents right now!"

She called Alyssa while Julia packed. Then, they both slipped into bed and tried to get to sleep.

* * *

The next morning, their dad energetically came into the room. "Time to get up, you two," he said, clapping his hands.

"No, no, too early," Lauren mumbled.

"Come on. You said you wanted to go. We need to get going," their dad persisted as he walked out of their room.

"Lauren, let's go. This is our chance, remember," Julia said. That statement struck a chord with Lauren, and she hopped up to get ready.

Julia checked the experiment and collected several samples from the bin. She took a few complete crystals that had signs of ooze beginning to form and put them in three small vials, then tucked the vials into her fanny pack.

A few minutes later, the girls came out fully dressed, yawning, with their luggage in tow.

"Wow! I'm impressed," their dad said, shoving a couple bowls of cereal in front of them. They ate without looking up, still struggling to wake up.

Before they could even get their empty bowls into the sink, their dad said, "Let's go!" And then he was out the door without looking back.

"Hold on!" Lauren yelled, running to catch up. Julia was right behind her.

When their dad went on work trips, he would fall into a zone where everything was rushed. The two sisters got the feeling they needed to pay closer attention to what was going on, as their dad wasn't going to offer much help, and if they fell behind they might get left behind.

The girls struggled to keep with their dad's pace down to the train station. He'd stop periodically and look back at them. "Come on, let's go, girls."

When they got to the spaceport, there was a short line for the ferry, as it was still pretty early. There were a few other business travelers and some construction workers headed to the other stations, but no other bleary-eyed kids.

They boarded the ferry with the other passengers and sat waiting to take off. Lauren remembered the feeling she got leaving the transport ship and braced herself for leaving the artificial gravity. Julia played a game on her phone, not paying attention to the launch.

"How can you do that?" Lauren frowned at her sister.

"Do what?" Julia questioned while she played her game.

"We're about to take off. Aren't you worried?" Lauren asked.

"What are you talking about? It's just a short, 30-minute shuttle," Julia shot back, trying to ignore her sister while she played her game.

Frustrated she didn't have anyone to share in her misery, Lauren let out a *humpf*, crossed her arms, and waited for her stomach to drop.

Shortly after that, the gut-wrenching twist away from gravity took her over. She clinched her armrests and gritted her teeth while Julia played her game on her phone.

Once free of gravity, Lauren felt a little nauseated, but she was able to keep from throwing up this time. The trip over to New Cielo was short. As they sped away from Cielo Prime, they could see New Cielo getting bigger.

New Cielo was a fantastical sight. The station was about halfway completed and was already as big as Cielo Prime. The monstrous structure was designed similarly to Cielo Prime, with a cylindrical shape but twice the circumference. The completed half had clusters of buildings around the shell just like Cielo Prime. They seemed like they were a little taller, but not by much. On the section still under construction, there were no buildings. Smooth steel plates skinned the cylindrical structure which had no distinguishable features.

“Dad, why aren’t there any buildings on that end?” Lauren asked, looking out the window.

“Well, you know, just like on Earth, people buy parts of grids on the station and build their own buildings. Since New Cielo is so new, people haven’t built on that end yet,” her dad answered.

The buildings transitioned into the raw skeleton where only the ribs of the station were exposed. Once complete, the skeleton would easily double the size of the existing structure.

Swarms of worker bots flew all around the skeleton, welding pieces of metal in place. Hot, glowing sparks made it look like a fireworks display. Lauren stared out the window in wonder.

Oblivious to all, Julia played her game without looking. Lauren elbowed her to get her attention.

“What? I’m almost finished with this level,” Julia said, agitated.

“Pause it! Look, this is amazing,” Lauren said.

Julia paused her game, then briefly looked out the window. She sighed, rolled her eyes and said, “Neat,” then went back to playing her game.

Lauren squinted at her sister then turned back to watch the station activity.

Moments later, the ferry slowed as it came closer to New Cielo, waiting in the queue to dock.

“OK . . . I have to work half the day talking to some people in the governor’s office. So I put you two in an activity for most of the morning and afternoon, then I’ll come pick you up. We’ll go look around the station a little bit, then we're staying at a hotel tonight and heading back tomorrow," their dad said.

"What are we doing?" Julia asked.

Their dad smiled broadly. "You'll see! I think you'll like it."

The girls looked at each other, wondering what entertainment New Cielo could possibly have in store for them that they couldn't do back on the other station.

By now, the traffic congestion thinned and the ferry proceeded to the dock for a landing. The dock was much busier than Cielo Prime's central station.

Similar to when they arrived at Cielo Prime, there were customs gates where lines of people waited. But this time they went through the Residents line, which went a lot faster.

New Cielo was much more frantic than Cielo Prime, too. The excessive activity outside the station was matched inside. Everybody on the station seemed to be going somewhere or doing something as fast as they possibly could.

Their dad pulled them toward a small kiosk shaped like a large box that had a wire hopper next to it. An automated attendant's voice asked, "Where are you staying?"

"The Intergalactic," their dad said, placing his finger in a small recess on the side.

"Please place your bags in the bin," the attendant said as their dad put their bags up on the shelf.

"Done," their dad said. "There, that'll deliver our bags to the room so we don't have to carry them around with us all day."

In the hustle of the morning, the girls had forgotten all their troubles and just went with the flow. They felt completely at ease, following their dad as he made his way through the crowd toward the train. He seemed to know where he was going.

The girls walked after him, still bleary eyed from the morning trip as he wove in and out of the crowd. Julia trailed Lauren, who was right behind their dad. He bumped into something and they heard him say, "Oh, sorry, young man, I didn't see you."

As their dad moved aside, Lauren's heart leapt into her throat. The young man was not a young man at all, but a Zeb. She couldn't speak. She stood frozen, dead in her tracks as she came face to face with the Zeb. Her heart pounded faster and faster. She heard every beat amplified in her burning ears. Blood drained from her face as it turned a pale white. The Zeb looked straight into her eyes for a moment, then continued past her.

Julia shrieked as she saw the Zeb, grabbing Lauren's arm in a death grip. When she did, Lauren snapped out of her daze and yanked Julia forward.

Their dad hadn't stopped walking and didn't notice that the girls lagged. They caught up to him and tugged at his arm.

"Dad, did you notice anything strange about that boy?" Lauren asked.

"What?" he asked, still focused on where he was going.

"Dad, this is important. Did you notice anything strange about that boy?"

"What do you mean? He was just a teenage boy. A little short, but nothing strange." He crossed into a main intersection of the station and pulled the girls along, then ducked into a door that read "Spaceport station."

Lauren shot Julia a glance as they struggled to keep up with him. When they arrived at the train, he finally stopped as they waited for the next train to come.

"Seriously, Dad, nothing about that boy?" Julia probed further.

"What are you two talking about? Nothing strange. Please quit asking me about it, I'm trying to figure out where this place is," he said, starting to sound annoyed.

As the train arrived, the passengers spilled off the train from several doors. From the adjacent door, another Zeb hopped off the train. He didn't notice the girls as they stared at him.

Julia pulled her dad's hand, saying quietly. "Dad, look at THAT boy. Does HE look strange?"

Their dad turned to look at the boy, then stepped back, startled.

Julia's eyes lit up excitedly. "You can see?"

"Yes, yes. Look at him!" their dad whispered back to her. "How could I not have noticed that before? His fangs, they're huge! And those horns? How does he not bump into things with those?"

Puzzled, Julia looked over at the Zeb again. Scratching her head and crinkling her nose, she looked up at her dad. "Horns?"

Lauren straightened her arms at her side and growled, "Julia, he's making fun of us!"

"No, I'm not, girls. I can see his monkey tail, too. He must have gone through a lot of mods. I wonder if his parents know about that? Do you two know about mods?" he said mockingly.

"Argh!" Julia grumbled.

Their dad dropped the charade. "You girls, I have no idea what you're talking about. That kid looks perfectly normal, too. Come on, we need to catch this train." He pulled them both onto the train as the doors closed.

Chapter 14

Spacewalk

On the train, Julia and Lauren decided it was best they pretend they didn't see the Zebs. Otherwise, their dad might take them to a psychologist instead of doing the fun thing he had planned. It seemed the Zebs weren't bugging anyone. They were just walking around the station minding their own business, right?

As the train accelerated, the girls insisted in unison, "What are we doing?"

"I'm not telling. You'll find out soon enough!" their dad said as they sat down. "It's just a couple stops from here."

He took his phone from his pocket and tapped it a few times. "OK, I'm going to drop you two off at the place, and when you're done go straight back to the hotel. I've already checked us in, so just go to the room and it will let you in. Here, Julia, let me see your phone."

Julia, who was sitting next to him, hunted for her phone in her fanny pack. She patted the vial with the treatment, reminding herself to check it later. At the bottom of the pack, she found her phone and handed her it to her dad. He tapped a few things on it and then held it up for both of the girls to see.

"This is the hotel. Go straight there when you're done. I've got a tracer on you two to monitor where you are, so if you don't go back to the room, I'll know!" he said, half kidding and half serious.

"We know, we know. We'll go straight back. We promise!" Julia smiled back, knowing full well that as soon as they were away from their dad, Lauren would immediately disable the tracer. They had an agenda here on New Cielo and couldn't let a tracer get in the way.

The train came to its third stop. Their dad hopped up. "Here we are!"

"Look at that!" Julia pointed out the window.

A huge sign, which said: "Spacepark! The one and only!" spanned the platform.

"Awesome!" the girls shouted, as they put both hands on the window and peered out. Their dad had to peel them off to get them out of the train.

"Let's go!" he said pulling them both.

A whole imaginary world of holographic images greeted them.

"Ah!" Lauren screamed as a real-life roller coaster swooped down in front of them with kids screaming, stretching their arms out in sheer joy.

It looked so real, Julia reached out to touch it, but her hand went straight through it.

They walked through the image and saw the star attraction, "The Monster." The famous roller coaster shot straight up into the middle of the station, rolling around as riders free-floated in the cars within a glass tube, then shot back down to the station surface. The Monster was something they never could have done on Earth.

The girls had definitely heard of Spacepark before. Kids talked about it all the time on Cielo Prime, but their family wasn't into theme parks back on Earth, so they hadn't thought too much about it here. But this was a one-of-a-kind theme park built as part of the grand vision of New Cielo that could never be duplicated on Earth.

"Come on, Dad, let's go!" they both shouted back to him.

Speed walking after them, he shouted, “Hold on, I’m coming!”

At the gate, their dad paid by waving his hand over the automated teller and saying, “Three passes.”

The automated teller responded as the gates opened, “Thank you. Please proceed.”

Through the gates, the girls stopped, waiting for their dad. “I thought you had to work today?” Lauren asked.

“I do. I’ll get you settled here, then I have to go,” he said.

“Are we going to stay here alone?” Julia asked, eyebrows uplifted.

“Well, glad you asked! This state of the art theme park comes with automated chaperones,” he said.

Lauren sighed, “Ah, man! Like the ones at school?”

“They’re a little different here. This one will act as your guide and will make sure you’re safe. It stays with you the whole time. It’s like a robot dad! It will even escort you to the hotel room once you’re done,” he said, beaming.

The girls crossed their arms, staring at him in offended disbelief.

Their dad walked over to a covered vestibule, said, “One chaperone,” and put his finger inside a nook by the window.

After a second, a cylindrically shaped machine with a domed top rolled forward out of the vestibule. The dome rose from the body, revealing a robot face that looked cartoonish, with big eyes, broad lips, and a rounded nose. It said, “How can I help you today? My name is Arnold. You can call me Arnie.”

The bot had a faint oval outline of where its arms would be and other than that, not a single feature on the outside of its shell. It looked like one solid piece of polished metal.

Their dad said, "Arnie, this is Lauren and Julia. Escort them through the theme park and then take them back to the hotel when they're done."

The chaperone robot said, "Nice to meet you, Lauren and Julia." Its arms popped out of the shell, then extended to shake each of their hands.

Lauren reached out and shook the robot's hand. Julia did the same.

"Dad, you can't leave us here with this thing! We're old enough to watch out for ourselves!" Lauren objected.

"I beg your pardon. I come from the most advanced line of automated chaperones on the market today! I'm equipped with the latest safety technology and even a personality module guaranteed to make this the most memorable theme park experience you have ever had!" the offended robot retorted. Its mechanical lips pointed downward on the sides, and its mechanical eyebrows lowered, too.

"Hmph! I still don't like the idea. We can take care of ourselves," Lauren grumbled.

"Lauren, this is a new station and you don't know your way around. This is the way it is going to be. Do you understand?" their dad directed.

"Yes," Lauren agreed, with her eyes rolled upward and her hands in fists at her sides.

"Julia?" he turned to her sister.

Julia wasn't paying attention. She was looking at the rides right in front of them. She batted her eyes and looked up at their dad. "Sure."

"OK, I'm going to head to my meetings now. Arnie will give me updates every 15 minutes and tell me if anything is wrong. If something does happen, it's equipped to protect you and take you immediately to park security, where I will come pick you up. Clear?" he asked.

"Yep," they both said.

The kids immediately bolted for the first ride they saw. Luckily, since it was a school day, the park wasn't very crowded and they could go straight up to the front of almost all the lines. Arnie hovered after them. The front of the ride had a hologram of an ancient-style cannon floating above the entrance with the giant name "The Monster!" shooting out of the barrel.

"Come on, Lauren!" Julia screamed, putting her hands to her face and laughing. She took a short skip and ran off to the front of the line.

Shortly after, the roller coaster cars came to a stop. The two quickly boarded. Arnie assured them, "I'll wait for you at the exit when you're done."

Barely acknowledging the robot, the girls said, "OK," and buckled in.

The coaster took off like a rocket, twisting and turning in a series of spine-chilling maneuvers that had the girls too terrified to scream. One short break later, eyes wide, they caught their breath enough to let out some slight whimpers. The cars were just slowing down for the finale. The cars paused for a second then with a jolt shot up to the very center of the station. For a few moments, the girls and cars floated effortlessly in space, encased in a glass tube like a centipede suspended in water. Then it ripped them back down in a horrifying plunge to the surface.

At the end of the ride, the restraints let go, and the girls plopped out wobbly and disoriented, barely able to stand, as if they had just spun around in a hundred dizzying circles.

Arnie waited for them as they stepped out, helping steady them as they walked.

"Whoa," Julia giggled, trying to walk. "That was cool!"

Lauren grabbed a rail to stabilize herself, gingerly staggering down the exit ramp, "I think I'm going to be sick!" she said, holding her stomach.

Lauren leaned over the rail and lost her breakfast on the pavement. It splattered on Julia's feet, and Julia jumped backward trying to avoid getting splashed with more.

A small worker bot meandered in, blinking. With a whoosh and a slurping sound, the vomit was gone just as quickly as Lauren had deposited it there. Apparently, that wasn't the first time this had happened!

"Much better," Lauren said, wiping her mouth with her arm

That was just the beginning. The two stormed the theme park with energy that only a couple of kids could muster, moving from ride to ride, always with the chaperone bot in tow.

After too many rides to count and a pause for a breath of air, the two settled down to eat lunch.

"Wow!" Julia said. "This is one of the most fun days I've had in my life!"

"No kidding, this is awesome!" Lauren agreed.

While munching on a bite of sandwich, Julia spotted a sign above a door across the food court that said, "Spacewalk." It immediately intrigued her.

"Lauren, look!" she said, pointing to the sign.

"What? What is it?" Lauren turned to look.

"A spacewalk! That'd be so cool!" Julia said hopping up and running toward the door without finishing her sandwich. The line wasn't too long when she opened the door. There were only a few dozen people in the room.

"Come on, Lauren, let's go!" she yelled.

Lauren ran after her sister with Arnie the chaperone close behind.

Inside, the group waiting was a mixture of young adults, all older than Lauren and Julia. There was a check-in booth where an older, college-age kid sat. An instructor stood at the side of the room, tapping on her phone.

The kid in the booth looked at them and asked, "Did you two want to do the spacewalk?"

"Yes, definitely," Julia said.

"There are a couple of spots left," he said, opening the gate. "Go sit in there and listen to the instructor."

The instructor addressed the group. She was also a college-age kid, with an athletic build. She had more piercings than most people—one in her nose and a few in her ears—with a complement of colorful tattoos on her neck and right arm.

"OK, most of you probably haven't done this before. Has anyone floated freely in space?"

The people in the group looked at each other blankly. Nobody had been up there before.

"OK, it's a completely new experience. You've all been on a ferry, right?"

They all nodded.

"Here are the suits you'll wear. Each suit has two joysticks on it—one on each hand. You can turn around with your right hand and move up and down with your left hand," she explained.

Many different sizes of suits were situated along the wall in the order of smallest to largest. On the side of the room was a small chamber that had a platform with seats and buckles inside it.

The girls walked over to appropriately-sized suits and slipped them on. It was simple enough. The fabric seemed too thin to protect them out in space, but as soon as they put it on, it pressurized and got stiffer. Their helmets had clear visors, and when they put them on, they could clearly hear all the other people in the group through the helmets' speakers.

"OK, come over and get strapped in," the instructor said, motioning to the chamber.

The girls complied, walking straight-legged over to the platform. As they sat down, overhead bars fell over their suits, locking them in.

The instructor continued, "Thrusters are in the feet. To go, kick your feet down a little. To go fast, kick them all the way down."

As soon as everyone was ready, the platform sped up the tube into the center of the station. As they climbed, they felt gravity losing its grip.

At the center, they could see the station rotating around them, making them dizzy. The platform stopped inside a massive area bordered by thick nets so they couldn't just fly off into space.

Julia started fumbling with her controls. The jets on the suit fired, sending her spinning off uncontrollably away from the group.

Lauren moved to try and catch her, but she too went off in a different direction. The instructor smoothly coasted over to Julia, righting her.

"Let's try this again. What is your name?" she asked, looking calmly through the visor at Julia. Julia was clearly frightened, gasping rapidly for air.

"Julia," she stammered, gulping.

"Julia, calm down," the instructor said. "Now, let's try this." The instructor put Julia's feet on top of hers and clasped her hands. "Now pull your right joystick to the right."

Julia did as she was told, and the suit gently swiveled to the right.

"Now, to the left," the instructor said. Julia did, and the suit again responded.

"All right, now kick your feet down a little," the instructor said. Julia complied and the suit thrust her quickly toward the net. "A little less," the instructor cautioned. "There, are you getting the hang of it?"

Julia nodded. "Yes." With that, the instructor kicked her feet, zipping up, arching her back, and doing a complete circle, gliding back toward the platform.

Julia felt much better about it and gained control. Now that she had calmed down, she realized how intuitive the controls were. In no time at all, she was floating around with ease.

In the meantime, Lauren had powered her way through learning the controls and now had a good handle on the suit. The two flew back and forth, springing from side to side of the net for what seemed like an hour.

Bringing their enthusiasm to a halt, the instructor said, "15 minutes."

The last few minutes went by much too fast for the girls. Along with everyone else, they softly landed on the platform and the seats responded, strapping them in. The platform dropped back to the surface, reengaging gravity.

They exited the platform room, hobbling over to the racks to take off the suits. Julia pressed the release button and her suit decompressed, allowing her to unhook the straps. She unzipped the front and stepped out. The suit was surprisingly light, given that it protected them from the vacuum in space and had to withstand the normal air pressure that humans were used to.

The girls hung up their suits, said thank you to the instructor, and walked out the building. Their chaperone bot sat waiting with its arms, head, and rollers rescinded into its small package, making the bot almost indistinguishable from the trashcan it sat by.

“Wow, that’s it. Let’s end it with that. That was the most incredible thing—ever!” Julia said to her sister.

“Good idea,” Lauren agreed and turned to their bot, Arnie. “Can you show us the way to the hotel now?”

Arnie’s head popped out, and its arms, too. “Greetings, girls, did you have fun?”

“Yes, we did. It was a blast!” Julia said.

“It’s this way to the exit,” Arnie said, rolling past the food court.

Julia eyed the cupcake stand as they went by, almost stopping.

“Julia, come on!” Lauren said, tugging at her arm.

The group left the amusement park and boarded the train.

Chapter 15

Discovered

The hotel wasn't too far from the amusement park. The two sat engrossed in thought the whole way there. They got off the train, and it was a short walk to the hotel. They walked into the elaborate hotel, which had ornate arches and columns throughout the lobby, with luxurious fabric drapes adorning the walls.

"You're in room 321. This way," their chaperone robot said, rolling in the direction of the elevators.

The excitement still hadn't worn off yet as the girls arrived at the room. They parted ways with Arnie at the door. The robot collapsed its domed head into its body, and its arms retreated as well, making it look like a hovering trash can as it rolled away.

"Wow. That spacewalk was incredible!" Julia said clapping her hands.

"It sure was. I wish we could do that on Cielo Prime," Lauren added.

Lauren waved her hand beside the door, where there was a small panel recessed in the wall. The panel glowed a pale blue and the door opened.

A voice overhead soothingly said, "Welcome to the Intergalactic on New Cielo." As the girls entered, they kept chatting, ignoring the voice as it continued. "We at Intergalactic Hotels strive to make your stay as enjoyable as possible. If there is anything we can do to make your visit better, please don't hesitate to ask."

The girls glanced around the room. The small room didn't have much to offer, having just a couple mid-sized beds and a bathroom.

The girls would share one bed and their dad would sleep in the other.

Julia plopped down on one of the beds and called to the screen on the opposite wall, "Screen on." The screen flashed on. "Show my program list." The screen promptly displayed a list of shows and other things Julia liked to watch. "Scroll down. Stop. There, play *Space Girls*." The show started playing.

There was a large bay window on the far wall, hidden behind a curtain. Lauren walked over to the wall, saying, "Open curtain." The curtain gradually opened, revealing a magnificent view of the unfinished portion of the station.

"Incredible. Julia, look at this."

Julia joined Lauren at the window. "Oh, that's amazing."

The concave circumference of the station looming on the horizon looked deceptively flat. The structure mirrored the tubular shape of the finished station, but the unfinished piece was simply a steel skeleton. The construction zone looked like a fireworks display, with sparks of all colors flying off the steel structure, from brilliant white almost as bright as the sun to cool blue. Worker bots flew around the structure with definite purpose, welding and fastening. Huge plates of steel floated in the middle of the station, waiting for worker bots to retrieve them and bolt them in place.

A couple minutes into Julia's show, a hologram of a lady appeared behind them beside the screen. The *Space Girls* show faded to all grey tones and paused. The hologram got bigger while talking, "Looking for dinner tonight? Why don't you try Saturn Burgers? We've got the best burgers on the station. Or looking for pizza? Try Mandola's, just upstairs from where you are."

Julia turned to look at the hologram. "I am getting hungry. Where do you think Dad is?"

"He said he'd be late, but let's try to call him anyway to see if he'd like to go to dinner," Lauren said.

Lauren picked up her phone. "Call Dad," she spoke into it.

The phone displayed "Not available" on the screen.

Then she said, "Locate Dad," and the phone displayed a map of the station with a blinking light where their dad was.

Not reading too much into it, Lauren said, "Hmm. Wonder why he didn't pick up? He must be busy."

She paused, "Well, if he's going to be a while, you know we still have some unfinished business here . . . we need to track down the source of where that intrusion on your blog came from," Lauren said, setting her phone on the table with the screen side up.

"Are you sure we should do that?" Julia asked. "What if it's dangerous?"

"Well, let's just go find it. We don't have to go in or anything," Lauren said, trying to alleviate her sister's fears.

She then spoke to her phone, "Show tracer map of New Cielo." The phone projected a hologram view of the station above it almost the size of the table. The image was a perfect replica of the station, including the construction zone. A path illuminated from their hotel room to where the tracer had been tracked. The location was in a remote corner close to the unfinished structure.

"Oh, look," Lauren said. "I think it's just right up there." She walked to the window and pointed across to the other side of the station.

Then she turned, thinking, "Wait a second. I think that's close to where Dad was . . . phone, overlay with Dad's location."

The phone displayed their father's location pretty close to the source of the intruder's trace.

Julia looked at Lauren. "I don't know Lauren. I don't like this."

"Julia, we have to go. We don't have a choice now. Dad might be in trouble, too. And this is the only way to find out who is doing this to us," Lauren insisted. "I'm leaving now. If you don't want to come, fine, you can stay here." Lauren headed out the door.

Julia hesitated a moment, shook her head, growling, then grabbed her fanny pack and followed her sister.

The girls followed the path down to where the tracer came from and into the construction zone. The construction zone was a maze of empty, unfinished halls. The space looked as if it was almost ready for people to move in, but there were only a handful of people around. Wires still hung from the ceiling, walls had gaping spots that revealed supports, and many spots in the ceiling were open so they could see all the air ducts and wires.

The tracer path took them down a newly constructed hall and then turned left down a dimly lit narrower hall.

The two peeked down the narrow hall.

"I don't know about this, Lauren." Julia stepped back into the bigger hall.

"No, this is it. Let's go," Lauren said.

At the end of the narrow hall, there was a generic door that looked like all the other doors.

"That is where it is coming from. Come on, there's no one around," she said as she slunk down the hall.

Suddenly, the door opened and the girls came face to face with a larger-than-normal Zeb coming out the door.

The Zeb stared at them, not moving. He cautiously reached his hand behind his back and motioned inside the door to another Zeb.

Lauren and Julia stood frozen, wanting to move but not able to. The Zeb motioned with his hands in a calming motion, not making any sudden movements. The two didn't know if he knew they could see through his guise, so they decided to feign ignorance.

Julia started, "Oh, sorry, we're lost. Can you tell us how to get back to the main part of the station?"

"Drop the charade, girls. We know who you are," he said, glaring at them as the other Zeb joined him.

The girls' jaws dropped as they both slowly walked backward toward the main hall.

"Stop! We would like to talk to you," the Zeb said.

The girls didn't stick around to listen to anything else as they sprinted away as fast as their legs could carry them. Not looking where they were going or to see if the Zebs were following, they ran through the halls, looking for any hiding place.

The first dark hall they came to, they ducked in and flattened themselves against the wall. The Zebs ran past them a moment later and turned into a hall on the opposite side. They were there for a minute then came back to the main hall.

"Do you see them?" one of them said.

"No, not in here," the shorter Zeb said in a gruff voice.

The two Zebs continued down the main hall out of sight.

Lauren whispered to Julia, "If they just searched there, I don't think they'll come back there. Come on, let's go."

"Good idea," Julia said as she followed her sister across the hall.

The well-lit hall went straight back, and at the end there was an open door.

"Quick, in here," Lauren said.

The two jumped through the open door. It closed quickly behind them. They found themselves in a prep room for workers and robots heading out to work on the station. It didn't look like many people used it.

"Julia, look," Lauren whispered, pointing at the suits. "They're not for grown humans. I bet the Zebs use this room to go out and inspect the station."

Julia wasn't paying attention. She'd taken her phone out of her fanny pack.

"What are you doing?" Lauren asked.

"Trying to call Dad . . . still no answer," Julia answered.

Before they could think much more about it, they heard the voices in the hall.

The two looked at each other in horror. "Quick! Into the suits," Lauren said as she frantically suited up. It didn't quite fit, but it was good enough. The suits were smart enough to compensate for different-sized individuals, and it tightened around her.

Julia stuffed her phone back into her fanny pack. As she did, one of the vials of the treatment fell out. Scared, she fumbled, trying to pick it up and accidentally stepped on it, smashing the glass.

"Oops," she said.

"Hurry, forget about it. We don't have time!" Lauren shrieked.

The familiar foul smell seeped into the room. Ignoring the vial, Julia did as Lauren said, zipping into her suit. They hobbled into the airlock room and flipped their helmet visors down.

Lauren tapped her wrist control to turn her microphone on. “Can you hear me?”

Julia nodded, “Yep.”

The airlock was a small room with a bench and an airtight seal to protect people in the prep room. It had a small circular portal so they could see inside the prep room.

Julia poked her head up into the portal to see if the Zebs had come into the room. As she did, she saw them entering the room, wincing at the rank smell from the treatment. They spotted her in the portal. She stumbled backward in the awkward suit.

Quickly, Lauren punched the airlock control and the space door opened, sucking them both out into the vacuum. Tumbling end over end, they both maneuvered to right themselves. The emptiness of space engulfed them with complete calm. They looked at each other with fearfully wide eyes, unable to cry and wondering if this would be the end of them.

Lauren shook her head, coming to her senses as they found themselves at the fringe of a construction zone. Worker bots buzzed off in the distance, back and forth, riveting bolts and welding metal together on the station. The bots were piecing the next enormous sections of the cylindrical shape into place. The massive project was almost too much to absorb.

“We need to get out of here. Those Zebs will be here any minute. Let’s head over to that construction area,” Lauren said.

The controls on the suit were the same as the suits in the theme park. With a kick of their feet, the two jetted off to the construction zone, hoping to get lost in the commotion.

Moments later, the Zebs appeared at the entrance to the airlock, jetting off in the direction of the girls.

After 10 minutes at full speed, Lauren and Julia reached the construction zone. As they drifted over, they gently shifted their feet forward to stop their momentum. A small automated transport moving materials narrowly missed them as it whizzed by. The two scooted behind a long, massive metal girder, then turned around to see how close the Zebs were following. Sure enough, the Zebs were close behind.

Lauren motioned to Julia to follow her. The two traversed the length of a girder blocking the Zebs' view. They took a sharp right into a newly constructed building shell attached to the end of the massive girder. Sparks flew all around. Metal rods swung back and forth, barely missing them.

On the other side of the building structure was a trash net where all the scraps were placed. Lauren pointed toward the net and the two jetted over to hide and wait behind it.

Once there, they floated, waiting to see what the Zebs would do. Lauren looked around to see if she could see another airlock. Just on the other side of the girder, she saw the largest ports where bots came in and out. She pointed it out to Julia, then motioned that she was going to check on the Zebs. Rather than use the jet pack on the suit, she climbed the netting, positioning herself to catch a glimpse. She peeked over the top, looking through the construction zone, but couldn't see them anywhere.

All of a sudden she heard a shriek and "Lauren, help!" in her headset. She looked down to see the Zebs tugging at Julia's arms.

She looked around for any weapon in the trash heap, finding a long steel bar loose in the debris. Using it like a lance, she gripped it tightly under her arm and kicked her feet, fully engaging her jets. Her aim was dead on, striking one the Zebs in the chest. Shocked and hurt, he looked up at Lauren in agony. His face contorted through the visor, staring back at Lauren. For a moment, she thought she saw a hint of remorse in his face.

Short on breath, the Zeb wheezed, "Stop, we're not trying to hurt you!" He doubled over in pain but didn't release his grip on Julia. The force of the blow sent the two spiraling off into the construction mayhem.

The other Zeb lunged for Lauren. She dodged to the left and whacked him with the rod, sending him floating in the other direction.

Julia and the Zeb drifted right in between two worker bots riveting bolts onto the girder. Lauren sped over to them, grabbing Julia's arm and then flipping her feet around and kicking the thrusters on again.

The force of the thrusters knocked the Zeb backward just as a worker bot was pounding a rivet into the girder. The rivet punched through the Zeb's space suit, trapping him. Lauren and Julia didn't stick around to see his fate, blasting off to the port Lauren spotted earlier.

Machines flew in and out of the bay doors, swarming the entrance. A queue of machines waited to enter in orderly fashion just outside the dock. Rather than fly in themselves, the two decided to hitch a ride on one of the bots waiting in line. The second bot in line was big enough for them to latch on. As they grabbed hold, the bot's thrusters kicked in, taking them with it.

The bot rapidly accelerated, scaring the girls for a second and causing them to tighten their grip. As it glided into the bay, they got their first view of the massive outfit needed to build the station. The giant bay housed a honeycomb of several smaller cubbies where the bots landed, picking up supplies, then returning to the construction site.

Their bot flew into one of the holes, gently landing as the door slid shut. The girls jumped off, feeling gravity once again as they headed for the only door in the bay. The door slid open and closed, pressurizing the space as it did. The two shed their suits and exited the chamber as quickly as they could. The chamber opened into a maze of shafts, scaffolding, pipes, and tubing.

"Hold on, let me see where we are," Lauren said, picking up her phone and speaking into it. "Display map."

Immediately, the phone displayed a map of this section of the station with a blinking red light where they stood.

"Show directions to hotel room," she said next. The phone traced a path through the labyrinth showing them where to go.

"All right, let's go this way," she said as she began to run. Julia followed as they picked up their pace.

"Turn right. Turn left. Go straight." The phone guided the two through the area.

Lauren stopped to wait for Julia and catch her breath. "You OK?" she asked her sister.

"Yes," Julia stopped too, putting her hands on her knees. "Let's . . . take . . . a . . . break," she stammered, sliding down against the wall to take a seat.

The girls sat for a few moments gathering their composure, looking at each other and panting. They didn't notice a figure coming in their direction.

"What in the world?" the figure said as he approached the two. "What are you two doing here and how did you get here?"

The two surprised girls looked up, relieved to see a human.

Chapter 16

The Trip Home

The man who found the girls took them to the control room overlooking the massive construction bay. On the other side of the room was a large window where the controllers could survey the entire bay operation. There were a few rough-looking workers who weren't paying any attention to them looking out the window.

"You two wait here," the man said. "We need to find your dad. He's not answering his phone."

He walked over to the control console, rapping his fingers on the counter.

The man spun around to address the girls. "You two are in a lot of trouble. You know how dangerous it is out there?" He paused, not really expecting an answer. "How did you get there, anyway?" he asked, folding his arms in front of him. He was completely unaware they had just done a spacewalk clear across the construction zone.

"Uh, we were just looking for our dad," Lauren thought quickly. "We can't find him, either."

"Hmm. You know we should call the police. It's really dangerous out there and you all shouldn't have been in there," he mumbled with a frown, not believing them.

"Please, sir, we weren't trying to break anything. We don't live here. We live on Cielo Prime, and we were trying to find our dad. We traced him to somewhere over here," Julia said.

"See, look." Lauren held up her phone with the map locating her dad.

"Well, I won't call the police. But it's weird how you didn't trip any of the security alarms," he said under his breath.

Just as he spoke, Lauren's phone rang and she picked it up. "Dad? Is that you? . . . . Yes, we're on the other side of the station . . . no, they're not happy about it . . . yes, they want you to come get us . . . yes, we're in trouble."

The man who detained them stood in front of them, perplexed. He wasn't sure what to do with the two, as they didn't have visitors very frequently and certainly not a couple of young girls. He had been inspecting the machinery when he found the girls and was covered head to toe in grease. He obviously wanted to get back to work and appeared agitated that he had to watch after the girls until their dad got there.

He yelled to one of the guys at the control window, "Charlie, I've got to get back to work. Can you watch these two until their dad comes?" He didn't wait for the guy to answer and just left the room.

"Sure," the gruff man at the window replied without turning around. He reached for his cup of coffee, hunched to blow on it, then took a drink.

The girls couldn't see his face, but they could tell he was older. They could see his silvery hair sprawling out of his beat up old baseball cap.

Julia and Lauren both approached him, peering out the window with interest. "Wow! Look at that!" Julia said when she could see.

The man looked down at the girls, surprised, but not agitated like the other man. "Hey, did you all want to see?"

"Definitely," Julia said, taking a step up on a bench.

"See here, these are all the bots fixing up the station." He turned, putting his hand up to his mouth to cough.

"That there giant one, see—" He pointed at the largest bot in the bay. "It comes in here and picks up all these ginormous metal plates and takes it out there." He waved his hand in the general direction of the construction.

"Wow! That's what makes the outside of the station?" Julia asked.

"Yep. Then you got your welding bots, and your electrical bots, and your inspector bots. They all know what they're doin'. We're just watchin' and waitin' for somethin' to break down. Then we fix it," he said, then coughed.

The girls just stood observing, mesmerized by all the orchestrated chaos. Just then, a loud buzz came overhead. The man reached down and punched a button. "Yes?"

The girls heard their dad's voice. "I'm here to pick up my kids."

"Come on up," the man said, hitting another button.

A few moments later, their dad arrived. Immediately, the girls could tell something was wrong with him. Devoid of emotion, he said to the man in a monotone, "Sorry for the trouble." Then to the girls, "Come on, let's go."

The congenial old man waved to the girls as they walked out. "Thanks for the company!"

Outside the control room, Lauren looked at her dad. "Dad, are you OK?"

"Yes, I'm fine," he said abruptly without looking at them.

"Did you talk to the governor's office?" she asked.

"Yes, it's all OK. We'll keep bringing back the rocks. We'll go to the hotel room now," he said.

"And what were you doing down by the new construction area, Dad?" Lauren asked.

"I wasn't there. I was in the governor's office," he said.

"What? We tracked you over there," she said.

"Must have been an error. I wasn't there," he repeated. Lauren and Julia looked at each other in doubt, wondering if the Zebs had gotten to him.

"Let's get back to the hotel room," he said.

"But we haven't eaten yet," Julia protested.

"We'll get room service," was all he said. From there to the room, he didn't say another thing. The girls just rode along glumly. Strangely, he didn't even mention the episode in the control room. The girls didn't mind, but they did think it was odd.

Back at the hotel room, their dad sat down in the chair next to one of the beds, looking at his phone. The girls looked at each other and shrugged. Julia opened her fanny pack and surveyed the contents. She found the vial with the treatment. It was ready. She knew this was the right time and caught Lauren's attention.

Lauren gave her a nod. Julia pulled the vial out of fanny pack, shook it, and unscrewed the lid. Almost immediately, a distinct foul smell filled the room.

Their dad instantly crinkled his nose, holding it, saying, "What is that horrible smell?"

Lauren twitched her nose and Julia was already holding hers. Julia twisted the cap back on the vial and placed it back in her fanny pack.

"I don't know. That's awful," Lauren said walking into the bathroom and turning the fan on.

Their dad said, "Air conditioning fan on, high," and the fan whirled on, sucking the air from the room. After several minutes, the smell still lingered.

"Let's go get some food," their dad said, putting his phone in his pocket.

"Good idea," Julia said. "There's lots of places up on the first floor. We saw a commercial earlier about the restaurants near the lobby."

The three left to go eat. They found a good Thai restaurant and each of them had their favorite curry. Lauren's was Musman, Julia's Penang, and their dad's some sort of green curry.

After an hour outside the room, they figured the smell should have subsided enough that they could return.

Back at the room, the girls were beat and wanted to go to sleep immediately.

Their dad still was still acting strangely and wasn't talking much. But they knew it was just a matter of time before the treatment started to work.

* * *

"Ugh!" their dad flew out of bed and into the bathroom, expunging his dinner into the toilet.

The commotion woke Lauren. "Dad? Are you OK?"

Julia stirred, but didn't wake up.

Lauren shook her. "Julia, wake up!"

Julia snorted, then rubbed her eyes. "What?"

"Ugh!" Their dad threw up again.

"Oh!" The two smiled at each other, then Julia rolled back over and went to sleep.

Lauren looked at the clock: 2AM

"Dad, are you OK?"

"Yes, Lauren, I must have a stomach virus or something," he said from the bathroom. "Go back to sleep . . . I'll be OK."

Lauren smiled to herself, pulled her covers up higher and went back to sleep.

Early in the morning, the girls woke somewhat refreshed. Their dad was slumped over the toilet in the bathroom, asleep.

Lauren walked in and poked her dad. "Dad, I don't think we should stay here any longer. I miss Mom. Can we go home?"

"What?" he said waking up. "I'm not feeling too well, anyway." He struggled to his feet on wobbly legs.

They packed in a hurry and were out the door in a flash. Their dad hobbled along behind them, clutching his stomach.

Julia turned to Lauren, grinning. "He's holding up pretty well. By now, we were out cold!"

Lauren chuckled back, "Yep. Now let's get him home so he can rest."

The trip home was uneventful other than their dad having to stop periodically, leaning against a wall or rail.

They barged in at home, their dad struggling behind. Their mom greeted them, surprised.

“Hey, you guys are here early. Did you have a good time?”

“Definitely, but he’s not doing too well.” Lauren looked back at her dad behind them.

“What happened?” their mom asked.

“I have no idea. I must have gotten something,” their dad said, wobbling in.

“Do you want me to call the doctor?” their mom wondered.

“No, I think I’m OK. I just need to rest a while,” he said.

The girls felt relieved, knowing the call to the doctor may have tipped off the Zebs before. Their dad just retreated to their parents’ bedroom and collapsed into the bed.

The next few days followed the same pattern that the girls had experienced. Their dad slept a lot, threw up some more, then slept again.

A few days later, he was feeling much better, just as had happened with the girls, but a little quicker. It was Friday and the family was up for family pizza night at the plaza.

After school, their mother greeted them as usual and the family headed home. The girls were anxious to see how their dad was doing. To their relief, he was back to his old self.

“Hey kiddos, ready to go get some pizza tonight?” he asked them when they walked in the door.

Maia and Evan started chanting, “Ya, ya, ya, ya!”

“Yep,” Lauren said.

Julia nodded in agreement, eyes gleaming.

"OK, well, then let's go."

The girls and their brother and sister set their bags down and ran toward the door.

"Why don't we walk today?" their dad asked.

Their mom said, "Sounds good." And they were off.

The family strolled along on the short walk. Everything was getting back to normal. Evan and Maia walked ahead, talking to each other and generally getting along.

The older girls stayed back, walking with their mom. Their dad walked behind, just happy that he was feeling better.

At the plaza, they went through their typical routine, getting pizza with pepperoni and black olives.

Lauren looked at her dad. "Are you feeling a lot better?"

"Yes, much. It's good to get out and walk," he said.

After pizza, their dad asked, "Do you all want some ice cream?"

"Yep," Julia said.

"Julia, Lauren, can you two help me?" he asked.

They walked up to order their ice cream at the window. Their dad looked around the plaza then stopped and squinted at some bushes.

"What?" Lauren asked.

"What is that?" he asked. "Have you ever seen one of those things before?"

Lauren looked back in the bushes and saw two monkoons. Her sister saw them, too. The two smiled at each other, knowing their plan had worked.

Part III: A New Alliance

Chapter 17

Our New Allies

"Dad, there's something we have to tell you," Lauren said, tugging at her dad's elbow.

"What, Lauren? What is it?" he asked, staring at the monkoons in the flowerbeds.

"The reason you can see that creature is because we gave you a treatment that made you sick," Lauren said.

"What are you talking about, Lauren?" he asked, as they shuffled up one slot in line to get ice cream.

"You got sick, remember?" she said.

"Well, yeah, of course I remember," he answered, looking back at the creature.

"Did you have a bad dream when you were sick?" she asked.

He turned his gaze down to her. "What do you mean?"

"As in, did you dream about a strange ship you went to, went through the halls, and ended up right in front of some pulsing blob?" Lauren put her arms at her side, akimbo.

Their dad's face went white. "Excuse me?"

"Yes, it happened to both Julia and me," she said. Julia stood behind her, nodding her head several times.

"What do you mean?" he asked.

“Like I said, we gave you a treatment. The treatment lets you see these things. That’s not all, either,” Lauren continued.

“What do you mean?” he repeated with a more stern voice, frowning.

“You know all those conspiracy theories about some alien life form living here, controlling us?” she said.

“Yes. But those are all stories. Made up by some wackos,” he answered, returning his gaze to the monkoons.

“They’re not stories. They’re true. We’ve seen them,” she insisted, stomping her foot on the floor.

“Seen what?” he asked looking back at her.

“The creatures. They’re a little taller than us and frighteningly ugly!” She scrunched her face and shivered as she spoke.

“What do you mean? Those things over there don’t look like that,” he said, nodding in the direction of the creatures.

“Trust me, dad, these creatures are just the tip of the iceberg. The other ones are real, too. They’re scary. We didn’t know what else to do, so we gave you the treatment,” she explained.

“What treatment? What are you talking about?” he asked, raising his voice with his face flushing red.

“The treatment. Julia had a science experiment and she dropped one of those rocks in it that you brought back from the asteroid belt. Something happened to it and it made that stinky smell. You remember? When we were in the hotel on New Cielo? That stinky smell?” Lauren asked.

“Yes, I remember,” he confirmed.

"That was the treatment that Julia made. Somehow, the microorganisms change us so that we can see these things and everyone else can't," she said.

He laughed an uneasy chuckle. "Wow, you all really had me going! That's some story." He got the ice cream and started walking toward the table.

Lauren grabbed his elbow again, pulling him back. "Dad, we're not kidding."

He grinned, "Sure! That was a good story. But I'd still like to know how you found out about my dream. Did Mom tell you?" he asked as he continued walking back to the table.

Lauren stopped, folding her arms in front of her.

Looking ahead, Julia didn't see her sister stop and bumped into her.

When their dad was out of earshot, Julia piped up, "What do we do now?"

"You sure were a lot of help! You didn't say a thing!" Lauren accused her sister.

"Well, you seemed to have it covered," Julia said, shrugging.

"Thanks a lot!" Lauren grumbled back.

"Girls, come eat. Your ice cream's melting," their mom called to them.

The two sauntered back to the table, wondering what to do next. Their dad's phone started beeping. He pulled it out of his pocket and held it up to his ear.

"Yello," he said, followed by a pause. His smile disintegrated to a frown. "OK, I'll come out there first thing in the morning." He hung up.

"What is it?" their mom asked.

"I have to go out to the asteroid belt. Some of the guys are having trouble out there. Production is down," he said.

"What! You just got better and now you have to go?" Their mom set her ice cream cone down.

"Well, I was gone for over a week. They're kind of a rough crowd out there and need supervision," he defended.

"All right, I guess it has to be that way." She looked around at her brood. "Are you all ready to go?"

"Yep!" Evan jumped up, licking his sticky lips. Maia got up behind him, ready as well.

Lauren and Julia lingered a second longer, still wondering what they could do.

* * *

The next morning, their dad was gone early. He was well on his way to the asteroid belt by the time the girls got up, as the trip out there took about half a day. It was Saturday, though, so the kids didn't have school and slept in later than usual.

About 10AM, Lauren and Julia rolled out of their bedroom into the living room. Lauren rubbed her eyes, stumbling to the couch. Julia was a little more alert, but looked wild with frizzled hair shooting in all directions.

"Well, look who's finally up!" their mom said. Evan and Maia looked over from the TV in the living room. Evan was playing a video game and Maia was watching.

A second later, Evan set the controls down. "Lauren, you said we could do something today!"

Lauren rubbed her face with her hands. "Maybe later, Evan."

"Lauren, you promised!" Evan pleaded.

"Are you two feeling OK?" their mom asked, studying them.

"We're fine!" Lauren shot back with a glare.

"Whoa . . . somebody got up on the wrong side of the bed this morning," their mom said. "Listen, you two need to get it together. I'm not sure what's wrong, but you need to figure it out. I'm taking Evan and Maia out to shop for school clothes and I expect you two to shape up by the time I get back."

Julia rolled her eyes. "OK, OK."

A few minutes later, Evan and Maia emerged from their room dressed and ready to go. Their mom stood at the door waiting for them.

"Girls?" Their mom looked at them.

No response.

"Girls!" she tried again.

"What? Huh?" Lauren shook her head.

"We're leaving."

"OK," Julia acknowledged.

As soon as they had left, Lauren hopped up, going back into her room to lie on her bed, drifting back to sleep.

Julia plopped in front of the television and turned on one of her shows.

After Julia's show was over, she sat up, wondering what to do next. She turned the TV off and lay back on the couch, staring at the ceiling. "Ring, ring." She was startled by the doorbell.

"Hmm, I wonder who that could be?" she asked herself as she went to see.

She opened the door, completely unprepared for what stood in the hall. Her jaw dropped almost to the floor. Taking steps backward toward her room, she stammered, "Lauren," in a low trembling voice.

Lauren stirred, blinking when she heard her sister. Immediately, a chill went down her spine, followed by a twinge in the pit of her stomach. She rolled out of bed, rushing to the aid of her sister.

Her anxiety quickly turned to fear when she saw two Zebs standing in the doorway. She recognized them as the ones that chased them on New Cielo. Her legs wobbled, barely holding her up.

"Girls, we're not here to hurt you," the larger Zeb said as he reached a hand out to help steady Lauren. "We're here to help." His lips didn't match the words he spoke.

Lauren refused his hand, stepping backward. The Zebs retreated, standing with their arms at their sides in the hall.

Lauren stood straight, stiffening her stance, scowling. "How could you help us?"

"You may not realize it, but you've already helped us greatly. My human name is Ankit. And this is Raja," he pointed at his companion.

Still in shock, Julia stood with her mouth open. Lauren didn't waiver, staring straight at them. "How did we help you? You chased us all around New Cielo and now you're trying to help us?"

"Yes, that was unfortunate. But you must understand, until now we had no free will. We were under its control," he said.

"Whose control?" Julia blurted out.

"You see, when you exposed us to those microorganisms on New Cielo, it had a similar effect on us as it did you," he continued.

"The what?" Lauren questioned.

"You mean the treatment," Julia answered.

"Yes, is that what you call it? The treatment?" he said. "We are under the influence of it, too, just like the human population. But the treatment somehow breaks the bond for us, like it does you."

"It was an accident. I had no idea it would do that!" Julia defended herself.

"No, you don't understand. It helped us break the bond," he restated.

"What bond? What are you talking about?" Lauren folded her arms, still scowling.

"We don't have a name in your language for it. This . . . this being . . . it controls our minds. It grabs control and makes us do things we don't want to do," he said in his low, calm voice. His words still weren't in sync with his mouth, almost as if something was translating for him as he spoke.

Seeing the look of confusion on their faces, Ankit offered an explanation. "You notice our mouths aren't matching what we're saying . . . when you all boarded the station, we injected you with a number of things, including nanobots that translate our language into yours. They attach themselves to your inner ear canal and do the translation."

Lauren stuffed her finger in her ear, twisting as if she was trying to dislodge the foreign objects.

Julia shook her head, then asked, “What is this thing?”

“It resides on the far side of New Cielo. You haven’t seen it before because you haven’t been over there. And all the other humans who do go there can’t see it because they’re under its control.” He paused.

“These things . . . that’s how they live . . . they travel from solar system to solar system. They’re like insects here on Cielo. They have hard shells . . . what do you call it? Exoskeleton? Yes, their exoskeleton protects them from space. Then, we can walk around inside,” he continued.

“In the middle of it is a large, pulsing mass that controls the ship. This . . . this is what controls us, too. It’s the brains of the monster,” he stopped again, taking a deeper breath than normal. “Forgive me . . . we have trouble with the atmosphere here.”

For the first time, Lauren noticed the strange suits the two Zebs wore. The suits fit tightly around their bodies, with ribs of fabric running vertically up the sides. A tube pushed a vapor up toward their mouths when they breathed.

The four of them quieted down when a mother and her three small children walked by. Lauren didn’t recognize them, but said “Hi” anyway and smiled.

Julia hadn’t seen a thing, lost in thought. Her eyes widened in horror, remembering Lauren and their collective dream. “Lauren, it is real!” She looked at Lauren, who just had the same revelation.

“Our dream! That brain thing! That big blob in the middle of the ship! When you look at it, it flashes lights like a squid,” Julia said.

"Yes, that is it. How did you know this?" the other Zeb, Raja, asked in a deep, croaking voice.

Lauren explained, "When we smelled the treatment, we got violently ill. We both had this horrible dream, where we traveled to that ship. We walked around through a maze and ended up right in front of this brain. It felt like it dug into our heads, then in a flash it was over. We both woke up."

"Strange," Raja said. "Maybe this is how the bond is broken."

"We had another dream, too," Julia said, not elaborating on the horrifying experience.

Ankit spoke again, "Once the bond is severed, then it can't find you. It doesn't know where you are, but sometimes it can reach out to try and scare you into revealing yourself. It doesn't know where we are now, either. We've been in hiding."

"How do you hide?" Lauren asked.

"Grid 2. We can stay there. So many people have mods, we can blend in. Our people don't have much of a presence on this station, either. Just a small mining operation," he said.

"Mining? You must be talking about the factory, where you take the crystals," Lauren said.

"Yes, how do you know about that?" he wondered.

"We found it. One day we ran into the woods and saw some people going in. Then we followed them to see where they went. We saw a huge conveyer belt, giant buckets, and huge hammers," Julia said with her eyes gleaming.

"These two have seen it all, then. It has no idea how much they've learned," Raja spoke to Ankit.

Another family passed by, and this time the girls recognized them. "Hi, Mrs. Smith. How are you today?"

"Just out doing some shopping," she said, looking at the two disguised Zebs out of the corner of her eye. She continued past them to her apartment.

Lauren looked up and down the hall. A few more people were coming by. They waited until they passed to ask more questions.

"Why do you need those crystals?" Julia asked.

"We don't. It does," Ankit said. "It feeds on the crystals. The factory breaks apart the rocks and extracts the crystals. Then we take them to it."

"Where we come from, these creatures have ravaged our civilization. They have an elaborate web of control. Each one controls some part of our people. They search for new unsuspecting civilizations all the time. They found your solar system about 50 years ago. They will try to do the same here that they did to us. They brought us here to mine the crystals. It uses some of the crystals, then keeps what it doesn't use, so they can bring more of its kind here," Raja added.

"More?" Lauren asked.

"Yes, that's how they live. They want to control whomever they can, wherever they can, to get more of the crystals. And the crystals give them power," Raja continued.

"And you can't stop them?" Julia looked horrified.

"No, we can't. The crystals make them too powerful," Ankit said.

"Our people are at war with these creatures. We came to know them as *Gr-awl-toltz*," Raja growled the first syllables, followed by a high-pitched ending.

"Translated, it means *those who vanquish us*," Ankit muttered while looking around the hallway.

"Growlts? Hmm, how about we just call them the Squids, because that's what they look like and I can't pronounce that anyway," Julia said, waving her arms.

Lauren mused, "Yeah, that's what they remind me of—a squid or a cuttlefish or something. Remember that show we saw on cuttlefish, Julia? They were amazing. They could change colors in a flash. They were smart, too . . ."

"Well, whatever you call them, they are bad. Very bad. Your analogy . . . sounds right. They're animals, not as advanced as us. They hunt and act on instinct. No compassion," Raja said.

"And we have nobody to blame but ourselves," Ankit added. "Hundreds of years ago, our civilization found these creatures in space. They weren't as advanced as they are now. We herded them in space, using them for mining asteroids to help establish new space colonies." He paused, folding his hands together, reflecting.

"Before, the creatures weren't threatening, just blissfully wandering in space. They would talk to each other using blinking lights, like we said before. Then, we decided to genetically modify the creatures to make them more 'controllable.' We modified them so we could more easily communicate with them directly to their minds using these crystals," Ankit explained.

"Then the creatures found out the reverse was possible, too," Raja interrupted. "They found they could control us. The more crystals they consumed, the easier it was to control us."

Ankit stood straight, fumbling for something in his front breast pocket. He pulled out a rectangular object that resembled one of the girls' phones.

"May I? This will explain a lot," he said, holding the device in the palms of his hands.

"What is it? I'm not sure what its going to do . . ." Lauren stopped herself mid-sentence as their surroundings transformed into another world.

In an instant, everything swirled, changing to a scene from a distant galaxy. Images flashed before the girls, depicting a few snippets of history from the Zeb culture. But more than that, they could feel the thoughts and pains of the Zebs they saw.

They took a mini-journey from when the Zebs first began herding the Gr-awl-toltz, to modifying their DNA, to eventual domination by the monsters. The rush of emotions overwhelmed the girls when the images stopped. It wasn't enough information to know their exact history, as the images blurred from their memories immediately after they experienced them, but the emotions remained.

Lauren asked, "What in the world did you just do?"

"Remember the nanobots we told you about?" Ankit asked. "They can hijack your senses. Using this device, we can show you anything."

This time Julia pounded on the side of her head as if trying to get water out of her ear. "Wow. I never could have imagined. I'm not sure I like having those things in my head."

"Well, what about the other Zebs? Can't they use that to get us?" Lauren asked.

"No, the nanobots only have a very short range. And the Gr-awl-toltz can only sense and control emotions. It can't see you," Raja answered.

"The Gr-awl-toltz are monsters. When they have no more use for you, they destroy you by overloading your mind with shrieking pain, eventually killing you," Ankit added. "Or they'll turn your own people against you to do the dirty work."

Julia frowned, shivering. "That sounds awful . . ."

After thinking for a second, Lauren asked, "What are these crystals and how did they get here?"

"The crystals—that was our undoing," Raja snarled.

"The crystals are organic crystalline structures we created in our world," Ankit continued. "You see, your solar system isn't that different than ours. As with here, our crystals grow in our asteroid belt. We seed them, and they grow. Then we farm them like you do, although you don't know you do it. When we first came here, we seeded your asteroid belt and they've been growing since then."

"How did these creatures get here?" Lauren asked.

"We've known about your civilization for some time. Radio waves, television, they all reach our solar system. They're not easily detectable, but we found them years ago. Our solar system is about 75 light years away," Ankit explained.

"We studied your solar system, finding it resembled ours—rocky planets close to a warm sun, gas giants, and, importantly, the asteroid belt on the fringes," Ankit said.

"Immediately, the Gr-awl-toltz found out and sent us out here to seed your asteroid belt. We were to establish a base, and then take control of Cielo." Ankit stopped, looking at the girls.

Lauren felt a tingle run up and down her spine. She'd had no idea how complicated the problem was and how grave the situation was.

"For us, it's different than it is for you," Ankit explained. "When we are under its control, we can think and know exactly what we are doing, but we can't resist. For you humans, you're blind to the atrocities it makes you do. When humans are under control and it tells you to do something, you block it out of your memory. I wish we could do that, too."

Raja continued, "We found that the further away you are from them, the less control they have. Some of our people broke free. They live beyond their control. Your treatment can help them."

Looking up, Julia asked, "How do you mean?"

"The treatment—with it, we can resist. We can get close enough to the monsters to strike!" Raja declared, raising his voice and hitting his fist in the palm of his other hand.

"Yes, with the treatment, we have hope!" Ankit confirmed.

Lauren looked at them, squinting one eye, then folded her arms in front of her chest.

Lauren felt a new kinship with these alien beings now that she understood their century-long plight. Realizing they were still standing in the hallway, Lauren looked up and down, seeing more passersby on their way down the hall. She still didn't know if she trusted them and would much rather be in a public place.

"Should we go to the plaza to talk more?" she asked them.

"Yes, that would be good," Ankit said and they left.

Chapter 18

More of the Treatment

The four of them chose to walk to the plaza instead of riding the train, giving them a chance to talk more in private. There weren't many people walking, as it was mid-morning and not quite time for lunch yet, but there were enough people to help the girls feel comfortable should something happen.

Lauren felt it was a better idea to be in a public place since they didn't really know the Zebs. No humans knew them, and they had no idea how they would act or if they were unpredictable ogres that would devour them in half a second.

"So do you all have Indian names?" Julia asked.

"Yes," Ankit answered, "when we researched your culture, people of Indian decent composed of 30% of the human population, and we suspected we would blend in better."

"I guess that's true," Julia said. "And do you have jobs on the station?" she asked.

"Yes, when it serves a strategic purpose, such as in a government entity or out on the mines or in the station maintenance," he said.

Lauren wanted to know more about the controlling mechanism, so she probed, "I still don't understand."

"Understand what?" Ankit asked.

"How EVERYBODY on the station is controlled," Lauren said, scrunching her eyebrows together, thinking about what they had just learned.

“Well, the Gr-awl-toltz can control some people just on their own after we modified them genetically, but when they’re given the crystals, it amplifies their ability exponentially,” he said. “There’s also an extra injection of the crystalline substance that can be given to humans, which gives the Gr-awl-toltz enhanced control.”

“I KNEW it!” Lauren exclaimed. “When I got that shot, it just felt like poison coursing through my veins.”

“No, that was only the nanobots,” Raja interjected in a deep, rough voice.

Julia scratched her head. “So the people in the factory, did they have the extra serum?”

“That’s right, they get an extra dose of the serum. It allows the Gr-awl-toltz to put them in a zombie state so they don’t remember anything,” Ankit answered.

“That sounds horrible,” Julia said, looking at them. She stumbled and recovered while they walked.

“Yes, it is. And we have to stop it. We do not want them to turn your whole world into slaves like they did us!” Ankit said.

There was an uneasy pause as the girls let the new revelation soak in. They kept walking and had arrived at the plaza.

Scanning the crowd, Lauren found the most secluded table she could and directed the group to sit down. She felt more comfortable now that they were around more people.

“What would you like?” Ankit asked.

“Oh, pepperoni pizza is fine,” Lauren said.

“Yes, for me, too,” Julia said.

Raja and Ankit walked off to get the food, leaving the girls at the table.

Lauren looked at her sister in disbelief. It was almost too much for her. Who would have ever thought she and her sister would be having pizza with two aliens from a distant galaxy and talking about the fate of humanity?

"So you eat pizza?" Julia asked when Raja and Ankit returned with four slices of pepperoni pizza.

"It's not like our food from home, but we're getting used to it. It's sustenance," Raja said.

"So what do we do now?" Lauren asked, looking at Ankit with a blank face.

Ankit sat, putting his hand on his forehead. "We need more of that treatment. That's clear."

"How much more?" Lauren questioned.

"Quite a bit. If we want to defeat it, we're going to need a lot. Roughly about this much, I suspect," Ankit said, while describing with his hands the dimensions of a small box.

"That's impossible!" Julia blurted out with her eyes wide open. "We can't make that much! We'd have to fill a room with equipment. Where are we going to get all of that and not be noticed?"

Raja grinned, a snaggletooth grin. "Never say impossible!"

"You're right, it is going to be difficult. We don't have many of our tools here . . . if we just had . . . we could get it done in a couple of days," Ankit muttered to himself.

"Had what?" Julia asked.

"Oh, nothing, some of our equipment. It's much more advanced than your primitive tools," Ankit said.

"Well, primitive or not, I used an electrophoresis chamber when I did it here, but there's better stuff at the mod shop—it just costs a lot more." Julia tilted her forehead, shooting a stern gaze at Ankit.

"Money isn't a problem. We can pay for it. We have access to all kinds of untraceable credits," Raja replied.

"Well, what are we going to do with it?" Julia asked.

"With what?" Ankit asked.
"The treatment!" Lauren answered back.

"We need to free more of our people. I think with more of our people we can defeat it," Ankit said.

"You think? You don't know?" Lauren asked, with a gaping mouth and crooked neck. The two now felt more comfortable speaking freely and acting insolent like they would with their parents.

"Well . . . it's happened so fast, I haven't had time to think it all through," Ankit muttered through his snaggled teeth.

"I'm sorry, but that doesn't give me a lot of confidence!" Lauren shot back.

"It's our only hope," Raja interrupted. "If we get a small enough group, we can wrest control from it. It would take much more than that to saturate the entire station to inoculate the humans."

"Well, then I guess we'll have to try that. Who do we inoculate first?" Lauren questioned further.

"I'm not sure," Ankit responded.

"Well, that's some plan you have!" Lauren accused.

“I’m still working on it.” Ankit shifted back in his seat.

“Come on, let’s go to Grid 2. We’ll need to hurry to get back home before Mom notices. We’ll need to stop by our apartment and get some more of those crystals,” Julia said, standing up.

Ankit and Raja stood up, joining Julia on the walk to the train station.

Lauren muttered, “I’m not sure I like this. There’s no plan.” She folded her arms and stayed in her seat. The she picked up her phone. “Call Mom.”

Her mom answered a moment later. “Mom, Julia and I are going down to Grid 11 to get more supplies for her project.”

Pause.

“Yes, we’ll be back a little after you get home. Love you!” Lauren disconnected and ran to catch up with her sister.

The girls knew they would have to be quick. Their mother was out with their two younger siblings and they had only a couple of hours to get the crystals, buy the equipment, and get it set up.

Their apartment was a quick stop away. Julia ran back home while the rest of the group waited in the train station. She gathered a number of the crystals that already had the treatment on them and put them into a sealed bag and grabbed as many of the unexposed crystals as she could carry.

Lauren saw her sister struggling with the bag of rocks in the hall and ran up to help her. The two of them lugged the bag up to the train and handed it to Raja, who effortlessly slung it over his shoulder.

“You humans are weaklings,” he said, grinning at them.

Julia laughed.

The next train pulled into the station and the group hopped on. The four seated themselves away from the other passengers.

Ankit glanced around the train at the other passengers, making sure they were beyond earshot. “There’s something we haven’t shared with you yet.”

Lauren looked up. “What? What is it?”

“We have the technology to travel through space much faster than the speed of light,” he admitted.

“OK,” Lauren said.

“There’s a problem . . . it took us over 60 years to get here from the outer boundary of our territory We traveled at the speed of light in a caravan from our solar system, all the while under control of the Gr-awl-toltz. We were put in hibernation, so we didn’t age. All of our family back home is much older now . . . maybe gone.”

Lauren stared at him with wide eyes. “I’m sorry. That must be hard.”

“It is. I had two little girls about your ages when they coerced me, forcing me on this expedition. I’m afraid I will never see them again.” Ankit looked away.

“Well, can’t you get back now that you’re free from its control?” Julia asked.

“That’s what we haven’t told you . . . the technology we have is a star gate. It’s a wormhole. It lets us travel instantaneously between two points in space,” Ankit said.

“That’s great! Then you can get home!” Julia blurted out.

“It’s not that easy. When we came here, we brought all the plans to build the gate. It is too big and fragile to move. It’s a massive undertaking. Most of our people are dedicated to building the gate.

We take a lot of the material intended for New Cielo and use it in the star gate," he continued.

"What do you mean?" Lauren questioned, looking more anxious.

"I think you know what I'm getting at . . ." Ankit said.

Julia crinkled her nose with a puzzled look, but Lauren understood, "You're building it to bring the rest of them here . . ."

Ankit nodded, confirming her fear. Julia pursed her lips into a concerned "oh."

"They're coming?" Julia asked.

"Yes, they're coming, Julia, why do you think they're building that thing?" Lauren frowned at her sister. She looked back at Ankit. "How much time do we have?"

"Weeks . . . maybe. They're ahead of schedule. It's getting close," Ankit replied. "Maybe that's what we should do with the little bit of treatment we can get. We could expose our people at the star gate to the treatment and try to get control of it."

"But it will take at least several days or a week to make enough of it! Even with the better equipment!" Julia protested.

Some of the people sitting at the other end of the train car looked down at them when Julia's voice rose.

Raja lowered his voice, huddling close to the others. "We have no time to lose. We need to start making it tonight."

"Where is this star gate? How come no one has seen it before?" Lauren asked.

"It orbits Jupiter now. That was the best place to put it to keep it undetected from Earth. On Cielo, it's easier to control the people since they are under the influence of the Gr-awl-toltz, so they cannot see it," Ankit answered.

"Jupiter? It'd take weeks to get there from here!" Julia said.

"No, with our technology it's mere hours. Our thrusters accelerate much faster than the technology humans have today," Raja interjected.

"Wait, how does the Gr-awl-toltz control you from that far away?" Lauren asked.

"Good question," Ankit said. "There's a neuro-repeater at the star gate that can relay the neuro-transmissions. It extends their reach when they aren't close enough."

"What are you talking about?" Julia asked.

"These devices can re-transmit the Gr-awl-toltz brain waves allowing them to control us at great distances," Raja added.

"Here we are," Ankit said, standing up as the train arrived at the Grid 2 station.

Julia led the other three through the narrow maze of hallways leading to Morrison's mod shop. They rounded the last corner with a hot, humid gust of air greeting them.

Julia looked down, rubbing her forearms as the moist air condensed on her arm. She looked back to make sure the rest of the group was following. As they came up to the shop, she noticed the light was still broken outside the shop, as it was when they had been there before.

They walked through the dimly lit doorway, looking around. The girls squinted. They recognized the man whose reptilian form and gangly arms draped over the counter. Low light reflected from his part-human skin, part-lizard scales.

Morrison recognized them, too, turning a side of his mouth up, smirking, “What are you . . . sss . . . two doing back here?”

He didn’t acknowledge their two companions.

The girls walked up to the counter. Julia asked, “Remember us?”

“Not too many kidssss your age coming in here . . . ssss . . . how can I help you today?”

“We need some equipment,” Julia said, slapping her phone on the counter and showing him the screen.

“Still feissssty assss ever,” Morrison said, eyeing the phone from a distance. He picked it up, bringing it closer to his face.

“Hmm . . . how . . . ssss . . . are you kidssss going to . . . pay for . . . thissss?” he asked, looking back at the two.

Lauren motioned to Ankit behind her. He stepped forward out of the shadows, extending his closed hand over the counter and dropping a handful of credits.

“Untracablesssss,” Morrison said, licking his lips. He narrowed his eyes at Ankit.

Ankit retracted his hand, clasping it with his other hand in front of his body, not a trace of emotion crossing his face.

Morrison looked at the credits, then back at Ankit. “You’re not one of them, are you? Sssss.”

Lauren’s face flushed. She turned away, diverting her gaze out the door. Morrison didn’t notice. Julia just stared at the equipment behind the counter.

“Them?” Ankit inquired, his eyebrow lifting slightly on one side. Lauren and Julia couldn’t see what Morrison saw, since they could see through Ankit's disguise now and hoped it was still fooling Morrison.

Morrison smiled, showing his needle-like teeth. "No matter, these creditssss are good," he said, swiping the credits up into his hand walking to the back of his store.

Lauren and Julia looked at each other, then back to their two companions. Ankit shuffled slightly, then winked at the two.

After about 10 minutes, Morrison returned, carrying a box of equipment. "Here'ssss the first box." He went to the back of the store again.

The next box was a little bigger than the first. Raja picked up one box, setting it on his shoulder without as much as a grunt. Ankit picked up the bigger one, then turned to leave the store.

"Now that we have this equipment, where is your hideout? We need to get started," Julia said to Ankit.

"Hideout, huh? Never thought of it like that, but I guess it is. Yes, follow us," he said, shifting the box on his shoulder.

They weaved through some more hallways, this time with Raja leading the way.

"It's deeper into Grid 2—about five minutes from here," Ankit said after a few minutes of walking.

"Can you make it carrying all that stuff?" Lauren asked.

Raja simply said, "Yes," picking up his pace.

As they ventured deeper into Grid 2, the people's mods got more and more spectacular. By now, the two thought they were used to just about any mod they could imagine, but they weren't prepared for some of the stranger ones.

A large man, about six feet tall at his shoulders, turned a corner in front of them. The girls looked up, seeing a part-bull, part-human head sitting on top of the man's shoulders, with large horns extending out from the sides of his head. Snot and mist blew from his nostrils as he made his way through the crowd. His angry eyes focused only on the direction he was going.

The two had read about the Minotaur in Greek mythology, but never had they thought they'd see one in person. They both glanced up, and the man's eyes met theirs for a split second. Julia and Lauren hid their eyes, looking down at the ground.

The girls weaved through the crowds, following their new Zeb companions, careful not to look up again for fear of seeing another unusual mod. Raja and Ankit carried the equipment ahead of them.

As with the rest of Grid 2, dim lights flickered on and off and moisture filled the air. Lauren twitched her nose. A foul stench permeated the halls.

Julia covered her mouth gagging. “What is that smell?”

Shortly after, Raja and Ankit turned down a narrow hallway next to a large storage facility. They stopped in front of a nondescript door at the back of the alley. Lauren looked around while they waited to go inside.

Rusty metal plates covered the walls and ceilings all around them. Most of the structures in Grid 2 were like this—built out of necessity rather than with a master plan. This apartment was no exception, tucked away in this alley. Lauren supposed someone had probably needed a hideout to avoid raising suspicion, which is exactly what Ankit and Raja needed, too.

“How did you find this place?” Lauren asked, muffled, not really expecting an answer.

Ankit waved his hand in front of the door. It opened, revealing a large living room with a couple of doors in the back. A small kitchenette was off to the right of the door. Tables lined the walls, with some leftover containers they could only assume was lunch.

“Welcome to our humble apartment. This is where we will set up our workshop,” Ankit said, setting his box of equipment down.

Lauren looked around. No pictures or personal items lined the walls or furniture. It was definitely Spartan, she thought, but they hadn’t been here that long, either.

“Looks homey,” she said, forcing a smile.

“Ha ha,” Ankit chuckled. “You don’t have to be that polite. This is temporary.”

“Oh, whew, I can’t fib very well.”

“No kidding?” Raja shot a crooked grin at her.

Ankit walked over to a table bumped up against the wall where a computer screen sat. “Here’s where I get access to the system. I can see what is going on at all times here.”

“Like what?” Lauren asked, walking closer.

“Well, as Zebs, we have control of all the systems on the station. I still have access because I stole one of the other guy’s codes before we left. He doesn’t know I have access yet.”

“So you can see everything?” Lauren asked, widening her eyes.

“Yep, take a look here.” He showed the station schematics. “Show Zeb factory.” The map zoomed in where the factory was and highlighted the section that wasn’t normally visible.

“Well, let’s get this stuff set up,” Julia said, clearing some space on the tables.

There were seven chambers she furiously started to assemble. They were much more automatic than the manual chambers she had before. This time she could just put all the materials in the chambers, enter the instructions, and it would do the rest.

She pulled together the crystals, jellyfish material, and the secret crud she had from back at her home, putting them in each of the chambers. She entered the instructions, then sat back in her chair.

“All done,” she said.

“That’s it? It took a lot longer last time,” Lauren said.

“I know! This equipment is great! But it will still take another week or so to cook,” Julia answered.

“I had enough to jump start this one from the previous experiment, but these have to go from scratch,” she said motioning to the first chamber.

“All right, well, I guess that’s all we can do now,” Lauren said. She wanted to get out of there. She still didn’t trust Raja and Ankit fully yet and wanted to get back home. They grabbed their things, heading for the door.

“I guess we’ll see you in a few days. I need to come back and check them,” Julia said.

Ankit got up to see them out. He grabbed Lauren gently by the forearm. “Thank you. I’m not sure you two realize yet what you’ve done.”

“You’re right. We don’t. It’s like we’re living in a science fiction story right now,” Lauren answered. She and Julia turned to walk down the hallway and catch the train back to their apartment.

Chapter 19

Flying out to Jupiter

It had been a few days since they went to the hideout, but Julia needed to check the ooze to see how it was progressing. So after school the two girls headed down to Grid 2. As usual, they told their mother they needed something for school. They thought she was starting to get suspicious.

"We need to come up with a better excuse," Lauren said to Julia on the way out.

"Yeah, I think Mom is catching on to us," Julia said.

The two hopped onto the train and rode down to Grid 2. Grid 2 was certainly not a place for two young kids, but the two of them walked through it like they were pros. Avoiding eye contact, lying low, they navigated the halls and ended up in front of the storage facility hiding their new friends' quaint home.

They walked down the alley, up to the hidden apartment. Lauren waved her hand in front of the door. They heard a faint ring in the room that must have been a doorbell. The door opened.

"Girls, we don't have as much time as we thought," Ankit said as they entered the apartment.

"What do you mean?" Lauren asked, setting her bag down and putting her hands on her hips.

"It's almost done. We have to act now."

"The gate? What could we possibly do?"

"We need to get out there and try something," Ankit said.

"But we don't have enough of the treatment. We won't be able to inoculate all of them!" Julia protested.

"That's a chance we have to take," he said.

"Well, how are you even going to get there? You two are fugitives!"

"Yes. Yes, we are," he said looking down at the ground.

Raja cleared his throat. "We will have to surrender."

"What do you mean?" Julia asked.

"You're right, Raja, that's the only way," Ankit confirmed. "We will surrender and hope we can release the treatment somewhere inside the gate."

"Won't they just shoot you out of the sky?" Julia asked.

"Again, that's a chance we'll have to take."

"They wouldn't shoot you if we were with you. They want us as prisoners," Lauren said, staring at Ankit.

"No, no. We don't need to do that."

They all sat trying thinking of alternatives.

"We're in this together," Lauren said. "There's no way the two of you can make it there alive. They'd blow you out of space. You know it's true. With us, they'd want to keep us captive and wait for instructions from the Gr-awl-toltz. There's just too much at stake to do anything less!"

"You know she's right," Raja said. "They would buy us enough time to get the treatment distributed to several of our people. Then we could disable the neuro-repeater."

Ankit didn't say anything for a moment. He just sat looking ahead.

"Fine. You can go."

Lauren didn't know if she should smile or get sick to her stomach. Thinking about flying in a ship out to Jupiter was amazing, but the dire circumstances were enough to make her ill.

"When do we go?" she asked.

"As soon as we can," he said.

Julia walked over to the chambers situated throughout the room. She looked through the glass on each one, peering at the crystals and looking for the telltale ooze.

"Looks like there's some ready in these three." She pointed at three boxes on the far table, then went to look at the rest of the chambers on the kitchen table. "Part of these two are ready over here."

"OK, what do we do with this now?" she asked. "I usually scrape it off and put it in vials, but there's too much to do that now."

"Here." Ankit stepped toward her, holding a small canister in the palms of his hands.

"It won't all fit in there."

"It will compress," he said.

He carefully opened the lid on one of the chambers and reached in with the canister. With the touch of a button, the end of the canister opened and sucked in the ooze from the crystal. He went to the next chamber, picking up the rest of the ooze that was ready, and to the next one.

Once done, he turned and handed the canister to Julia. "This canister is undetectable when they scan you. Put it in your fanny pack." He nodded toward her pack. "Then, when I give you the signal, press this button and drop it on the floor."

Julia took the canister and tucked it into her fanny pack, nodding.

"What do you mean it's undetectable?" she asked.

"We can modify signatures of things. I've changed this so that when they scan it, it will look like a canister of water, which would not be unusual for you to carry. So they wouldn't suspect anything."

"We have to call Mom and tell her something," Lauren interrupted.

"Call her and tell her we're spending the night at Alyssa's," Julia said.

Lauren picked up her phone. "Call Mom."

A second later, she spoke into it, "Mom, can we spend the night at Alyssa's tonight? We're at her apartment now."

Pause.

"Yes, both of us. She went with us down to Grid 11 to pick up the stuff and wanted us to stay."

Pause.

"Uh, let me check where she is. Hold on." She put her hand over the phone and whispered to the group. "She's asking for Alyssa's mom!"

Ankit reached for the phone. "Let me speak to her."

Lauren frowned at him, but handed the phone to him anyway.

"What is your mother's name?" he asked.

"Kathryn."

He put the phone to his mouth and spoke, but when he spoke it sounded like Alyssa's mom, "Hello? Oh, hi, how are you, Kathryn?"

Pause.

“Of course it’s no problem. They can stay until tomorrow afternoon.”

He listened for a second longer. “Yes, of course. Here she is.”

Lauren grabbed the phone, covering the mouthpiece again. “You’re going to have to tell me how you did that. That was cool.” Then she spoke again to her mother.

“Yes, Mom. OK, we’ll see you tomorrow.” She slipped her phone back in her pocket. “OK, we’re ready.”

“How do we get there?” Julia asked.

Raja smiled. “Now we get to show you some real technology.”

“We have a number of hidden ports up and down the station. We have our ship at one that hasn’t been used in a while,” Ankit answered Julia.

“Ports? What do you mean ports?” Lauren asked.

“They’re small rooms we had converted to be undetected by humans, but they allow us access to fly in and out of the station whenever we want,” Ankit said.

“This, I have to see! Let’s get going,” Julia said.

The four left the apartment again, losing themselves in the Grid 2 crowd. Ankit and Raja took them to the other side of Grid 2, where they hadn’t been before. Ducking behind some garbage collection areas, they found a small steel plate that looked like a riveted patch instead of a door. Ankit waved his hand in front of it and it opened. They looked to make sure no one was watching them and walked in. A small ship occupied the space.

“Wow!” Lauren said, walking up and caressing the side of the gleaming ship.

The angular shape flared out toward the back, making the ship look like a bullet. A chiseled groove wrapped around the sides of the ship, separating the body from the windshield. Strange runes they couldn't understand were written on the side.

"What does that say?" Julia asked.

"Nothing really, just a name and number," Raja said in a monotone voice.

Ankit stepped up to it and the door split open, with the top swinging up and the bottom down. The four of them stepped in. There was room enough to walk in between the seats, but there were only four seats in the craft.

"OK, you two sit back here." Ankit pointed to the seats in the back.

Julia and Lauren strapped themselves in. Ankit grabbed the controls, lifting the ship up. The dock opened behind them, and he backed it out. In a flash, they were out into space, flying toward Jupiter.

The ship was small inside. There was room enough for them to get up and stretch their legs beside their seats, but not much more. Lauren wasn't sure what to do if she had to go to the bathroom. It didn't look like there was one on the ship.

Ankit swung around to talk to the girls. "OK, the trip will take about four hours. We're out in space, so if you have to get up and move around, you're going to float. Are you OK?"

Julia had already pulled out her phone and was playing a game. Lauren stared out the window.

"Yes, we're good," Lauren said.

Julia just nodded.

Lauren drifted off to sleep, thinking about all that had transpired. Her eyes twitched as she recalled the harrowing experiences. Julia played her game, then went to sleep, frowning with concern. At least the ride in space was peaceful and quiet.

"Girls! We're almost there," Ankit said, leaning back.

The enormous planet Jupiter occupied the entire view. The vivid bands of clouds swirled and swayed on its surface, soothing the girls. Io, one of Jupiter's moons, floated in front of them, an eerie greenish color. They could see hundreds of big volcanoes projecting from the surface. One of them fumed a yellowish gas. Over the top of Io, they saw a sliver of the star gate. Each kilometer they sped closer, the gate got bigger and bigger.

Lauren stared at it in awe, "My God!" Her face went white as the gate came into full view. The two sisters leaned forward to see it better.

The star gate was an enormous steel ring anchored by a base attached to the bottom. From their ship it looked complete. A few bots welded pieces of metal here and there with flashes of light around the ring, but there weren't any major gaps or holes around it.

Floating some distance from the ring was a large structure that Lauren could only think looked like the control station. It was many times larger than the base and seemed to be the destination they were headed for.

Julia pointed to it. "Is that where we are going?"

"Yes," was all Ankit said as he adjusted some of the controls.

The two girls settled back into their seats, looking at each other. Then, just as they started feeling comfortable, sparks gathered around the perimeter of the ring, crackling against the structure.

The sparks grew more intense, reaching toward the center in a brilliant flash, surrounding a solid black core in the center.

"No! They're in final test mode. They're only days away!" Ankit said.

Ankit guided their ship closer to the base of the gate. As they approached a hanger, he pressed a button on the control panel in front of him, "This is *Fra-si-tot* requesting access to land."

The voice on the other end responded, but Ankit had headphones on, so the girls couldn't hear it.

Ankit turned to the girls. "They're letting us land. They don't yet realize this ship is compromised. Be prepared. Once we land, they will immediately know. They'll take us into custody and lead us to the detention center. When we get there, you know what to do . . . Are you ready?"

The girls stared straight ahead. Their mouths clinched. Lauren glanced at their new friend, saying, "We're ready."

Julia's body trembled for a moment. She shook it off, then grasped her sister's hand.

Lauren clasped her hand over her sister's, caressing it. She leaned over and said to her sister, "Whatever happens here . . ."

"No, we're going to be fine," Julia returned, with her eyes welling up with tears.

"All right, let's do this," Ankit said, and he pulled the ship into the dock.

There were no doors on the space dock. It looked like the whole dock was exposed to space. But Zebs still walked around on the deck without getting sucked out into the vacuum. When the ship crossed the bay threshold, a purple electric haze encircled the ship.

"Why aren't there any doors on the dock?" Julia asked, leaning forward.

"You see that electric field?" Raja pointed to the haze.

"Yes," Julia answered.

"It keeps the air in and space out."

She sat back, satisfied with the answer.

The control center station didn't rotate like one of the human-built space stations, and as soon as they landed, gravity took hold. Lauren peered out the window.

"Why isn't everything floating?" she asked.

"Ah . . . we have much more advanced technology. On our stations, we employ gravity balancers that generate their own gravity pull on each deck," Ankit said, smiling. "Now, you won't be used to this. Our gravity is a little stronger than yours and our atmosphere a little wetter, so it will take some time to get used to."

The ship sailed into the dock and came to a stop. The door to the ship split in half, with the top section shifting up and the bottom section settling down on the dock's floor. As it touched, the smooth surface of the door expanded into steps.

The four stood. Just as Ankit had warned, Lauren and Julia felt the stronger gravity immediately. Julia shook her legs, getting used to the new tug, then the two followed Ankit and Raja down the steps. The humid air seeped into their lungs, making them feel like they were in a swamp.

A couple of Zebs in uniforms came to greet them. As they approached, they lost their smiles of greeting and looked shocked.

The older of the pair approached, asking Ankit, "Uh, what are these human children doing here?"

Ankit put his hand on Lauren's shoulder. "I am Ankit. They are with me."

"Ankit!" the Zeb said, surprised. Immediately, something invisible pulled at the Zeb. He strained, resisting, but something forced him to grab his weapon and point it at Ankit.

The younger Zeb tapped his shoulder. "Control, we have Captain Ankit and he's brought two human children with him."

The Zeb listened to something, holding his hand over his ear.

"Understood, I will bring them to you right away."

The muscles in his neck clinched as he said, "Come . . . with me."

"It is OK. Do not resist, my friend," Ankit said to the Zeb guard.

The other guard took out a baton-like device and moved it up and down in front of Ankit. He then looked at it, nodded to the other Zeb, and did the same to Raja.

"That must be a scanner," Lauren whispered to Julia.

Julia held her breath as he scanned her, but just like with Ankit and Raja, he looked at the screen and nodded to the other guard.

He scanned Lauren, then extended his arm, pointing toward the bay exit. The guard in front guided Ankit, Raja, and the girls toward the door.

Inside, the walls were bare and grey, giving the whole station a military feel. The ceilings were lower than on human stations, but otherwise, it looked remarkably similar to the new construction section of New Cielo.

Their entourage marched through the halls, winding through the lower floor and arriving at an elevator that took them up a couple more floors to an open gallery. Zebs they passed stopped to stare, not sure what to think about two human girls being paraded around the star gate as prisoners.

In the larger gallery, Zebs scurried about, moving equipment or themselves from one part of the gate to the other.

One of the Zebs pointed to a corner hall. They started walking in that direction when Ankit grabbed his chest, stumbled, and fell to one leg. The two Zeb guards went to help him up, the older one saying, “Come on, get up. Let’s get to detention.”

Lauren stopped, putting her hand on his shoulder. Ankit looked up at her, whispering, “Now.”

Lauren looked back at Julia, who immediately knew what to do. She turned slightly so neither guard could see her. She opened her fanny pack and pulled the treatment canister out. She flipped the lid, pressed the button on the side, then rolled it on the floor into the middle of the room.

The familiar foul stench permeated the room. Each and every Zeb clutched their mouths and noses, trying to avoid the smell. Even the girls, who were used to the smell, had trouble given the amount of treatment spilling out of the canister. The two guards held their noses, pulling Ankit to his feet.

“What is that smell?” the younger guard screamed. He pushed the group along. “Let’s go, move it. Keep going.” He pointed toward the other side of the room, grimacing and trying to cover his nose.

Raja lingered back next to Julia in the group. “Good job. Now we wait.”

On the other side of the gallery, there was a detention area where the guards deposited them. “I don’t know what you were trying to pull with that foul smell, but it didn’t work. Stay here until we figure out what to do with you.”

The young guard stayed in the room while the older one left. He came back a few minutes later.

“Is that smell gone?” the young guard asked.

“Yes, it’s gone. Somebody picked up that canister the little human girl dropped and disposed of it,” the older guard said.

“Good, that was terrible.” The young one waved his hands around his nose.

“The General said we should leave them here in detention until he figures out what to do with them,” the older Zeb said, fiddling with his fingers, looking at their prisoners.

The room was small, but functional. A small table with chairs lined one wall and a couple of bed-like benches lined the other walls.

At the door, there was a panel with buttons and a strange language inscribed on the keypad, symbols similar to the ones on Ankit’s ship. One of the Zeb guards punched some of the buttons, making beeping noises. They left, with the door sliding shut.

“Like I said, now we wait,” Raja said, lying down on one of the benches. He folded his arms on his chest and closed his eyes.

“How is he so calm?” Lauren asked Ankit. “We’re in a prison cell on a star gate that’s about to flood our solar system with a ton of those squid monsters, and we’re trapped here!”

“You see, shortly after we were affected by the treatment, we blacked out. We both woke a day later with the bond broken. Much quicker than what happened with you,” Ankit assured Lauren.

“A whole day? I’m starving! If they black out, they won’t feed us!” Julia protested.

Ankit smiled, looking at Julia. “I don’t think you’d like what we eat.”

“Oh, man!” Julia complained sitting down on the other bench.

Lauren sat down at the table, taking her phone out of her pocket. She started tapping on the screen.

"What are you doing?" Julia asked her.

"Playing a game . . . what else am I going to do?" Lauren responded.

"Does the phone work?" Julia asked.

Lauren tapped a few more buttons and held it up to her head. "No, nothing."

"You wouldn't be able to get any signal out here anyway," Ankit said.

Julia pulled out her phone and started to play a game, too. Hours passed. Mostly Lauren and Julia played games on their phones. Ankit would pace around, then sit. Raja drifted in and out of sleep on one of the daybeds.

"I'm bored," Julia said.

"We're prisoners. You're supposed to be bored," Ankit said.

Julia nodded in acknowledgement to Ankit, sighed, and went over to the other daybed to lie down.

Julia flipped and flopped on the daybed, then propped herself up on her arm. "So why don't you use your Zeb name?" she asked.

"Oh, we've been using our human names for so long, we've almost forgotten our Zeb names," Ankit replied.

Julia looked up at him. "What is your Zeb name?"

"Ah . . ." Ankit sighed, "My name was Tosh-ka."

Julia tried to pronounce it the way Ankit did, but mangled the second syllable.

Ankit laughed, “Almost.”

Shortly thereafter, Julia drifted off to sleep.

An hour later, Lauren slumped over in her chair, asleep.

* * *

Julia stirred, blinking her eyes. She lay on the daybed, trying to decide if she should get up or just lie there staring at the ceiling. She looked over at her sister, who was sitting asleep in a chair. She looked for Ankit and Raja, but she didn’t see them in the room.

“That’s strange. Where are they?” she said aloud. She sat up and said, “Lauren, are you awake?”

Lauren snorted and rubbed her face but didn’t wake up.

Julia walked over to her and shook her. “Lauren?”

This time, Lauren blinked her eyes, then rubbed them. “What?”

“Ankit and Raja aren’t here,” she said, then walked over to the door and looked out the window. Everything was brighter and whiter than she remembered it, looking very sterile. She put her hand on the door and it slid opened.

“Lauren, look, the door’s open.”

Lauren got up, walking over to look out the door.

“That’s strange,” she said.

The two ventured out into the hall. The makeshift prison cell was right off the main hall, but no Zebs seemed to be around. The room was empty.

“This is really strange,” they both said at the same time.

“Jinx,” Lauren said.

Julia just glared at her sister.

“Well, let’s look around,” Lauren said.

They walked across the room to the other side to what looked like a cafeteria. Food preparation machines littered the space, all of them were completely clean and abandoned. The girls walked further in.

Julia absently picked up a whisk, examining it.

Boom! Screech!

The noise from their last dream pierced their ears.

“Oh, God, it’s another dream! It must be the Gr-awl-toltz coming after us again!” Lauren said.

“What do we do?” Julia asked.

“How should I know? It’s a dream! But that thing can still hurt us,” Lauren shot back.

They both peeked out the kitchen door. The brightness that had persisted before was eclipsed by a dark presence.

“Come on, let’s go this way,” Lauren said, running to the back of the kitchen. There were supply closets lining the walls.

The screeching noise rang in their ears again, this time closer. They sensed it was in the kitchen.

“Quick, in here,” Julia said, opening one of the doors. They ducked into an empty room and closed the door. They both slid to the ground, huddling in fear. The light shone through the door cracks.

Julia buried her head in her hands. “Wake up, wake up, this isn’t happening.”

Lauren simply hugged her knees.

The noise got closer, hurting them again. Both girls closed their eyes, trying to ward off the sound. The light shining through the cracks dimmed. The noise stopped.

Julia looked at her sister, whispering, "Is it gone?"

As Julia spoke, Lauren saw the faint outline of what she thought was a tentacle creep toward her sister. Before she could say anything, a tentacle wrapped itself around her neck, coming from the other side of the door.

Julia's eyes widened. Before she could move, the other tentacle wrapped itself around Julia's neck, then her body. Like a python squeezing the life out of its prey, with each breath the girls took, the tentacle compressed more. Their breaths got shallower and shallower as the grip from the tentacle slowly killed them. Lauren reached out to grab Julia's hand on the floor. Julia squeezed her fingers, then they both blacked out.

* * *

"Julia! Julia, wake up." Lauren shook her sister.

"What, what?" Julia jumped up, startled. She patted herself, making sure all her parts were there, then reached up to feel her neck.

"We're alive. I'm not sure why, but we are," Lauren said.

Julia took a deep breath.

Ankit walked over to them. "What happened? Are you two OK?"

"Another dream . . . I thought we were going to die this time," Lauren said.

"What kind of dream?" Ankit asked.

"I don't want to talk about it or think about it," Lauren said.

“It must have been the Gr-awl-toltz,” Raja said sitting up.

“How long has it been?” Julia asked.

“It’s been about 24 hrs since you dropped the treatment,” Ankit said.

The girls sat, regaining their composure until the door suddenly opened. The older of the two guards who had apprehended them came in. “I don’t know how you did it, but the bond is broken with some of us.” A smile appeared as he spoke.

“I am Ramesh.” He walked forward, patting Ankit on his shoulder.

“It was only a matter of time, my friend,” Ankit said smiling back.

“How?” Ramesh asked.

Ankit turned and pointed at both Lauren and Julia. “You have these two to thank. They are the ones who discovered the treatment.”

Ramesh stepped forward, outstretching his hand. “You two have no idea what this means for us.”

Lauren reached to shake Ramesh’s hand. “Uh, you’re welcome?”

“Well, you can explain it to me later.” Ramesh’s smile melted to a longer face. “The treatment only worked on half of our people. There are a number still under its control. We have to expose them, too.”

“That’s impossible! We used all the treatment yesterday,” Julia said, joining the conversation.

“They’re trying to open the gate,” Ramesh said, looking at Ankit. “They have barricaded themselves in the control room.”

“Hurry, we have to destroy the neuro-repeater,” Ankit said.

"We did that for this section, but it's too strong on the other side of the station," Ramesh said. "Come, we must go."

The four Zebs rushed out of the room.

Raja turned when he got to the door and said to the girls, "You two stay here. It could get dangerous."

Lauren and Julia looked at him with wide eyes. He left the door open, so they weren't prisoners, but they stayed put like he told them to—at least initially.

"That must have been what saved us, when they blocked the neuro-transmitter," Lauren said.

"We got lucky," Julia said.

Lauren paced around the room not saying anything. Julia sat back down on the bench.

After ten minutes or so, Lauren couldn't stand it anymore, "We can't just stay here. If they open that gate, that's the end of the station. Maybe even Earth!"

Julia shook her head. "They said to stay right here! I'm not going anywhere."

"Well, you can stay here. I'm going to go out there to see how I can help," Lauren said, stomping out the door.

"Ugh! She always does this!" Julia muttered to herself, then adjusted her fanny pack and ran toward the door.

Out of the detention cell, they found themselves back in the large gallery filled with Zebs. There was so much commotion that the two girls went unnoticed. Zebs were running in all directions.

Then an older Zeb saw the girls and stopped what he was doing. "You two are the human girls who were with Ankit?"

Lauren looked up at him. He was only a little bit taller than she was. "I guess so."

"I want to shake your hand! That's what you humans do, isn't it?" he said, extending his hand smiling.

Lauren reached out, grabbing his hand, and then Julia did the same.

"You girls have no idea what this means for us," he said.

"We've heard," Lauren said.

"Our people back home. This is the first step to freeing our people back home! All because of you! You're going to be famous in our world one day," he said, walking off to continue what he was doing.

Lauren looked at Julia, shaking her head, "What is he talking about?"

"I don't know," Julia shrugged.

In the big hall, the back wall was a large window. They could see the star gate ring hovering in the distance. All of a sudden, giant sparks of electricity crackled around the perimeter of the ring, just as it had done when they arrived. But this time, the intensity increased.

All the Zebs in the hall stopped what they were doing and looked at it. Most of them were completely speechless, staring with gaping mouths.

Lauren stopped one of the Zebs rushing by, grabbing him by his elbow. He looked over at her, surprised at first.

Lauren said, "Yes, we're the two human girls you've heard about . . ."

His eyebrow cocked up while he looked at them, then he grinned. "Yes, I assumed."

"What is going on here?" Lauren asked.

"The Zebs that didn't get your treatment . . . they're trying to open the gate," he said.

"Can't we stop them?" she asked.

"The General and Ankit are trying to stop them," he answered.

"You know Ankit, too?" Julia asked.

"Of course. He's our one of our most revered Captains! It caused quite a stir when he broke his bond!" he said. "If you'll excuse me, I have to go help them." He ran off into the crowd.

The other Zebs stood for a few moments longer, then broke into chaos again, running around like ants that just had their mound destroyed.

The girls kept staring at the gate. In the center, a black ball appeared. It got bigger and bigger, almost reaching the edge of the ring.

The girls looked into the blackness expecting to see a void. Instead it was one of the most horrifying visions they could have imagined.

Julia gasped, then reached into her fanny pack and pulled out her microscope. Her trusted device could magnify anything, not just microscopic organisms. She pushed a few buttons, then held it up in between her and the window. She motioned with her fingers in a flicking motion. The view on the screen zoomed in.

Lauren looked at the screen, terrified. Julia's hand shook. In the view, they could clearly see thousands of Gr-awl-toltz creatures waiting on the other side of the star gate, their squid-like tentacles flailing in space, flashing lights parading over their exoskeletons in a brilliant display. Mesmerized, the girls just stared.

A handful of the Gr-awl-toltz monsters broke rank, surging forward to the star gate. They got bigger and bigger as they approached the gate, forming a single-file line, ready to jump through.

The first one in line reached a massive tentacle through the gate, then as quickly as the black void appeared, it shrunk back to nothing and the electric sparks stopped. As the sparks receded, the enormous tentacle that had breeched the gate was severed from the Gr-awl-toltz's body. It had momentum and floated by the control ship, flailing like a lizard tail that had just gotten pulled off.

Blood-like liquid coagulated into balls behind the tentacle. As it floated by, one of the blood balls splattered the window with a big thud. As it did, every Zeb in the hall jumped up with their hands in the air, cheering.

Moment later, they could see the other end of the tentacle whipping around, heading straight for the station. The massive limb struck the station with an enormous force strong enough to knock the girls off their feet.

They looked up. The tentacle had smashed a hole in the window they were looking out of. There were narrow walkways around the perimeter of the room where a couple of Zebs were working on repairs. The two next to the smashed window floated up and out into space.

The girls could feel the air getting thinner as it got sucked out of the room. Then a purple haze of electricity formed around the hole and the whishing sound stopped. The girls stood, holding each other, staring at the gaping hole

Chapter 20

Space Ship Pilots

"Come on!" Lauren tugged at Julia's arm. "We need to find Ankit and Raja. And we need call Mom and Dad. I'm sure they're worried about us!"

Julia nodded.

The two didn't know where to start, so they just started wandering around the halls, asking if anyone knew were Ankit and Raja were. Most of the Zebs had heard about the girls, but they were still taken aback by seeing the two in person.

"Have you seen Ankit or Raja?" Lauren asked one of the Zebs walking by.

The Zeb stopped, startled. "Yes, they're on the upper deck with the General."

"Thanks!" she shouted to his back as he kept walking.

"Where's the upper deck?" Julia asked her sister.

"How should I know?"

"Well, let's ask someone," Julia said.

Lauren shook her head, feigning frustration, and stopped the next Zeb walking by.

"How do we get to the upper deck?" she asked.

He pointed over to some double doors, "There, that's the elevator. Get on and say *Upper Deck*. It will take you there."

The girls did as he said, boarding the elevator. “Upper Deck.”

Nothing happened.

“Upper Deck,” Lauren said again.

Again, nothing happened.

A Zeb boarded the elevator and said, “Upper Deck,” eyeing the girls.

The elevator closed the doors and went up.

“That’s weird, why didn’t it work for us,” Julia asked.

“Because you’re not speaking Zeb,” the Zeb said.

“What do you mean? We said ‘Upper Deck’,” Lauren said.

“Yes, but you said it in your native language. The nano-bots translate language for your ears, so you hear us speaking your language, but we’re actually speaking our language,” he said with a smile.

A half a minute later, the doors opened, revealing a scene of Zebs running in all directions. At the center of the fray, Ankit stood next to an older Zeb who was giving orders to a group. The group disbanded.

Lauren and Julia walked toward him.

Ankit looked up. “What are you two doing up here?”

“We came to help!” Julia said, snapping to attention.

“And we need to call our parents,” Lauren added.

“Yes, I’m sure they’re concerned,” Ankit said.

“Let’s call Dad first. If we try to explain it to him, he can calm Mom down,” Julia said.

"Here, let's go over to this room." Ankit led the way to a room in the corner.

In the room, there was a screen on the table.

Ankit waved his hand in front of the screen and it turned on. "It's tied in to all the systems in the Cielo complex."

Raja came in, looking around. "Everything OK?"

"Yes, they just wanted to call their parents," Ankit responded.

"Call Dad," Lauren said into the screen.

A message flashed on the screen, "Locating . . ." Then the picture flashed on to their dad.

"Where are you two?" their dad said, looking at them through the phone.

"Well, that's kind of hard to explain, Dad," Lauren muttered.

"Hard to explain, huh?" He frowned at her. "Well, you two were right. I've seen them."

"Seen what?" Lauren asked.

"Seen those creatures. The ones that are kind of like us."

"You mean the Zebs?"

"Yes, they're all over out here. I thought we just had a bunch of short workers, but many of them are Zebs," he said.

"You mean they're out there mining the asteroids?" Julia asked.

"Yes! I tried contacting you two earlier, but I couldn't get through. Which is strange because I could talk to your mother. I haven't talked to her since last night. She said you were spending the night at Alyssa's," he said.

"Where are you now?" Lauren asked.

"We're on a little ship coming back to the station. No Zebs are on here. I checked," he responded. "Where are you?"

"Well, we're kind of out near Jupiter," Lauren said, rolling her eyes, looking up at the ceiling, and smiling.

Julia jumped in, bumping her sister out of the way. "Yeah, Dad, we're out here close to Jupiter. You have NO idea what's gone on out here, but don't worry, it will all be fine now."

"JUPITER! What! How! That's impossible. How did you get out there? Does your mom know where you are?" he shouted.

"Dad, we're fine. I promise! We have a LOT to tell you. I wish you would have believed us before . . ." Lauren said.

"Well, do you blame me? I couldn't have believed you without seeing it myself. But I'd believe anything now," he responded.

Overhead alarms sounded on their dad's transport ship. He turned around to see what it was.

"What is that?" Lauren asked.

"Not sure. Hold on one sec." He floated back out of the room, pulling on the door jamb with his hands. The small transport ships didn't have gravity, as they were used just for moving people back and forth between stations. He was gone for a couple of minutes and came back. "Girls, I have to go. There's some strange space ship coming right at us!"

"Wait, hold on! What does it look like?" Lauren asked. Her skin flashed hot, burning.

Her fears were confirmed when their dad responded, "It's strange. I've never seen this type of ship before. Strange markings on the side of it."

Raja was listening in the background said, "That sounds like one of our ships. They're coming for your dad. The Gr-awl-toltz wants revenge!"

Lauren turned around, looking at Raja with wide eyes. "What?"

"Who said that?" their dad asked.

She whipped around to address her dad. "I'll have to explain later, Dad." Then she asked Raja again, "What are you talking about?"

Raja said, "It knows about you. They might be primitive, but they understand revenge. It's going after your dad to get to you because it senses a connection."

The blood drained out of Lauren's face as she turned back to the phone.

Her dad asked, "What's the matter?"

"Dad, I think they're coming for you," she said.

Just then, the girls heard a loud clunk from the phone.

"What was that?" Julia asked her dad.

"I'm not sure. It sounds like they are docking onto us," he said with his voice quivering slightly. "Girls, I will be OK."

The phone picture went black.

"Dad!? Dad!?" Lauren screamed, shaking the phone.

Julia buried her head in her hands.

Ankit spoke. "Girls, the Zebs won't kill him."

When Ankit said "kill" Julia burst into tears. She sank back in her chair, the corners of her mouth turned down. Tears streamed from her eyes as she stared blankly at the ceiling.

Lauren's mouth gaped wide open. A tremor shot through her. "No, no, no," was all she could say, pounding her fists on the table.

"It's my fault," Julia said. "If I hadn't ever discovered this treatment, we wouldn't be in this mess and Dad would be safe."

Ankit looked at her sternly. "Julia, had you never found the treatment, that brigade of monsters on the other side of the star gate would be streaming their way here by now. It's because of the treatment that we can now help your father."

Julia glanced up at him, brushing her tears away.

Lauren gained her composure again, remembering she was the older sister and patted her sibling on the back.

Lauren turned to Ankit, "How do we help him now?"

Ankit scrunched his eyes, staring off in the distance. "Well, we've tested the treatment . . . it looks like it could affect the Gr-awl-toltz, but we don't know how long it would take. It could take minutes or it could be hours."

Raja interrupted, "How do we get it inside the Gr-awl-toltz? We cannot go near it. It would know we were there."

Ankit nodded, then sat down in the chair next to him.

Lauren stayed quiet for a moment longer, then sniffled and spoke in a quiet voice, "You can't . . . but we can."

"What do you mean?" he asked.

"You can't get close to it, but we can. It wants to punish us. We could go right up to it," Lauren said.

"No, it's too dangerous." Ankit shook his head at her.

"She's right. It's the only way. It wants to terminate you up close. I can almost feel its rage," Raja said, shifting his gaze to Ankit.

"Terminate?" Julia asked.

"Yes, Julia! Terminate. That thing wants to kill us! It wants us dead! And from the sound of it, it wants to torture us first!" Lauren shouted.

Julia shivered, burying her head in her knees, then looked up. "But we have to do it."

"You said the Zebs won't kill our dad. It won't kill us either until it knows it has hurt us," Lauren said.

"She's right. It would want them right next to it, so it could break through the treatment barrier. Then it would tear their minds apart," Raja said.

Julia shot a glance up to Raja. "That doesn't sound very pleasant."

"Well, that is, if the treatment doesn't work on it . . . ," Ankit said.

"We don't have any of the treatment left," Lauren said. "It would take another week to get enough."

"Not necessarily," Raja interrupted. "Here at the star gate, we have access to a lot of our technology. We have ways of accelerating the process. We could take the accelerators back to Cielo Prime."

"Yes, of course," Ankit said, turning to Raja. "Go get the General. We don't have any time to lose."

Raja ran out of the room faster than the girls had ever seen him run.

Moments later, the older Zeb Ankit had been standing next to out in the control room came to join them.

"General Santosh!" Ankit addressed the Zeb.

"Ankit, what can I do for you?" he asked.

“Biological accelerators—we need seven to take back to Cielo Prime,” Ankit said.

“What do you need them for?” the General asked.

“We can accelerate growth of the treatment with them, but the only samples we have are back on Cielo Prime.”

“Let me have them loaded onto your ship.” General Santosh excused himself from the room while he talked in to his wrist. Lauren thought it was strange, but then wondered if there was some communication device there.

“Get ready, girls. We need to go back to Cielo Prime . . . fast!” Ankit said to them.

The girls were still worrying about their father as they marched off to the ship with Ankit and Raja.

When they arrived at the dock, a number of Zebs were loading supplies into a compartment at the back of the ship. They were also outfitting the ship with what looked like missiles and other armaments.

“What’s all that stuff?” Julia asked.

“Just a few things we might need,” Raja said to her. “Now hop in. We need to get going.”

The girls boarded the ship first, then Ankit and Raja. The doors closed behind them. The Zebs finished loading the storage compartment with supplies, then backed up, giving Ankit a signal. Ankit waved back at them, firing the engines.

Ankit gently raised the ship, then did a 180-degree turn. The purple electric haze slid over the ship as it crossed the threshold to space.

“OK, you two, settle in for a little bit, then we have a surprise for you,” Ankit said to the two girls.

Lauren and Julia looked at each other. Julia asked, "What is it?"

"You'll find out!" was all he said.

The anticipation interested the girls as they sped past Io. The beautiful moon showed off its yellowish, greenish color.

"Look at that!" Julia pointed to the moon.

"What? What is it?" Lauren asked, looking where Julia was pointing.

"That, it's a lava flow. Can you see it?" Julia pulled her microscope out of her fanny pack. She held it up to the window and expanded the view.

"See! It's really cool." She held it so Lauren could see.

"Wow!" Lauren said, seeing the fast-moving lava on the surface.

Ankit wasn't paying attention to the girls. He was focused on navigating around the moon instead. Once past, he spun around addressing them.

"OK, here's your surprise," he said, clasping his hands together. "You two are going to fly the ship. I think it's something you need to know how to do."

"What? Really?" Julia said raising her voice.

"Awesome!" Lauren said.

"OK, let's switch places," Ankit said. He had put the ship on cruise control. "Lauren, you and I will switch first, then Julia and Raja."

Lauren and Ankit unbuckled, floating untethered in the ship. Lauren grabbed the seat in front of her, pulling herself out of Ankit's way as he took her seat. She then pulled herself around and strapped herself in the pilot's seat.

Julia did the same, switching with Raja, giggling the whole time, excited to fly a spaceship.

"Before we start, let me give you this." Ankit handed both Lauren and Julia small, round wristbands.

"We got these on the control ship. They can alter your body signature to make the ship think you are one of us. Wear it at all times. It doesn't just work on the ship, it works on the station too, getting you into the secret docks and other parts of the station."

They both took the wristbands and cinched them around their wrists. They didn't quite fit, but they were able to shove them up their arms to tighten them.

"Now, it's pretty easy. All the controls are where you think they should be, and they do what you think they should." He pointed to the joystick-like control on the dashboard.

"Move that around to go in the direction you want to go." Then he pointed to the accelerator control on the right. "And that control speeds you up or down."

Lauren took the controls, turning the joystick left with her hand. The ship rolled to the left.

"Whoa!" Lauren said as she moved the ship the other way. She eased the accelerator up and the ship sped faster, turning in a flat spin.

"Uh, I'm getting dizzy!" Julia said, holding her head.

Lauren laughed, trying to right the ship, then moved it around in all directions, making her passengers uncomfortable, but helping her master the controls.

"This is easy! It's just like a video game!" she laughed again as she did a barrel roll.

"OK, OK, we get it!" Ankit said. "You know how to fly the ship now."

She straightened the ship out again.

"Now, in open space like this, you can put it on autopilot, telling the ship where to go. For example, tap on that pad that looks like a map'"

Lauren scanned the dashboard. "This one?" she asked pointing to a button.

"Yes, that one."

Lauren touched the button and a map of Jupiter displayed in a holographic image by the windshield.

"Now, tap the right corner to zoom out and the left corner to zoom in," he said.

Lauren tapped the right corner of the pad.

The map zoomed out, showing Jupiter in one corner, the station complex in another corner, and asteroids in the middle.

"Good, see it's very intuitive!" Ankit said to her. "Now I can tell it to go to Cielo Prime. Go to Cielo Prime."

"Why can't I?" Lauren asked.

"You're not speaking our language," he said.

"Oh, that's right," Lauren said. "Well that's stupid! Why can't this thing speak English?"

The ship corrected its course, and on the map it showed the trajectory going to Cielo Prime.

Raja spoke to Julia. "OK, now it's your job to control the weapons."

"Yessss," Julia said, waggling her fingers, ready to grab the controls.

"Before firing the weapons, you have to engage them. You can do that by pressing that button." He pointed to a button on the control panel in front of her.

Julia pressed the button and a target cross appeared on the windshield.

"Now, move the target around until you find what you're trying to hit."

Julia moved the controls around, zeroing in on an asteroid off in the distance.

"Now, you can track the target by tapping once with your thumb or holding it down."

She tapped the button with her thumb and the target cross glowed yellow, following the targeted asteroid as the ship moved along.

"You can fire when ready with your index finger."

Julia pulled the trigger. A buzz got louder and louder for a second, then a blast of energy shot from the ship at the floating rock. Moments later the asteroid blew to bits in a cloud of dust.

"Awesome!" Julia shrieked as it blew up.

"You can fire freely by pulling the trigger, but the tracking lets you fire lots of times at the same place."

For the four hours it took to get back to Cielo Prime, the girls practiced flying and shooting. By the time they got back, Julia had shot 30 asteroids and Lauren had succeeded in making the rest of them sick.

Cielo Prime got closer and they slowed down almost to a crawl.

"OK, now that we're back at the station, tap on the map again" Ankit said to Lauren.

She tapped on the map pad and, the map of the station appeared.

Redicons circled the docks hidden around the station.

"All around the station, there are secret docks where you can land and store your ship safely," Ankit said, pointing to the dock at Grid 2, where they were headed. "Go to that one."

Ankit touched one of the docks circled in the holographic image on the windshield. The circle turned red.

Lauren guided the ship toward the dock circled in red. As she got closer, she decelerated. The doors opened when the ship approached the dock, allowing Lauren to pull the ship in. She carefully moved the ship in but nudged it too far, putting a small dent in the wall as she bumped it.

"Oops!" she said.

Ankit laughed. "Just pull it back a little."

Lauren nudged back a little and set the ship down. The doors closed behind them and the dock pressurized with air. The events of the past day and a half came crashing back, and the gravity of the situation almost paralyzed the girls. Lauren sat with her hands on the controls, staring at the wall in front of her. She shuddered.

Julia sat bleary eyed in the seat beside her. She patted Lauren on the arm. "Come on, we need to go make some more of the treatment."

Chapter 21

A New Plan

Lauren looked at her phone. "10 missed calls. Uh, oh. Looks like Mom is in panic mode," she said to her sister.

"What do we tell her?" Julia asked.

"Leave it to us," Ankit said. "But first, we need to get the treatment going."

They got out of the ship and Raja grabbed a cart. He started unloading the biological accelerators onto the cart, plus the other provisions. The four of them then headed to Ankit and Raja's apartment.

"What are we going to do about our mother?" Lauren asked Ankit.

"Whatever we do, it will be temporary. We just need to distract her for a few days. After that, if we're not successful, it's not going to matter," Ankit said.

"What can you do?" Julia asked.

"We can inject her with that serum that makes you somewhat catatonic," Ankit said. "She'd be functional, more agreeable, and not know why."

"You want to drug our mother?" Lauren said, looking at Ankit with raised eyebrows.

He paused and then said, "No, no, it's not a drug. It's not permanent. It's just a temporary microorganism that makes humans easier to control. They forget what happens during that period of time."

"We're not talking in generalities. We're talking about our mother," Lauren said.

"I don't see any other way of getting out of this," Julia said.

"I don't like it, but I guess we'll have to do it." Lauren frowned.

Back at the apartment, Raja quickly set up the equipment. They all transferred the current growing crystals into the accelerators with several new crystals. Ankit punched some buttons on them, and they appeared to work.

"All right, let's get you two back home. It will still be a couple of days before this is ready," Ankit said.

Ankit picked up a device from one of the boxes that Raja got from the ship, and they all headed out the door. The ride back to the girls' apartment was somber. The girls couldn't quit thinking about their dad and wondering if he was OK. All Ankit and Raja could do was console the girls.

They walked up to the girls' apartment and the door opened. Their mother stood in the kitchen. Her face crumbled when she saw the girls.

"Oh, God! There you are," she said, tears streaming down her face. "Where have you been?"

Before she got any further, Ankit reached over and tapped their mother on the back of her arm with the device. Almost immediately, her demeanor changed.

"Hello, girls, how are you?" She straightened her back, wiping the tears away. A fake-looking smile appeared on her face.

"Yuck. How Stepford is that?" Lauren said. "I hope this doesn't last very long. Reminds me of when Dad was like that on New Cielo."

"I'm sorry, girls. What is wrong?" Their mother's weird smile persisted.

"Nothing, Mom. We just want to go to bed," Julia said.

"And who are these nice men here?" she asked.

"We're no one," Ankit said, turning to leave.

"OK, well, thank you," their mom said, waving to them as they left.

The girls went to their room, fell on their beds, and went straight to sleep without changing their clothes.

The next day, the girls didn't go to school. They told their mother they were sick. With the serum, she didn't care and let them stay home. Mostly they tried to distract themselves throughout the day, but they couldn't. It was pure torture sitting and wondering what fate awaited their father. They hadn't heard anything about him or his ship.

In the morning, they went back to Ankit and Raja's apartment early. In a day and a half, the ooze had quadrupled. Julia was amazed at how quickly the ooze formed in the new chambers.

Peering into one of the new boxes, she spoke to the ooze as it were her friend, "Come on, little guys. You can do it, just a little more."

"Who are you talking to?" Lauren asked, glaring at her sister.

"It helps if you talk to the ooze," Julia said, smiling.

Ankit sat in the corner looking at a screen. He had been working on hiding their footprints within the Zeb system and had successfully covered most of their tracks.

Just then, the front door opened. Raja came in carrying a small bag he set on the counter. Lauren presumed it was food because it made the room stink.

Julia looked up. "That smells worse than the ooze!"

Raja chuckled deeply.

Ankit finished what he was doing, then turned to talk to the group. "Now that the ooze is coming along, we need to figure out the plan to help your father."

Lauren looked at him with a somber face. "Once again, we already know the answer. Julia and I have to go."

Julia shivered thinking about it.

"I don't like it one bit," Ankit said, "and I won't allow it. Not this time."

He took a deep breath. "I think the only option is for both Raja and me to go."

Raja spoke in a gruff voice, "We've run some simulations with the treatment and think that it will harm the Gr-awl-toltz pretty quickly. It looks like it envelops the crystals, and when it does that, the Gr-awl-toltz can't feed on them. The Gr-awl-toltz absorbs an astonishing amount, so it should affect it very quickly."

"Yes, it seems that the treatment will almost neutralize the crystals . . . BUT it must be applied directly to them, and they're in the same place as its brain," Ankit added.

"I don't like 'should'. And, how are you going to get this whole batch of treatment that close?" Lauren asked with her arms folded in front of her.

"There's a flaw in security. These masking devices we use to conceal our identity and voice to the human population can be used to hide us from it and the rest of the Zebs," Raja said.

"What do you mean?" Julia asked.

Ankit showed her the device he was wearing on his arm. "We gave these to you earlier . . . the signature modifiers. This tricks your brain to make you think we are human in the same way the Gr-awl-tolz influences you. We Zebs are suceptable, too, but no one ever thought that any of us would turn on the Gr-awl-toltz, so we didn't protect against someone using it on us."

"So we can use that to hide from the Zebs?" Julia asked.

"Yes, it can change your appearance in a hologram or it can make you disappear entirely," Ankit said.

"That's cool! So we could just walk around and they wouldn't notice us?" Lauren said. "How does it work?"

Ankit showed Lauren a sequence of buttons to push on the wristband.

"Since we all have the treatment, though, you wouldn't really know if it was working or not." Ankit pointed to an extra wristband sitting on the table. "But this is too dangerous for you two. We're going to do this alone."

"There's a supply ship that leaves every morning at 8 AM from the headquarters on New Cielo. We can hide on the ship with these devices, then board the Gr-awl-toltz and go up to it." Raja added.

"We have to go! They have our dad!" Julia objected.

"No! And that's final. I will not have your blood on my hands," Ankit said, staring at her.

"It's going to be challenging . . . but with these signature modifiers, we can trick their sensors into thinking we're friendly," Raja said.

Lauren had already checked out and wasn't paying attention anymore. She didn't want to delegate this and wanted to be there for their dad. He was their dad, she thought, and they should be there.

"Well . . . we need to go," Lauren said grabbing her bag, heading for the door.

Ankit looked at her, surprised, but just assuming they were disappointed about not being involved. "OK . . . well, we will head out tomorrow morning to get there."

Julia looked up, frowning. Lauren shot her a glance to be quiet.

Julia got up to join her sister walking out the door. She questioned her sister, "Why did you want to leave?"

"We have to go," Lauren said in a quiet voice, looking back at the apartment door while she walked.

"What are you talking about?" Julia asked.

"Ankit and Raja shouldn't do this. This is our dad!" she said.

"So what are you saying?" Julia asked.

"We have to go. We have to save dad!"

"What? How are we going to do that? Say we do get in there. Then what?" Julia asked, stopping and wrapping her arms around her waist.

"Just like they said, to them we'd be invisible. And, with those canisters, we can take the treatment right up to that thing and release it out all over it."

"OK, suppose that works, how would we ever get in there in the first place?"

"Well, just like Ankit said. I guess we can stow away on one of the supply ships. We already have the signature modifiers, we just need the treatment."

"The more I hear about this plan, the less I like it!" Julia said, shaking her head and starting to walk again.

Lauren followed, slightly behind her sister.

"The ooze is almost ready. Tomorrow there will be enough to fill the canister," Julia said.

"So tomorrow, we just come here early when they're not there, take the treatment, and head to New Cielo," Lauren said, catching up to her sister.

Back at their apartment in the safety of their room, Julia lay on her bed staring up at the ceiling. "I'm not sure I like this plan."

"I'm a little worried about it, too. Who knows what will happen to us if they find us," Lauren thought out loud.

Julia winced. "I don't like the sound of that, but you're right."

"So the plan is, we tell Mom we're going to school early, but then we go to Grid 2 instead. We'll call in sick, then collect the treatment and head directly for New Cielo. Once there, we'll stow away on the supply ship to get on the Gr-awl-toltz, then we'll release the treatment and wait to see what happens. Then we'll go find Dad." Lauren walked through the steps counting them off on her fingers.

She hesitated on the last step. She knew the plan was shaky, but she had no idea what else to do. She hoped that her insecurity wasn't obvious to Julia.

"Sounds right. We'd better get some sleep. We've got a big day tomorrow," Julia said, rolling over.

Neither of them slept very well that night. Both tossed and turned. By morning, they were ready to get the day over with.

The girls joined their family in the living room. Their mom and siblings were already up.

"You two are up early," their mom said. "What's going on?"

They didn't hear their mom, or pretended not to. They sat down next to their brother and sister on the floor.

Lauren sat staring off into space thinking about all the things they had to do that day. She suddenly realized she might not ever see any of them again. The stress was almost overwhelming. She looked around, then up to her mom.

"I love you, Mom," she said, and got up to hug her.

"Well, what's that for?" Her mom hugged her back.

Lauren sat back down, looking at her brother and sister and trying not to cry.

"Your dad called, by the way. He said he'd be another few days out there."

Lauren looked confused, then realized the Zebs must have fabricated the message so no alarms were raised.

"What's wrong with Mom?" Evan asked his sisters. "She's acting weird."

"How should we know?" Julia snapped.

"She's fine," Lauren said.

Julia was clearly agitated, fidgeting on the floor next to her brother. She scowled at the TV. "I don't want to watch that right now. Change it!"

"I was here first," Evan said, kicking his sister.

"Ow! Evan, I hate you!" Julia said, getting up from the floor.

She marched off to her room to grab some things and brush her teeth.

Lauren did the same. A moment later, they were at the door. Lauren yelled to her mom, "We're going early to do some things. We'll see you after school."

"OK. Love you!" their mom said, sitting down to join the two younger kids. Apparently, the serum was wearing down a bit, as she didn't seem so creepily cheerful this morning.

Both girls paused for a second, looking back. Lauren sniffled as the feelings swirled in her head. Julia grabbed her by the arm and dragged her out the door.

The plan was unfolding as expected. When they arrived at Ankit and Raja's hideout, they stood far enough away from the apartment so that Ankit and Raja wouldn't see them when they went out for breakfast.

After a 10-minute wait, Ankit and Raja emerged engrossed in conversation, oblivious to everything. They passed by and walked out to where the local food court was.

"Now, let's go," Lauren said, rushing over to their door. She waved her hand in front of the door and it opened.

Lauren rushed in. "We need to hurry."

Julia grabbed the canister and threw open the first box. Like a vacuum cleaner, the canister sucked up all the ooze. Then she went to the next box. She worked around the room, gathering all of the treatment.

"There, done. I can't believe it compresses so much," she said, flipping the top back on the canister and stuffing it into her fanny pack.

"Good, let's get out of here," Lauren said running for the door.

The two sprinted down the hall to the hidden dock. They stopped for a second to catch their breath and looked back behind them. Ankit and Raja were returning to their hideout, still talking.

"Come on, let's go," Lauren said.

The two weaved in and out of the crowd, eventually ending up at the small dock. Again, Lauren waved her hand in front of the camouflaged door, which opened immediately.

The two climbed in the ship, scanning the controls.

"Start engines," Lauren said aloud.

The doors shut and the engine started.

Behind the ship, the bay doors opened, exposing space.

Lauren grabbed the joystick with her left hand, backed the ship out, then twisted it clockwise. The ship did the same in unison with her movement. With her right hand, she nudged the accelerator slightly. The ship moved forward into space, hovering outside the space station.

"OK, let's go," Lauren said, accelerating and pointing the ship toward New Cielo.

"Head to the construction zone," Julia said.

"Yep, that's where I was going," her sister answered.

The trip over there was quick in this ship, only a few minutes. The ferries took 30 minutes.

Julia looked at her phone. “It’s 8:00. We need to hurry.”

Once there, Lauren tapped the map pad and the image overlaid a couple of dock icons around the construction zone.

“There,” Julia pointed. “Go to that one! It looks smaller. Then I bet that larger one is where the supply ship leaves from.”

Lauren rolled her left hand and accelerated with her right, whipping the ship around to the dock.

“Whoa! You’re getting pretty good at that,” Julia said.

Lauren didn’t answer, instead concentrating on landing the ship. The bay doors of the hidden dock opened, and she pulled the ship in and set it down.

“Here we go . . . are you ready?” she asked her sister.

Julia shivered. “I guess I have to be.”

“OK, turn on the signature modifier.” Lauren said, tapping the wristband.

“How can we make it so no one else can see us, again?” Julia asked staring at her wristband. There were six buttons in rows of three on the top of the band.

Lauren looked at hers, too. “I think it was this,” she tapping two of the buttons, then another.

Julia did the same, but nothing seemed to happen.

“Did it work?” Julia asked.

“I don’t know. I guess we’ll have to find someone to see,” Lauren said.

The two ventured forth into the construction area. They knew exactly where to find the Zebs and headed for the main hall they congregated in.

The two walked as quickly as they could, navigating the labyrinth, getting closer and closer to the hidden port. No one was around, so they didn't know if the signature modifier was working.

Finally, they saw a human man walking toward them. The two pretended to casually walk by. The man didn't notice them.

"Hold on," Lauren said, running back to where the man was. She waved her arm in front of him.

No response.

Lauren ran to catch up with her sister.

"Wow, it really does work!" Julia said.

The two kept looking for the hidden port.

"It should be right . . ." Lauren said, walking around a corner.

As soon as they rounded the corner, they stood face to face with a group of Zebs walking down the hall. Lauren and Julia stopped, staring at the group—neither breathed.

The group didn't notice the two and walked right past them and through the dock door.

Lauren grabbed her sister's hand and dragged her through the door.

The dock was bustling with activity. A mid-sized ship sat on the dock. Several Zebs were loading boxes full of supplies into the ship.

Lauren whispered to her sister, "That must be it. Let's find a way in."

The two circled the ship. On the far side, they found an open door and boarded. There were boxes of supplies all over the ship.

"Over here," Lauren said, pointing to a stack of boxes. Behind the boxes, there was enough space for the two of them to sit and peer out a window.

They sat for a few more minutes while the Zebs loaded the last of the supplies and waited for the ship to take off.

Chapter 22

Going into the Belly of the Beast

Two Zebs boarded the supply ship when it was finally loaded. They got into the cockpit and turned on the engines, then guided the ship out of the dock.

"I'm scared," Julia said to her sister.

Lauren just looked at her, thinking the same. She poised herself, saying, "We'll be OK."

The two sat in their hiding place aboard the Zeb transport ship. The ship was much larger than Ankit and Raja's ship. The girls just stared out their small circular portals into space. Lauren could see New Cielo getting smaller and smaller as the ship sped away.

Julia could see the Gr-awl-toltz in the distance getting larger and larger. She closed her eyes and shuddered. She patted her fanny pack, thinking of their plan. She had no idea if it would work, but it was the only chance they had to save their dad. So far, things were going as expected.

The supply ship accelerated as it closed in on the Gr-awl-toltz. The Gr-awl-toltz was enormous. There were tentacles spreading out from the center of the creature, which curved as the Gr-awl-toltz spun, making it look like a miniature galaxy.

The ship approached the belly of the monster. They felt a twinge of static in their brains, like a faint hum in the back of their thoughts. Lauren shook her head.

"I'm not sure this was a good idea," Julia said to her sister, cupping her hands over her ears. But it didn't help—the hum persisted.

Triangular-shaped flaps of the exoskeleton curled back like a mouth exposing the inside. The Zeb pilot guided the ship into the gaping hole.

As they entered, the flaps rescinded too, sealing them in its belly. Inside, there were thousands of smaller passageways that branched off this enormous cavity. The chamber pulsed like a living, breathing animal. Each of the passageways had a membrane-like flap that would open and close, seemingly at random.

The Zebs navigated their ship deeper into the monster, knowingly choosing each passageway. As they approached, a flap would open, allowing access. Then it would close after they went through it.

A dead calm persisted throughout the passageways, allowing the girls to reflect that they might be slowly riding toward their own execution.

Lauren wondered how the Zebs knew which way to go, as all the passageways looked mostly the same. Further in, the interior walls started flashing from bioluminescence, with pulses of blue, pink, purple, and white shooting through the monster's flesh.

Lauren's mind wandered back to the dream she and her sister had shared. It seemed years ago, but in reality it was just a few months back. She vaguely remembered it now, having tried to suppress it as best she could. The walls seemed familiar. She struggled to remember them from the dream. They looked fleshy to the touch. The air looked thick and soupy. The ship glided further into the innards, eventually navigating to a small chamber where a metal landing pad had been constructed. The landing pad connected to a door at one end of the room with a metal grate walkway.

Lauren looked up and glanced around the small dock. The metal doors and walkways were similar to what they had seen at the star gate, so she assumed the Zebs had put them here. Apparently, she thought, it didn't bother the Gr-awl-toltz too much, because the structures were everywhere.

The ship settled down on the landing pad with a loud clunk. The exterior door opened, exposing them to the damp air. The faint hum invading their thoughts grew louder. The two Zeb pilots got up out of their seats and exited the ship.

A group of Zebs came out of the door, marching down the walkway. The two Zeb pilots spoke to the group, and then they started unloading the supplies onto some small carts.

Lauren and Julia stayed quiet, watching them. The Zebs came and left, carrying boxes.

"There's no one here now. Let's get moving," Lauren said, standing up and walking to the center of the ship.

Julia sat fumbling with her fanny pack. She had opened it to get a snack on the ride and was zipping it shut. When she set her hand down to get up, she noticed a wristband lying on the ground next to her. Immediately, she looked over at Lauren, who was peering out the door of the ship, and saw she wasn't wearing her wristband.

"Lauren!" Julia whispered, cupping her hands around her mouth.

Lauren waved her off.

Just then, two Zebs were walking up the ramp to get onto the ship and stopped, gawking at Lauren.

"What in the world?" one of the Zebs said.

The other one said, "Grab her!"

Lauren looked down and noticed her wristband was gone. She froze.

Julia didn't know what to do. She stood staring at her sister with her mouth wide open.

One of the Zebs grabbed Lauren by the arm.

She didn't struggle. She knew there was nowhere to go. She motioned to her sister to stay hidden.

Lauren plodded along with two Zebs in front and two in back. None of them spoke to her. She just stared ahead with a glum look. Lauren took comfort knowing that her sister was right behind her.

Julia followed the group, keeping enough distance so that the Zebs didn't suspect she was there.

The door opened, exposing a long hallway that resembled the same hallway they floated through in their horrific dream. The images from her dream raced back to Lauren, causing her to pause before entering the door. For a moment, the hum escalated, almost throbbing, then receded. Stepping aside, Lauren grasped the door frame with one hand and her chest with the other. She whimpered, then stumbled forward a couple steps.

Julia's vision narrowed as she almost blacked out. She reached over and grasped the rail beside her.

The Zebs behind Lauren stopped abruptly, noticing her reaction. "Keep moving," one of the Zebs in back said in a low monotone. Then he gently nudged her forward.

Lauren stopped, frowning. "When do I get to see my dad? I know he's here."

"Soon enough," one of the Zebs said. "Let's keep moving."

They marched for what seemed like a long time on the winding walkway. The air was still thick and humid, making it difficult to breathe. The air condensed on the girls' foreheads like beads of sweat. The walls of the hall pulsed and shivered. Every now and then, they heard a low grumbling.

There was a simple elevator at the end of the hall. It wasn't fully enclosed. The sides were short rails with chain link around the perimeter of the platform. The elevator was attached to a tall metal column that drove the platform up and down. The shaft where the elevator resided was a huge open cavern whose sides pulsed in and out. With every pulse, a quick gust of air blasted on anyone inside.

The platform was just big enough for four Zebs and Lauren. They boarded while Julia looked on. The elevator started inching upward. Lauren's eyes widened, seeing that her sister was about to be left behind.

Julia ran to the side of the platform and jumped onto an outside ledge, holding firmly to the rail just as the platform shot upward. She lost her footing and hung suspended as the elevator ascended.

Lauren gasped, looking at her sister out of the corner of her eye.

"What's the problem?" a snaggle-toothed Zeb asked, grinning. "Lose your stomach?"

Lauren just glared at him, not saying anything.

Julia regained her footing and stood back up on the outside of the platform.

The sides of the cavern heaved in and out, forcing air up the shaft. With each blast of air, Julia tightened her grip on the railing, making her knuckles turn white.

At the top of the steel column, the elevator stopped abruptly. One of the Zebs flung the cage door open. Lauren and the Zebs got off the elevator, standing in another chamber.

Julia quietly jumped over the side and stood behind them.

The hum buzzing in the girls' heads escalated again to an almost excruciating level. Directly in front of them, they saw the brain of the Gr-awl-toltz—fleshy, grey, and stinky. The smell was almost unbearable. For a moment, the stench took the girls' attention off the painful hum.

In the middle of the room, columns of flesh supported the ceiling with a large blob-like membrane in the middle. Flashes of light crackled like lightning over the membrane. As it did, the pain surged. With every pulse, the pain intensified.

Lauren shrieked, "Ahhhhhhh!" She grabbed her temples. Tears trickled down her cheeks.

"Come on," one Zeb said, grabbing Lauren by the elbow. She ripped her arm from his grasp, stomping forward.

"Dad!" Lauren shouted. Near the membrane blob, their dad stood blindfolded by some sort of visor.

He reached out. "Lauren? Is that you?" The Zeb guarding him shoved him to his knees.

The Zebs pushing Lauren forced her forward, not letting her check on her father. They moved her directly in front of the brain. This close, the Gr-awl-toltz's power could subdue the barrier from the treatment.

Julia rubbed her forehead, her mouth contorting to fend off the pain. She knew that if she shrieked, she'd give away her position. It became unbearable. Blood trickled out of her nose. She reached up to wipe it, but the pain was too much. She grasped her head and screamed.

"What? What is that?" one of the Zebs said.

“It came from there,” another one said. They gang tackled the spot, landing on Julia, ripping the signature modifier off her arm. She reappeared under the pile, her arms pinned down.

Lauren could feel and sense the Gr-awl-toltz, but it couldn’t control her. It pushed further, probing her mind, trying to dig like a worm pushing through earth. The hum had graduated to a shrieking pain. Lauren looked over at her sister. They had stood her up, holding her by her arms. Blood trickled from her ears, too, as she winced in pain.

Lauren ripped her hand away from the guard who had hold of her and ran over to Julia, jumping on one of the guards with all her weight. They fell to the ground in a ball.

“Julia . . . now!” Lauren screamed.

Julia plunged her hand into her fanny pack, grabbing the canister. She aimed it at the brain’s membrane and pressed the button on the side of the apparatus.

The familiar foul stench permeated the air. The ooze spewed onto the surface membrane. Almost immediately, the pulsing lights where the ooze touched dimmed. The Zebs holding her released their grip, covering their mouths and noses.

Julia immediately ran closer to the membrane, canvassing the flesh with the canister’s contents. The grip the Gr-awl-toltz had on the Zebs started to fade. Julia ran around the perimeter of the brain, holding the canister out, eventually tossing it as high as she could onto the blob.

Lauren ran to help her dad. She ripped off the visor. Her dad looked at her, surprised.

“Dad? Are you OK?” she asked.

Stunned, he just looked at her, not saying anything for a moment. Then he came to. “We’ve got to get out of here.”

Julia sprinted over to them. “Come on!” She didn’t stop, running past them toward the elevator.

Lauren helped her dad scramble to his feet, and they hobbled after Julia. The great monster rumbled with an enormous tremor. The floor heaved up to the ceiling, almost flattening them.

The elevator creaked and groaned under the stress. Julia opened the elevator, waiting for her sister and father, waving them on and peering between the flaps of flesh that formed the floor and ceiling.

“Come on! We have to get out of here!” she yelled.

The monster relaxed for a moment, which returned the cavity back to normal and gave Lauren and her dad just enough time to get to the elevator.

The pressure from the tremor bent the elevator shaft. The metal creaked and groaned as it flexed.

“I’m not sure it will work,” Julia said, pressing a down symbol.

The elevator moved down slowly, rubbing metal on metal and screeching all the way down. Julia’s teeth tingled, almost as if someone had run their fingernails down an old-fashioned chalkboard.

The elevator started and stopped, finally coming to rest at the bottom of the shaft. They stepped out into the first hall where they’d started. The Gr-awl-toltz heaved again. This time the elevator shaft crashed behind them, sending a shockwave down the metal walkway and hurling the three in the air.

The girls crashed on the walkway, bouncing and then settling down on the twisted steel. Their dad wasn’t so lucky. The fatigued steel finally snapped, exposing serrated edges. The exposed steel sliced deep into their dad's leg when he fell back to the floor.

"Ugh," Lauren and Julia looked back to see their dad suspended in the air with his leg caught on the jutting steel. Blood dripped down onto the steel grate.

A low bellow erupted from the monster, almost seeming like a laugh.

"Dad!" Lauren shrieked, jumping up to help him, ignoring the gash on her own head.

Julia jumped up. On seeing the exposed wound, she dry heaved, "Blah . . . blah." She turned to hide her horror.

"Argh," their dad said, grabbing his leg with one hand. He reached up, finding a stray metal rail, then tugged as hard as he could. The metal dagger slid several inches out of his leg, covered in blood and leaving bits of skin.

Gritting his teeth, he said, "Keep going." He pulled off a belt from his clothes and buckled it around his leg as quickly as he could.

Lauren put his arm around her shoulders, helping him hobble to the end of the hall. The door had been tossed aside by the upheaval.

The walkway to the ship had been upturned, but luckily the ship was still in one piece. The squishy floor of the landing cavity slowed them down, but they made it out to the ship without too much more trouble. Once there, they climbed in.

"What now?" their dad asked, gritting his teeth and holding his leg.

"Get in. Fasten your seatbelt, Dad," Lauren commanded.

"You . . . know . . . how?" he tried to get out.

"Relax, we got it covered," Julia cut him off.

"OK." Lauren looked around the cockpit. She slid her hand over the left panel on the dashboard. The engines fired with a low roar but didn't start. She tried again, but it didn't start. All of a sudden the Gr-awl-toltz collapsed the chamber, squashing the ship against the floor and ceiling. It relented for a moment. Lauren tried starting the engines again. This time the low roar crescendoed, growing louder. She grabbed the joystick with her left hand. The ship immediately responded, hovering above the ground.

The Gr-awl-toltz heaved again, forcing the ship to bump the ceiling. As Lauren struggled to gain control, the ship weaved and bobbed through the tunnels. The pulsing lights of the walls almost blinded them as she guided the ship out of the maze, eventually entering the enormous chamber they thought was the stomach.

"Sealed shut," Lauren said, looking out the window and circling the exit.

"No problem," Julia said, smiling now that it was her turn. "I knew the target practice on the asteroids would come in useful!"

With a flick of a switch, Julia armed the weapons. The powering up of what she could only assume was a capacitor hummed loudly over the sound of the engines.

Lauren banked the ship around and flew directly toward the center of the mouth.

"Fire!" she shouted.

Julia pulled the trigger, releasing an energy blast from the front of the ship. The pulse exploded a hole in one of the flaps big enough for the ship to escape. Bits and pieces of the shell splattered everywhere, some onto the window of the ship.

Lauren threaded the ship through the hole and out into space. Outside, she kicked in the thrusters, accelerating away from the Gr-awl-toltz.

They looked back to see the tentacles flaying in space. Its mouth gaped open now, as if it were trying to swallow them.

Minutes later, with the monster safely behind them, Lauren slowed the ship down.

She looked back at her dad. “How are you doing?”

Their dad coughed, clasping his leg. “Not so well, kiddos.”

Julia looked back to look, too. Her eyes widened when she saw the gash in her dad’s leg. “Lauren, hurry, we need to get him back!”

Lauren accelerated considerably, leaving the Gr-awl-toltz far behind. Soon they couldn’t see the monster behind them anymore. As they approached Cielo Prime, the vast field of farms and other satellite stations appeared. Lauren backed off the accelerator so she could navigate through the farms.

Julia looked back again. Their dad was shivering, still holding his leg.

“Lauren, hurry,” Julia said with a slight quiver in her voice.

“I’m going as fast as I can!” Lauren growled.

Lauren weaved in and out of the farms.

She headed towards their apartment building and tapped the map pad when she got close.

The window displayed a couple icons on the station, highlighting where the hidden docks were.

“There!” Julia pointed to one of them.

Lauren moved the ship close to the dock Julia pointed to, slowing down as she approached.

Since the ship was invisible to all the systems on the station, she was able to float completely undetected into the small makeshift port. The door slid open as she approached, and she gently glided the ship into the small port. The doors shut behind them as quickly as they'd opened. Air filled the dock with loud swishing sounds. The indicator light flashed on the dashboard, indicating it was safe to exit the ship, so the girls opened the door.

"Come on, Dad. Can you make it down?" Lauren asked, hopping out of the ship.

"I . . . think . . . so," he said, struggling to take off the seat belt.

Julia helped him click out of the seat belt and then braced his arm while he tried to maneuver to the steps on the ship.

Lauren stood outside the ship, giving him her shoulder for support as he labored down the stairs.

Once he was off the ship, the three hobbled to the exit and out into a vacant hall. They were in their neighborhood, but didn't recognize this particular spot. Worker bots strolled by, ignoring them.

"Julia, call for help," Lauren said.

Julia unzipped her fanny pack, pulling her phone out. She spoke into it. "Emergency, emergency, we need an ambulance."

An automated response came back, "We have isolated your location and will be there shortly."

A few moments later, an ambulance cart arrived. It was a small, box-shaped vehicle with a door on the back, just small enough to get through the halls and elevators. A sliding compartment at the front of the cart opened and two medical bots emerged. They had arms and short stubby robotic legs. Immediately, they moved over to look at their dad's leg. One of the bots pulled a device from its chest and waved it over their dad's wound. The weeping wound stopped bleeding.

The bots then extended their arms up to help their dad. He transferred his weight to them, using them like crutches. The side of the cart opened, revealing a bed right at knee height. Their dad sat down on the bed, reclining. As he did, the door shut.

The girls hopped onto a back platform big enough for them to stand on, and the cart whisked them away to the closest hospital.

Chapter 23

Attack of the Killer Monster

When they arrived at the hospital, a doctor came out to look at their dad's wound and then rushed him into an operating room. After about 30 minutes, the doctor came out to speak with the girls.

"He's going to be OK," the doctor said. "He's lost a lot of blood, but we're replacing that now, we repaired the wound."

The doctor paused, then asked, "What happened to him? I don't see wounds like that up here on the space station. I haven't seen something like that since I left Earth."

The girls avoided answering the question. "When can we see him?" they asked in unison.

"He's just getting a transfusion now," the doctor said, leading the way to the room their dad was in.

The doctor stopped at a doorway to room 3B, knocking on the open doorframe. "Here you go, girls."

Their dad was sitting up in bed, rubbing his leg, looking at it. He had a tube running from his forearm and leading up to a flattened bag that surrounded his upper arm. When the girls came in, he looked up, smiling.

"Girls, come here," he said, opening his arms up.

"Dad!" The girls ran to his bedside.

"How are you?" Lauren asked.

"A little light-headed, but doing OK. You two have a LOT to tell me," he said to them.

Julia smiled an impish smile. Lauren just laughed.

"Yes, LOTS," Lauren said.

Julia started from the beginning, not stopping for a breath, waving her hands wildly, curly hair bobbing as she talked. Their dad listened, frowning, then smiling. Just as she started to describe their trip to the star gate, a loud crash rocked the station. Medical supplies flew off the shelves.

Another crash. A nurse ran by their room. Lauren ran out, yelling at her to stop. "Hey, what's going on?"

The nurse looked at her with pleading eyes. "Turn on your TV. We're being attacked . . ."

Lauren picked up her phone, saying, "Show local news."

The phone turned on, showing an image on the screen. They heard screams, then the newscaster talking. "There are reports . . . we're being attacked. We don't know by what . . ." He turned to his production manager. "Show the footage."

The screen showed the monstrous Gr-awl-toltz latched onto the station, raising a tentacle and crashing it down.

"Oh, God! We have to get to the ship to see what's happening out there," Lauren said, putting her phone back in her pocket.

"Dad, can you move?" Julia asked him.

"I think so." He moved his legs off the side of the bed and got to his feet. He had a severe limp, but he was in much better shape than when they had gotten there.

He left the blood running but pulled other leads off of himself and started getting dressed. As soon as he did, a nurse ran in.

"What are you doing? You can't do that!" the nurse said to him.

He looked at her, lifting his eyebrows, "Did you hear that thump out there? Do you want to stay?"

The nurse stepped aside, letting them leave. The hidden dock with the ship wasn't far.

"Here, this way," Lauren said, running ahead.

Their dad was in better shape, but still hurting a lot. He struggled to keep up, hobbling along with a stiff leg.

They went several blocks before finding the maintenance facility where the hidden dock was.

BOOM. Another thundering blow rippled through the station. They staggered in the hall. Their dad fell and the girls helped him back to his feet.

"This is it," Lauren said, looking around.

"Yes, in here," Julia said, ducking down one of the halls.

The three came to the nondescript door where they had stashed their ship. Lauren waved the signature modification bracelet they had taken from Ankit in front of the doorway, opening it.

BOOM. Another blow.

The three boarded the ship. Lauren fired up the engines and the door opened. She rotated the ship around to jet out of the dock.

"Aaah!" Julia screamed and pointed out the door.

They could see the giant underside of the Gr-awl-toltz poised just outside. It moved slightly to the side, exposing a hole big enough for them to escape.

Lauren punched the accelerator, blasting the ship out of the dock. A huge tentacle looped around, trying to swat them as they emerged, but it was too slow for the quickness of the small ship.

Their dad in the back seat was still groggy. "Lauren, get some distance . . . fly out there . . . and turn around," he pointed as he spoke.

Lauren did what he said, accelerating, then turning the ship around for a better look.

From this better vantage point, they could see the Gr-awl-toltz spanned half the height of the station. It had attached itself to the station and was pummeling it with its tentacles. With every mighty crash, the station shook.

"God, no . . . that's home." Their dad pointed to the beast, barely able to lift his arm.

"Mom!" Julia shouted, a trickle of tears streaming down her cheeks.

"What can we do?" Lauren asked, shaking, looking at her dad for answers.

"I don't know . . . that thing is enormous . . . uhh," he said, pulling himself forward to get a better view.

"We can fight!" Julia said. "Get us closer, Lauren. I'll shoot it!"

"Maybe . . . we can distract . . . it," their dad said, his chest heaving with every breath.

Lauren accelerated the ship directly toward the beast. *This is a suicide mission*, she thought, but the monster wanted them, and them alone.

The ship buzzed by the Gr-awl-toltz. It ignored the flyby, continuing to pound the station.

“Do it again. I’ll get him this time,” Julia said.

Lauren maneuvered the ship out further for another pass. She banked the ship in a swift turn. As she did, the three of them felt the pressure of the centrifugal forces tugging at their bodies.

“Ungghh,” their dad groaned in the back seat.

Julia flipped the switch to the weapons. Again, they heard the power transfer to the weapons.

Lauren gave the ship one last boost of the accelerators to align the ship directly in the sights of the Gr-awl-toltz.

“Fire!”

Julia pulled the trigger. A burst of light shot from the sides of the ship, aimed at the Gr-awl-toltz. A split second later, the blast exploded on the surface of the monster, directly on its back. It was so small, they could barely see the hit. A small black cloud materialized from the spot.

The monster didn’t notice. It pounded the station again. The station shook. This time, as the monster retracted its tentacle, they could see a huge divot in the side of the station.

“Again!” Lauren said.

Julia fired once again. And again, the blast barely registered.

“No!” Julia shouted, tears welling in her eyes as she pounded her fists on the dashboard.

"Let's try again. Maybe we can get its attention," Lauren said.

"Be . . . careful," her dad managed.

Lauren pushed the accelerator faster, swinging in close to the monster. They could see the enormous beast hovering over them. A tentacle went up to beat the station again. Lauren dodged under it, buzzing around the creature like a fly.

"Julia, fire!" she said.

Julia complied, blasting as many shots as she could get off, hitting the monster around the perimeter of its body.

This time, the Gr-awl-toltz took notice. It detached its enormous body from the station, lifting up, but still holding on with its back tentacles. Its mouth flaps curled open in slow motion.

As the massive flaps widened, the ship's power supply stuttered. It briefly stopped, then started. As the mouth opened, the Gr-awl-toltz pulled the ship toward it, sucking them in somehow.

"What's happening?" Julia asked.

"I don't know," Lauren shot back. "It's pulling us in."

They could see the triangular-shaped mouth flap getting larger as they drifted in.

"Aaaaieee!" A voice came from the dashboard.

In unison with the voice, the Gr-awl-toltz reeled up, detaching from the station and pulling all tentacles close into its body. Blasts of light exploded all over the shell of the monster.

The girls' ship regained power. As soon as it did, Lauren punched the accelerator, flying the ship in the opposite direction.

Julia asked, "What was that?"

Lauren peered at the dashboard, pursing her lips. “Ankit?”

“The one and only! Need some help?” he asked.

“Ankit!” Lauren shouted. “What did you do?”

She swung the ship around and guided it back around to get a better look at the Gr-awl-toltz. Over the top of the monster’s body, explosions blasted, with towers of flames shooting from the shell. Just beyond the explosions, they could see a swarm of ships attacking the Gr-awl-toltz.

It released its grip from the station and drifted out to get in a better attack position.

Julia sat up in her seat, beaming a smile, eyes scrunched like crescents. “We’re not going to die!” She grabbed her sister by the shoulders, staring into her eyes, “We’re not going to die!”

Lauren screamed with her sister. They turned around, looking at their dad. He had sat back relaxing in his seat, but then he popped up, pointing out the front window. “Watch out!”

Lauren turned around just in time to see a large building looming in front of them. She pulled the controls up, dodging the building by a hair.

“Pull back, get away from here,” their dad said.

Lauren throttled the ship out a ways so they could see the battle from a distance.

The fireworks of the mêlée lit up space in all directions. The Zeb ships buzzed closer to the mighty monster as it swatted at them with its massive tentacles, missing each time.

Then, in one mighty strike, the Gr-awl-toltz hit one of the ships. Smoke trailed the wounded ship as it careened into the station.

The ship exploded on the side of the station, with a plume of smoke floating from the site of the crash.

Then, again, another ship hit. This time the injured ship swung directly into the Gr-awl-toltz's outer shell, exploding in a massive fireball. The blast subsided, revealing a gaping wound in the monster's shell and exposing its innards.

The remaining ships concentrated all their firepower on the open hole. One ship veered close to the opening and launched a torpedo. Moments later, the Gr-awl-toltz's shell ballooned, then imploded. The once mighty beast floated limp.

"Ankit?" Lauren asked in a low voice. "Are you there?"

"Yes, I'm here . . .," he said.

The girls said nothing, just sat looking at the motionless Gr-awl-toltz.

"Get us back to the station. We need to find your mom, Evan, and Maia. Fast!" their dad said, putting a hand on each of the girl's seats and pulling himself forward.

Blinking, Lauren snapped to attention. She whipped the ship around and headed toward the hidden dock they'd come from.

Lauren guided the ship to the secret Zeb port. The bay doors opened as they got closer. She gently set the ship down on the floor and the doors closed.

The three hopped out of the ship as quickly as they could. They were close to their building—it was only a few blocks away. Outside the maintenance area, it was utter chaos. People ran in all directions, many with bloody arms or legs, nursing their wounds. Medical bots dotted the crowds, administering basic care. Medical personnel mixed in the crowd placed tourniquets on people, doing what they could.

Lauren and Julia barely heard any of the screams as they navigated toward their apartment building. The surreal surroundings just blurred together. They finally made it to their train stop and went down the hall that read, "Alpha Centauri Landing."

Their dad hobbled behind, trying to keep up. Lauren's heart hung in her throat. She rounded the corner, looking at her sister, whose eyes were open wide. They hurdled panels strewn out on the floor deeper in the hall and arrived at two large girders that blocked the way. Cords hung, crackling with electricity.

"NO!" Lauren screamed, tugging at one of the girders. It wouldn't budge. She put both feet on a piece of metal and pulled harder.

"Julia, help!" she yelled back at her sister.

Julia stood motionless, staring at the mass of debris. "Evan?" she said, sniffling slightly, tears welling in her eyes. "Mom? Maia?"

Their dad caught up. "Oh, God, NO!"

He threw himself at the girder, trying with all his strength to pull it free. It inched up slightly. As it did, the other girder filled the gap, holding the remaining pieces firmly in place.

He slammed his back against the wall, bracing himself up for a second, then slid to the floor, crying.

This was the first time Lauren or Julia had ever seen their dad cry. Lauren slumped by her dad, cradling his arm, crying on his shoulder.

Julia fell to her knees, staring at the pile.

After what seemed like hours, their dad clasped Lauren's hand. "Kids, we need to get out of here. It's not safe."

Lauren nodded and helped her dad to his feet.

Her dad reached over, grabbing Julia's shoulder, pulling her up.

She brushed his hand away. “The last thing I told Evan was I hated him . . .”

“Julia . . . there was nothing we could do. You know he knew you loved him,” he pulled her close to his chest, hugging her.

The three turned, walking toward the stairs leading to the surface. People ran everywhere. The commotion was deafening, but the three didn’t hear anything. As they made their way up the stairs, their heavy steps slowed them down.

As they crested the top of the steps, the other half of their family stood huddled together, as scared as they were.

“Mom!” Lauren screamed, letting go of her father. Her dad caught himself on the top step when she let go.

Their mother looked up, teary eyes beaming. Maia and Evan started jumping up and down, screaming in joy.

“Evan!” Julia said, running to hug her little brother.

Their father struggled over to the group, giving the whole lot of them an enormous hug.

Chapter 24

Unlikely Heroes

Cielo Prime was at the tail end of a four-month massive clean-up effort, and life was beginning to return to normal on the station. The kids were back in school. While the reconstruction effort was underway, they had to live in a hotel and wear donated clothes from kind citizens around the station for a month. After that, they finally gained access to their apartment so they could get to all their things. Then they were able to get most of their clothes, but they still had to live in the hotel room until the apartment was safe to move back into.

The shock to the station was all that the kids at school talked about. The new alien life forms that had been the subject of so many conspiracy theories in the past were now a regular part of everyone's lives.

The task of integrating the Zebs into the station culture fell on the shoulders of Ankit. He was busier than ever now, working with the Cielo bureaucrats and trying to figure out how his people would fit into this new world. It was easier for the Zebs, since they'd been living among humans for so long, and a little more difficult for the humans who had to get used to them.

Dignitaries from all over Earth scrambled to visit Cielo, trying to put their stamp on inter-galactic relations in preparation for unveiling the star gate as the Zebs were furiously trying to get the gate operational. The star gate was the first step for humans to travel beyond the solar system and dignitaries were jockeying to be the first ones to go.

The girls' lives hadn't changed much, since their parents requested that their involvement remain private. But the Zebs knew, and every time a Zeb saw one of the girls, they would walk up to them with a big smile and give them a hug. The girls' friends vaguely suspected that they had played a part, but they really didn't treat them any differently.

This afternoon, the family was finally able to move back into their apartment. They walked up to the building for the first time since construction finished. The hall walls were new, and the decorations were new, too.

"Wow! They really spruced this up!" their mom said as she walked through the halls. She sniffed the air. "It even smells new!"

They approached their apartment door.

"And I've got a surprise for you!" their dad said, smiling when the door opened. He was still limping from the accident and hobbled into the apartment, waving his arms like it was a drum roll.

"Oh, wow, it's bigger!" their mom said as she charged in.

Evan ran in to see that he had his own room now. "Look! LOOK! I don't have to share a room with Maia!"

"How'd they do that?" their mother asked, walking to the window that was about 25 feet further out than it used to be.

"They cantilevered the room, extending it out the side of the building. They did that with several of the apartments," their dad said.

The girls' room was slightly larger, but relatively intact. Their dressers were still in the same place and their beds were, too. They just had a little more space.

Lauren walked into their room. "Finally! We get our room back!" she said walking to a dresser.

"I know what you mean," Julia said, observing their new room.

The two walked out to the living room and smiled at their mom and dad, who were sitting at the table. They now had a real living room, a dining area, and a larger playroom.

"Wow, this is nice!" Lauren said as she sat down at the table.

Both Lauren and Julia appreciated their family now more than ever. They had never really thought about it much until the recent events forced them to.

Julia grabbed a snack from the kitchen and plopped down on the living room couch. Their mother got up and walked over to join Julia. Evan and Maia were back in their new rooms looking around.

"What do you say we hang out here for a little longer, then we go up to the plaza and get pizza?" she asked.

"Yeah! That sounds great!" Julia said.

"It'll be just like old times," their mother said.

The girls got up to inspect the new game room and Maia and Evan's rooms. Evan was so happy he finally had a room of his own. His stuff was in a box on the side of his bed, and he had already started unpacking and carefully arranging his possessions on his desk.

They went over to Maia's room, where she lay on her bed whimpering. "I liked sharing a room with Evan."

After helping Maia get adjusted some, their mother called, "Come on, you all. Let's go."

They all marched out of the room through the new living room, then out the door. They decided to walk to the plaza, since it had been a while since they walked their neighborhood. They strolled along, taking it all in. A Zeb passed them on the path and waved and smiled at the girls as if to say "Thank you." The family waved back.

At the plaza, they did the usual. Their dad ordered pizza and the rest of them sat down at a table. There were several people sitting at other tables. A single Zeb was engaged in conversation with a human at one of the tables.

Their mother looked at the girls. "You know, that wouldn't have been possible without the two of you."

"We know!" Julia said, shaking her head, feigning exasperation, but deep down feeling proud.

Their dad came back to sit down with them.

The girls looked around at the plaza. Everything was in its place. Life had gotten back to normal . . . at least they thought it had!

11033765R00173

Made in the USA
Charleston, SC
25 January 2012